C000049917

Helen Larder was born in Yorkshire in 1958 and now lives in the north-west of England with her partner and child. *Treasure* is her first novel.

Treasure

HELEN LARDER

DIVA

To Joyce and Hayden, the loves of my life

'Pack up Your Troubles (In Your Old Kit Bag)' Words by George Asaf
and music by Felix Powell © 1915. Reproduced by permission of
Francis Day & Hunter Ltd, London WC2H 0QY.

All characters in this novel are fictitious and any resemblance
to real persons, living or dead, is purely coincidental.

First published 2003 by Diva Books,
an imprint of Millivres Prowler Limited, part of the Millivres Prowler Group,
Spectrum House Unit M, 32-34 Gordon House Road, London NW5 1LP
www.divamag.co.uk

Copyright © 2003 Helen Larder

Helen Larder has asserted her right to be identified as the author of this work
in accordance with the Copyright, Designs and Patents Act 1988

A catalogue record for this book is available from the British Library

ISBN 1-873741-81-2

All rights reserved. No part of this book may be reproduced, stored in
a retrieval system, or transmitted, in any form or by any means, including
mechanical, electronic, photocopying, recording or otherwise, without
the prior written permission of the publishers.

Printed and bound in Finland by WS Bookwell

Distributed in the UK and Europe by Airlift Book Company,
8 The Arena, Mollison Avenue,
Enfield, Middlesex EN3 7NJ
Telephone: 020 8804 0400

Distributed in North America by Consortium,
1045 Westgate Drive, St Paul, MN 55114-1065
Telephone: 1 800 283 3572

Distributed in Australia by Bulldog Books,
PO Box 300, Beaconsfield, NSW 2014

Acknowledgements

Many thanks to the following people for their advice and support: Kathleen Bryson, Sophie Hannah, Sue Harper, Liz Kessler, Jai Penna, Gillian Rodgerson, Helen Sandler, Michael Schmidt, Sandra Sinclair. Thanks also to all my friends and family for their love and help.

FRIDAY

One

I can hear them shagging. I want them to stop. Want to get in between. Megan's allowed. She must be on their bed. I can hear her throat grumbling and purring. If she can stay, they should let me. It's well snide. Sarah can't even stand cats, especially Megan. Probably too busy to notice.

Push the door. Just a bit. See what happens. Don't want to stay downstairs any more. The cartoons are boring. There's only fighting ones on. I could just walk in. But I might get in trouble. If I hide behind the door I could watch what they're doing. No, they'll see me. Just stay still and listen. It reminds me... reminds me of that new girl...

'Suck a fanny.' That's what she kept saying to me, before the holidays. 'You're a suck a fanny.' Her mouth drawn all straight and thin like a pencil line.

'No, I'm not.'

'You caught it at your house.'

I wanted to pound her head in, but went quiet instead. Jo says I have to feel sorry for her because she's from a hostel and she's a vicious circle.

'Where's your dad?'

'Haven't got one.'

'Everyone's got a dad, you muppet.' Her eyes went bulgy and her tongue pushed her chin into a mound, so everyone saw what she meant. Mong. 'You can't be born without one.'

'I've got a 'nonymous donor, right.'

Her straight mouth was right next to my nose. 'A what?'

'And I'm lucky, yeah, 'cos I've got two mums.' Saying that to her made my stomach squeeze. So I said it again, because I remembered something about talking like a broken record to shut stupid people up. This time I tried to sound lucky, like Sarah says I always did when I was little. She says I used to tell everyone everything, all the time. On buses. In the street. Everywhere. And in the middle, she'd ask me: 'Who you telling your life story to now, Derrie?' Not in an angry way. Sort of laughing. 'You'd talk to a dead dog.' She looked all red in the face when she pulled me away from people and whispered, 'You dead dogging again...?'

They're still doing that funny breathing. Got to look and see. Maybe I should leave them. Suppose it's better than them fighting. If I leave them alone, they might not wake me up in the night again, shouting. They might not split up. But it's not fair. I need cuddling too. Just push the door a bit. Only a bit.

Two

Poised over Sarah, Jo froze as she heard the door chafing against the carpet.

'When's Friday going to start?' Derrie asked. Hearing her voice, the cat jumped down and hid under the bed.

Trying to pull the duvet over them, Sarah screeched, *'Don't* come in.'

The door opened further. 'Why not?'

Calmly, Jo freed herself from the tangle of covers binding her long legs. 'We're just havin' some loving, an' that.' Her nasal Scouse still sounded easy-going.

Without hesitation, Derrie marched in and stood motionless, curiosity lighting her eyes.

'Just go downstairs for a minute,' Sarah pleaded.

In the hall below, the letterbox snapped shut. Derrie didn't move. Her stubborn pixie pout jutted from beneath an electric tangle of hair. White-gold hair, oddly angled by sleep. A defiant, iron-willed girl, just the way Sarah liked her. Loved her. Stalemate hung in the silence, making Sarah want to laugh, but she knew that would sabotage this hard-won moment with Jo. This chance at redemption.

She glanced at Jo to ask for help, but her eyes were already shut. Jo's once dark hair now looked silver, coarsened into bristles. Sarah still needed her – even more, now that she knew, with solid cold conviction, that Jo was working up to leaving her. Leaving her and Derrie. It didn't matter how much Jo denied it, Sarah could smell guilt on her. The suppressed laughter of seconds before twisted into a sore throat full of tears, which she knew she would be swallowing for weeks. Would keep swallowing for months, until they washed her into an incapable heap.

As if she sensed Sarah's lost focus, Derrie padded towards the bed, stretched over and doled out kisses equally. Before either of them could protest, she pushed their heads together to make them kiss each other. Then, scaling their bodies, she lifted the duvet and wriggled in between, carefully manoeuvring her tiny peach bottom into the curve of Sarah's spine.

'You petticoat,' Derrie muttered. 'Get up crumble lane.'

Sarah was caught. 'You what?' She tried to make sense of her daughter's words. Then she recognised them, extracted out of context from the book they'd read the night before.

Derrie chucked in another non sequitur. 'I know you are.'

Realising she couldn't hope for anything other than nonsensical one-liners, Sarah packed the duvet round her ears.

'Have a snooze, girl… ' Jo told Derrie sleepily. 'S'holidays… S'no need for you to get up so early.'

Derrie started printing ticklish kisses along Sarah's arm.

'Hmm,' Sarah murmured blissfully. Derrie's skinny tangle of limbs moved in.

This child's cheeks could be marketed. 'Extra soft, with a hint of apple.'

Against the pillow, Derrie began to plait wavy strands of her mother's hair through her own. She studied the erratic blonde pattern for a moment, then, knowing she had Sarah hooked, Derrie pressed home her advantage.

'Please can we get up now?'

'In a minute.'

'Yeah, right. It's never a minute.'

'Don't go on at Sarah like that.' Jo sealed herself into an irritable curl. 'You're not on. Anyway, it's my turn for a lie-in.'

Derrie stung. 'You've got a witch up your arse.'

Jo stiffened.

To prevent a fight, Sarah urged Derrie to name a scapegoat, 'Where did you get that from?'

'Probably your no-mark sister.' Jo sounded seriously awake, mention of Sarah's sister heightening her aggrieved Liverpudlian.

'No. Not from Auntie Ellie. From my brain. Like it's my fault.'

Jo let out a quick breath. 'Hey short-arse, I know exactly where you're headed.' She jutted her sharp chin towards the door. 'Go and get a bowl of cereal and give us a bit of peace, or I'm not taking you on that bike ride.'

Pressing her lips together, Derrie climbed over them, searching out handholds, as if they were rough terrain, and launched herself off the bed. Bouncing downstairs, she caused a shuddering impact through the house.

'I've found a weird letter on the floor,' Derrrie shouted up to them. 'Can I open it?'

Automatically, Sarah got up to follow her. 'Leave it, honey. I'll get it.' From the pile of clean clothes on the oak bedding-chest, she chose the sheerest white lace pants she could find and slid them on slowly. Well aware of Jo's interest, she reached for her dressing gown.

Jo sprang forwards, grabbed Sarah's arm as if it belonged to her and pulled her back into bed.

'She's big enough to get a bit of brekkie.'

'Yes, but –' Sarah made a move away again.

'C'mere.' Jo nuzzled her neck.

'You know what she's like.' Fine hairs stood up obediently where Jo's smile touched down. Fury flared in Sarah's chest – she might be able to manipulate me physically, but my mind's still stronger than hers. Determined to get away, she swung her legs over the side of the bed.

Instantly crushed under the weight of Jo's tight muscles, she heard her orders.

'Do as you're told. Or, I tell you what, there'll be big trouble.' Playfulness couldn't cover the conceit.

Sarah lay still, waiting. She knew they were already in bigger trouble than either of them could handle. Trouble that wouldn't go away just because Jo claimed it didn't exist.

Jo drew an unhurried line just inside the lace waistband, while the percussion section in the kitchen worked towards a crescendo, weaving its way into breakfast. As Jo traced her forefinger even more lazily under the lace around the top of her leg, Sarah identified milk bottles jangling together before the fridge door slammed shut. She could hear plates threatening to topple as they disengaged from the lopsided pile on the draining board.

Jo billowed the duvet, moving down her, grazing Sarah's plump stomach with biting kisses. Sarah considered pushing her off. Cracking her with a fist, so her ears rung. But then Jo would just get it somewhere else. Sarah held her breath as Jo caught lace between her teeth and tugged, squeezing her flesh into pulsing shocks. Well, let her go off, Sarah decided. Let her fuck off. She wasn't going to be blackmailed. A trickling taunt parted her legs. Molten. Wired. She was almost distracted enough to ignore the stainless steel crash of cutlery against a flying drawer. Her pants clung damp on the inside and wet on the outside from Jo's tongue, but the sudden peace downstairs worried Sarah even more than the noise. She imagined the hazardous scene in the kitchen. Star-shaped splatters of spilt milk, ready to skid on. Hot-plate dials accidentally knocked, standing by to sear a stray hand. With all that happening, sex stood no chance.

She wriggled from underneath Jo. 'I'll just make sure she's all right.'

'Stay here!' The hold on Sarah's wrist stung.

She lay back but her stare raged at Jo.

At the bottom of the stairs, chirping voices were accompanied by the tinny strains of spokes, as a wheel hit the front door open.

'We're ready.' Derrie's announcement rang round the hall. 'Adesua's got her bike.'

'When did you sneak out?' Sarah tried to sit up. 'Did you finish your breakfast?'

Jo lifted her head, eyes distracted. 'I'll be down in a minute, lovely girl.'

'That's what you said hours ago.' Derrie's tone remained just within the realms of patient reason.

'Has Adesua got a jacket?'

'No. She doesn't need one.'

Jo turned stern. 'Take her back next door and get her one, please. It might rain.'

'Okay.'

The high-pitched chattering became muffled and Sarah saw Jo's shoulders relax.

'I should think so, an' all.' As Jo arched one eyebrow at her, posing a silent, rhetorical question, thoughts of Derrie left Sarah's mind.

She tried to pull Jo over her. 'Come and lie on me.'

'No.' The corners of Jo's mouth moved, suggesting a smug smile, before she twisted onto her back and raised a taut thigh between Sarah's legs. 'You lie on me.' Her eyes teased with victory.

Sarah shifted over her, cunt scorching in rhythm as she gripped on. 'I don't know if I can now.' Now that Derrie will be back any second, Sarah thought. Now that I can't stand you. Now that you're killing this with lies. But she came in furious seconds.

Jo jumped out of bed, her grin self-satisfied. 'I'll have some of that later.' Who from? Sarah wondered, as she noted the hasty way Jo dressed. 'I'm on a promise to me daughter now.'

As soon as silence resonated around the house, Sarah got up. She knew they'd be gone for a while. For miles. The need for Jo to have her daily dose of endorphins drove her harder than any drug and Derrie would be desperate to keep up. She smiled sadly as she peeled off her wet pants and balled them in her fist, ready to throw in the washing machine.

Crossing the landing to the bathroom, something caught her attention at the bottom of the stairs. Something flashing gold, lying on the mat behind the front door. An envelope. Probably another birthday card for Jo. Intending to find out later, Sarah turned her head, but a gold wink stopped her and led her downstairs. The envelope lay face downwards with some kind of logo printed on the flap. She leaned over to see what it was. A beckoning hand, the crooked finger irresistible. When she flipped it over, the words made her start. Their address was there, but no name. Just a message. 'Looking for treasure? Dykes only.' She wondered if one of their friends could be having a joke with them, or whether this was just a clever marketing strategy. As she tore it open and slid out the shiny card, a shaft of early sunlight pierced the art deco windows. It stained the walls with blocks of curved emerald and yellow irises and swelled like liquid across the embossed message. Crouched on the bottom stair, still naked, Sarah ran the tip of her finger over the gilded indentations while she read.

'The hunt is on! Saturday 28th August.' Tomorrow. 'Come and have a go if you think you're smart enough! Win a surprise holiday. Dykes only. Access our web site now for first clue: treasurehunt66.co.uk.' She checked for a signature. Nothing. Maybe it was a joke. Someone she had invited to Jo's picnic. Would they have gone to that much trouble? Feeling confused, she hid the card in her cream linen jacket, hanging over the banister. *She* was supposed to be the one organising the surprise for Jo, not anyone else. Annoyed, she retrieved the card from her pocket and stormed into the living room to unplug the phone and connect to the Internet.

While the electronic dialling punctuated the quiet, she braved the kitchen. A trail of blackcurrant juice ran into cloudy pools where it mingled with milk along the white Formica top, then streamed down to the polished floorboards. A towel lay crumpled on the floor, dumped in a halfhearted attempt to mop up. Leaving everything as it was, Sarah determined to supervise Derrie in a cleaning mission the moment she stepped through the door.

As she punched in the web address, Sarah felt an inexplicable fizz in her stomach. Light the blue touchpaper and retire. She recalled the phrase from an early BBC safety film and could clearly hear the announcer's staid, measured delivery. 'Under no circumstances return to a lighted firework.' Something was about to go off. The graphics downloaded. A princess-cut diamond, at least 2 carats, shot bursts of crystal light at her. 'So, you think you're smart enough? Let's see if you're right. Cost: £40 per car. Dykes only. Fill in your credit card details in the space below to receive a print-out of the first clue.' Sarah sat back in the computer chair and sighed at the screen. This was decidedly odd. How could they hope to monitor that dykes-only stuff? And what if she gave them her credit card number and got nothing for it? Or worse. They could take much more than £40, couldn't they? She had never ventured to buy anything from the Internet because of that. Still, if it was real, it was a small price to pay for Jo's birthday. Everyone could come. It could be step one of her plan.

Jo had made Sarah promise not to organise anything. But Sarah couldn't leave her fortieth birthday unmarked. Without agonising any longer, she went to fetch her purse. It was time she tried courage. Time to cash in her lifetime all-risk cover. Rapidly typing in her credit card number, she fed herself as much self-help theory as she could remember and switched on the printer. Those who say no are rewarded with security, those who say yes are rewarded with adventure. Faint heart never won fair maid. Well, Jo wasn't fair exactly. More a tender-hearted butch. All legs and no sense.

The printer jarred into action.

Three

'That's only brand frigging new,' Jo complained to herself, as Derrie flung her bike down and raced to be first to the trees before her friend. Jo was about to lay into Derrie, when she remembered – at that age, she would've done exactly the same thing.

'We're climbing this one,' Derrie instructed.

While Adesua searched the trunk for a foothold, Derrie picked up one of her friend's braids.

'I want my hair like this. Will you do it for me, Jo?'

'Go way, I haven't got a clue about that sort of stuff, have I?'

'Well, maybe Sarah could.' Derrie caught Adesua's hand. 'Or your mum. D'you think she would?'

With an eloquent lift of one shoulder, Adesua shrugged. 'Maybe.'

Jo's fingers combed through Derrie's high-voltage hair. It occurred to her that this cute kid was going to be beautiful, just like her mother.

'Listen, honey girl, yours might not stay in. It's too fine, an' that.'

'It will.' Patting her own head, Derrie was certain.

'Stop acting soft. You don't wanna be copying Adesua.'

'I do. We're twins.' She sandwiched their faces together to prove her point.

Adesua's tolerant smile implied, 'She's missing the obvious, isn't she?' The six-month age gap between the girls felt more like years to Jo. Loving Derrie often landed a heavyweight jab to Jo's chest, but she couldn't make her out. Sometimes she said things that made her sound... like some kind of mystic. And other times she was so bleeding immature. Christ, she was nearly nine. She ought to have some sense by now. Jo knew she should stop being so down on the little scally. Especially now.

The branches of the tree were worn silk smooth from climbing and Adesua's soles slipped on the bark. She gripped one of her sandals by the heel, but before she could find a safe place to throw it, Derrie had already kicked her own trainers to the ground. Seeing their bare feet brought back flickering pictures of them both, much younger, in one of Sarah's first Super Eight experiments – the patio patterned with two pairs of miniature footprints and the kids working like maniacs to scoop all the water out of the paddling pool. Then, forgetting the camera, Derrie's arms went limp. She stared at her friend, trying to find words. When her mouth moved on the film, no sound came out. But Jo remembered...

'I want brown skin, like Adesua.'

Holding a towel out as an invitation to either of them, Jo spoke carefully. 'You can't choose, Derrie, all right? It depends how you're born.'

Adesua rewarded Jo's response with a single nod.

'But why?' Derrie whined. 'It's not fair. I don't want to be pink. It's nasty.'

Straight away, Sarah put the camera down and picked up a couple of plates. Her eyes launched a full-scale appeal at Jo, but her voice sounded artificially bright.

'Come on, girls. There's some sliced apple here for you.' She waited until they were settled inside their towels with their mouths full, then guided Jo into the privacy of the kitchen. 'Will you talk to her later? I don't want all the black kids thinking she's a creep. You know, some sycophantic little white nerd, following them everywhere and trying to imitate their every move.'

'Calm down, girl.' Jo folded her arms round Sarah, resting her palms on the curves of her behind. 'She'll sort out how to behave when she gets a bit older.' A breeze from the open door lifted one blonde wave of Sarah's hair in a game of kiss chase across both their cheeks. Jo's skin shimmered. Holding Sarah like this, all was well with the world.

Furrows appeared along Sarah's forehead. 'And what's all that stuff about her skin being nasty? D'you think she's got low self-esteem?'

'Oh, behave. She just sees the cool kids at school and wants to be like them, doesn't she? There used to be this bloody big gang of us, trailing after the cock of our estate, trying to bask in his glory. Didn't you ever do that?'

'I suppose so,' Sarah said doubtfully.

Jo poked two tickling forefingers under Sarah's armpits. 'My mistake. I forgot. You weren't ever a kid, were you?'

She saw Sarah's eyes darkening from blue to green, as she opened her mouth then closed it again. Even though she was rejecting the temptation to go into 'poor little me' mode, Jo could imagine her thinking 'Try being the oldest of five, with parents who were more interested in wife-swapping than children.' That, or some other variation on a theme...

Adesua's dress caught on a branch, yanking her back down to Derrie. Jo unhooked her and the little girl gathered the offending garment into her knickers before pushing herself high up into the tree.

'Wait for me,' Derrie begged.

A giggle erupted from below them and Jo saw the girls were being watched. From her pram, a frilly baby gave them a plump-faced smile. Her stringy mother stood, arm poised, so that the smoke from her cigarette wound into her daughter's eyes. Kicking off her lacy boots, the baby chuckled at Derrie and Adesua again.

The mother winced. 'She hasn't realised yet that life's not funny.' Then she spun round and wheeled the pram away.

Before Derrie spoke, Jo noticed that she had the social grace, for once, to wait till the woman was out of earshot. 'Why isn't it funny, Jo?'

'Take no notice.'

'She's probably tired,' Adesua offered.

'You're spot on, girl. Life's as funny as you make it.' But Jo didn't believe her own words any more. In the simple, shorthand speak of couples, it had always been accepted that Jo was the calm, optimistic one, but now itching nerves crawled round her neck. She wished Sarah hadn't organised this bloody picnic thing. Maybe she could get away with saying she was too ill to go. But she knew that one more lie might make all the rest spew out.

'Hey,' Derrie called, scrambling down. 'Check it. There's a wedding over there. I've got to get my picture taken.'

Not again. That girl was going be in every wedding album in South Manchester. Jo imagined friends and family pointing an accusing finger at the tiny Pigpen figure in half the shots, saying, 'Who's that again?' She'd be a talking point. A cute curiosity. Each couple convinced no one else had that jubilant stranger featuring on their big day.

Jo and Adesua followed, skirting the lawn as Derrie galloped across the manicured grass.

'Use the path,' Jo shouted ineffectually, knowing Derrie wouldn't listen.

Against a dry waterfall structure in the Victorian rock garden, the photographer arranged the bride's white satin gown into watery swirls between the alpines. Next, he manoeuvred the stiff young bridegroom into a familiar stance beside her, so that standing sideways, he was taller than her, courtesy of a conveniently placed rock. The photographer made sure it was hidden by the train of the wedding dress, before cupping the boy's hands in a begging attitude, palms upwards. The girl admired her rings as she took her cue and placed her fingers over his. A cluster of guests waited under the trees, the men with their fists jammed into their suit pockets while the women pulled at their hemlines and their hair.

Preparing himself for the first shot, the bridegroom extended his lips over the braces on his teeth. As the bride shook the veil away from her face, Jo saw that her orange foundation emphasised rather than disguised the acne bumping along her chin and forehead. I'll give it two years maximum, Jo thought, wondering which one would fuck it up. She'd known for a long time that most human beings had a real feel for built-in obsolescence – especially when it came to relationships. She witnessed the mentality at work, daily. Her caseload was full of carbon copies of the pair in front of her. Trash it and move on to the next one. Serial monogamy, the serial killer. Licence to litter the world with unwanted families.

With patience born of expert practice, Derrie stayed motionless until she heard the photographer's tone change, then she leapt into the frame, a muddy grin creasing her whole face.

That's an absolute classic, Jo thought. Even if she wasn't mine, even being totally objective, our girl will be the only thing that shines in that picture. At that moment, Jo realised that if she couldn't see Derrie everyday, a part of her would be severed. Butchered.

Taking advantage of the wedding party's blank surprise, Derrie scaled the layered rock, until she was above their heads.

How ironic was all this? If Sarah kicked her out, Jo could end up with one of her work-mates doing a court report on her and Derrie. Deciding if she was a fit enough parent for a residency order. No, that couldn't happen. They wouldn't send an officer she knew.

The photographer and the guests homed in on Jo and she realised she'd have to play at being an outraged parent.

'Come on, you little scally. Home.'

Before anyone could catch her, Derrie jumped into the bushes.

'One of these days,' Jo warned, 'Your reputation will precede you and someone'll report you.'

'She can run faster than *them*.' As she walked away, Adesua tilted her head towards the wedding party. 'She can run faster than any-body.'

'They looked daft.' Derrie reappeared in front of them on a small wooden bridge and draped her arm over Adesua's shoulder. 'I'm never getting married.'

Jo beckoned Adesua closer. 'When Derrie was four, she used to say she was going to marry me and Sarah and live with us forever. But by the time she was five, she'd changed her mind.' She paused for effect. 'She'd decided she was gonna marry her best mate, from next door.'

'Who?' Adesua asked, pleased. 'Me?'

Derrie dragged her friend towards the place where they had left their bikes. Their heads pressed close together and Jo tuned in on their murmuring.

'You know how first this summer you went to Jamaica with your dad,' Derrie asked, 'Then your mum took you to Paris Disney? Well, if Jo moves out, I'll get double holidays like you.'

Adesua flinched.

Jo lunged forward, grasping Derrie's upper arms. 'What are you on about? I'm going nowhere, girl.'

Four

'Carlton Car Hire. How can I help you?'

'Somoya, it's Sarah. Can you talk?'

'For a minute. Me new manager's really clampin' down on personal calls.' As Somoya abandoned her bland telephone voice, her broad Bolton vowels conjured up, for Sarah, a close-up of her friend's spiralling charcoal hair springing against the receiver. A gentle sip filtered down the phone as Somoya stopped to drink. 'An' I can't be doing with him making any more cracks about me face not fitting.'

An involuntary intake of breath choked Sarah's speech. 'You *what*? You've got to get him done for racial harassment before you leave. Sue him for constructive dismissal.'

A dead pause echoed down the line. 'I'm not leaving.'

'What d'you mean? Is there a problem with your course?'

'No.' Somoya lowered her voice to a murmur. 'I can't afford to pack in work just now.'

'I don't understand. You can't lose your university place, honey. Not after waiting so --'

'Look, Sarah, I'll have to get off the phone.'

'Hang on. This is a business call. I need to know if you've got a Porsche for hire?'

Somoya spluttered through a mouthful of drink. 'Yer jokin' me?'

'No, it's for the picnic. There's a dyke treasure hunt thing on to-morrow.' Still not dressed, Sarah wriggled on the bottom stair, trying to get comfortable, as the new jute carpet cut itchy imprints into the backs of her thighs. 'Have you heard about it?'

'No. But just how long have you been saving up? You must be made of money, pal. A Porsche, that's going to cost a packet –'

'I don't know why Jo makes such a big deal about them. As long as they get you from A to B. I'll phone you at home tonight, to see if you can get –'

'*No*,' Somoya's interruption sliced through Sarah's words un-characteristically. 'I'll phone you later.'

'Is something the matter?' What a stupid, obvious question, Sarah berated herself. She could easily imagine what it would take to rattle her like that: Jaz.

'It'll have to keep,' Sarah heard Somoya's throat constrict even more. 'Me android, I mean manager's, gawping. Damn cheek. It's not as if we're chock-a-block in here.'

'I'll write some anonymous hate mail about him and e-mail it to head office. Oh, before I forget, can you tell Jaz we need to meet an hour earlier at Marple Bridge, instead of our house? I've worked out the first clue and there's no point getting Andi to drive to our side of the city, just to head back out again.'

'Er... I meant to tell you. Jaz can't come. She's...' The split second delay grated. '... visiting her bloody nutty mother.' Somoya rushed on to avoid being challenged, 'So can I get a lift off you?'

'Any excuse to ride in a Porsche.'

'Listen, right,' Somoya sounded strangled, 'Are you sure about all this? Jo were only saying yesterday she didn't want any fuss making. Shouldn't we take her at her word? Don't want her stressing out.'

'Take no notice.' The basketwork scent of the carpet soured the air, as Sarah tried to breathe. 'Her fortieth has to be special.'

'I'm just saying, she might not be right chuffed. Couldn't we just have a cake and a quiet drink?'

Outside, children's shrieks sang down the street.

'What's all that stuff you keep telling me about Leos craving constant attention? Jo won't let us forget it if... Shh... that's her now. Listen, love, you look after yourself.' The full force of a bike wheel crashed into the front door, chipping the paintwork.

Nearby, she heard Jo trying to remain calm. 'Wait till I've opened it.'

Derrie burst through the door then jerked her bike to a sudden stop when she saw Sarah sitting naked on the hall floor.

Jo grinned appreciatively. 'Mmm. That's a nice sight.'

'Yes and it will be for the whole neighbourhood, if you two don't close the door.'

Jo noticed Sarah's hand still over the receiver. 'Who you ringing?'

'It's a secret. Never you mind.' As Sarah tapped the side of her nose, she saw Jo's smile dip. Sarah followed the neat herringbone design along the floor with her forefinger. Redesigning the house hadn't helped. She would rather have no carpets and Jo back to normal. She wondered whether the surprise she'd organised might stop Jo clouding over whenever she looked at her.

'Tell me the secret,' Derrie lowered her voice. 'Is it about sweets?'

'She's trying to get me to take her to the shops.' Lifting Derrie's bike clear of the hall, Jo swung it through to the kitchen.

'For a Pushpop,' Derrie clarified.

'I'll take her,' Sarah offered, putting the phone down. 'Change of shift. You have a rest, old lady.'

You're going to need it.

21

Five

Sod's law. As soon as Jo lowered herself into the scalding bath water, the phone rang. She contemplated leaving it. Then, knowing who it might be, she seized the nearest towel and trailed hot footprints down the stairs, hoping it wouldn't stop before she got to it.

'Yeah. It's me.'

Jo didn't know whether to feel relieved.

'Just wanna sort stuff out. About, you know,' Jaz's staccato style continued spitting down the line. 'About tomorrow. Can't get through to Somoya just now. Line's busy. Thought you could, you know, fill me in.'

Don't tempt me. 'How d'you mean?' Jo studied the dividing line across her body. Light tan above the waist. Bath-boiled skin below. Cradling the receiver between her cheek and shoulder, she struggled to wind the hand towel around her.

'You know. Times, etcetera, for tomorrow.'

Jo's conscience gave her a warning pinch. 'I'm not supposed to be in on it.' She told herself to stop stalling. Just give her what she wants and get rid of her. Some crappy birthday this was going to be. She didn't see why Sarah couldn't invite Somoya without that gobshite Jaz.

'It's just that, I'm staying at my mum's tonight. So I thought, I could meet you there.' In the street, a car alarm started up, a wounded wail that made Jaz's jerky speech virtually indecipherable.

'Hang on.' Jo dragged her hands dry along the towel and flicked through the message pad by the phone. Hidden inside the cardboard back cover, Sarah had written something. Without her contact lenses, it was hazy. She drew it level with her face and could just make out the looped scrawl merging into the flecked grey card, 'Ring Andi. 10.15 Marple Bridge.' A loose leaf of scribbled names was folded on top of the message. She almost smiled. Christ, Sarah was rubbish at keeping secrets. She repeated the information to Jaz, hung up and took the stairs two at a time back to the bath, still holding the list of names. She could see from the heavy lines scoring the page that a fair few had been crossed off.

In the heap of clothes on the bathroom floor, she felt for her glasses then stepped into the water. The lenses clouded on the end of her nose. Worse than useless. Tossing them back onto her crumpled T-shirt and jeans, she screwed her eyes up at the damp paper wilting in her hand. An inveterate list-maker, that was one of the things Sarah called herself. She had a knack for self-promotion. Full of sound-bites broadcasting acceptable versions of herself. That had to be one of her most irritating traits. Jo checked herself. There was no point blaming Sarah for the shit they were in, trying to kid herself that she didn't want her, didn't still want her like crazy. But she was too quick, that girl. Too quick to find fault.

She squinted to pull the words into focus and saw the bottom half of the page floating. Lifting it clear of the water, her own name mocked her. She deserved to be crossed off. Twelve pretty good years, close to being cancelled out.

Jo tried to stretch her cramped legs and, as usual, found them too long for the bath. The limp list laughed at her. There she was, right at the top. First the worst. Smudged. Then Derrie. Second the best. If she saw her name there in prime playground position, she'd be gloating, pointing at herself so no one could mistake who was undeniably, second the best. Our miracle girl. She still knows life's a joke.

Closing her eyes, Jo pressed at them, until the pain set off firework flashes. The rest of the rhyme taunted her. Third the dirty donkey. When she opened her eyes again, the driftwood cabinet moved in waves around the aquamarine walls and Sarah's display of holiday trophies wavered above the shelves. A filigree fan of coral: Christmas in Barbados. A chunk of lava rippled with tangerine lichen: Easter in Lanzarote. Barnacled sea-snail shells from summer in Southport. Holding the list high above the water, Jo submerged her head. The blood rushing in her ears amplified to a seashell roar. Sarah's collection could be as complete as it was ever going to get.

Blowing stinging water from her sinuses, she noticed that the next three names on the list had been slashed with an impatient pen. Friends who had already been claimed elsewhere, blurred and spread on the paper. The cooling water, grey with soap, lapped in a chilly rhythm against Jo's skin. She immersed as much of herself as possible under the surface. Ellie's name, fanning out inkily, was nearly indecipherable under scribble. She didn't understand how Sarah's sister had made it to the list in the first place, unless it was to deliberately wind Jo up. No, there was no way Sarah would do that with Derrie around. So, who did that leave? The last two names swelled in a pulpy blue sea. Somoya. Question mark. Somoya. Solid. As a rock. She'd be up there with the world's most wanted women, if it wasn't for Jaz. But Jaz's name wasn't on the list. Jo's muscles contracted involuntarily. What the hell had she done? She squeezed her eyes under a heavy thumb and forefinger, then read the last name.

Andi. Just about legible. Followed by another question mark. Sweet Andi. Sherbet lemon. Either Sarah wasn't sure if she was coming, or... This was the thinnest bleeding guest-list her birthday had produced for years. Fitting. Just deserts.

Six

The clear lemon of Jo's Acqua di Gio hung in the air. Sarah knew she had only seconds to decide what to say before Jo went out. A queasy thudding started against her breastbone. From the edge of their bed, Sarah stared as Jo stood in front of the mirror and dipped her finger into her contact-lens case. The tear-drop sliver balanced on her finger-tip and she leaned over to blink it in, while Sarah breathed the chemical taste of after-shave.

'Expensive perfume won't help.' The words were out of Sarah's mouth before she could censor them.

'You wha'? What you on about now?'

She could still smell lies prickling through Jo's sweat. Sarah warned herself to go easy.

'I could come with you.'

Tight shock registered on Jo's face. 'We haven't got a babysitter.'

Sarah was going to fight this. It would be an invisible brawl. No teeth. No nails. Just infinite perseverance. Anyway, there was Derrie. Jo wouldn't leave her. Not that Sarah would ever use her as a weapon. But, whoever this woman was, the three of them were going to out-live her.

'Ellie's always good at short notice. She could bring Becka over and put her to bed with Derrie.'

'The less your frigging sister's around Derrie, the better.'

'But they're mad about each other.'

'That's precisely the problem. How many times do we have to go over this? You sound like a BBC repeat. You know your sister can't be trusted. End of story.'

Sarah changed track. 'Is there another reason you don't want me to come with you?'

'Don't start, eh?' Her plaintive adenoidal tone made her sound adolescent and Sarah watched her pick up her comb, then put it down again when she realised she'd already run it through her hair.

Sarah waited to see if Jo could meet her eyes.

'Who's going to be there?'

'Not this again.' Jo shuffled through the notes in her wallet. 'You never used to get psychotic with jealousy.'

The top of Sarah's skull felt instantly open, sliced by a precision surgical instrument. She groped along to the top of the bed and leaned her back against the flat chill of the wall.

'You always used to give me straight answers,' she paused to lower her voice, aware of their sleeping girl in the next room. 'And don't give me any weak crack about gay answers. You're not funny.'

'It's a mystery to me why I haven't worked that out yet, since you've been telling me for years. I just thought... I didn't think you'd want to come with me. You always say clubs are too smoky and full of children.' Stone-faced, Jo stuffed money and keys into the back pocket of her pale jeans.

'Half of whom are my students.'

'Wouldn't do them any harm.' Jo sat down next to her, snaking an arm round Sarah and offering her neck a tentative, halfhearted kiss. 'Seeing their teacher enjoying herself.' The words 'for once' clung judgmentally to the end of the sentence.

'So, I'm coming with you, then?' It came out as a hiss.

Jo flicked a pained glance towards Derrie's bedroom, as if she could see her sleep being disturbed on the other side of the wall, while Sarah listened for clues in the dark pause.

'Well, you could. But Andi said she'd sorted out this special treat, or something, for me birthday.' She delivered the rest of her speech on the run and Sarah strained to hear as Jo took the stairs several at a time. 'She kind of sounded like she wanted us to spend some time on our own, since we haven't seen each other in weeks.'

The front door slammed.

'Not Andi,' Sarah whispered to herself. 'Surely it couldn't be Andi.'

Seven

Want to wee, but I'm too tired to... get up. Too tired to... Wish they'd be quiet. Sarah's too loud. I wanna sleep... wanna. I'm dead light now the duvet's fallen off... Floating. Can't see a thing... only tunnel dark. Have to feel my way, so I can speed into the white.

Auntie Ellie's there again. Her hair's like lightning. Yellow zigzags, waving at me.

'Glaring, bright as a desert,' she whispers and swipes at the strands crackling round her face. It's well weird when she starts hearing stuff in my head. 'About time,' she tells me off. 'I've been waiting ages. Thought Jo must've grounded you.' She does a sort of strange laugh. 'Kept you away from me, 'cos I'm *such* a bad influence.' I do breast-stroke through the air, pushing up higher towards her. 'See?' she asks me, 'we're over the threshold. Playing soaring euphoria.'

I'm not sure what that means. I know I'm flying, but I can't see my body.

She points underneath us. 'Got a bird's eye view of Sarah and Jo, down there by that pool.'

I've seen this before. They're much younger. Jo's hair's still black and Sarah's fat with me. The sun's hot on her belly, warming me. Holding me for Ellie. Mad bad Ellie. Well, that's what Ellie keeps saying.

'Once, we were moulded to each other like that.' She's pointing at Sarah's stomach. Her whispering is tickling the insides of my ears. Off again with her dorky talk. 'Me starting where you left off. Shuffled off...' Her throat sounds croaky. 'At least now, we can sometimes fit back together. But this time round you'll get a better deal and we can make up for dead time. Go back to blazing about.' I don't know why she keeps going on as if she's my real mum. I know it can't be true. I've seen the photos of when I first came out, with blood on my head, smearing onto Sarah's leg. 'Come on, you little runt, let's go down for a laugh. Wind those two up a bit.'

There's me, younger too. Skinnier. Reaching a lower pencil mark on the wall. The strings of this leopard-skin bikini keep slipping. It's far too big. Right. Got their attention. Made you look, made you stare, made the barber cut your hair.

'Tap Jo first,' Ellie says. 'She's always a soft touch.'

'Can I have an ice lolly yet?' My question makes Jo's forehead ripple, 'cos she doesn't understand what I've got to do with her. Makes me want to laugh, so I have to hold my breath to stop it.

She swims up to me and snorts water out of her nose, between her thumb and finger.

'I don't mind getting you one, girl, but you better ask your mum, eh?'

'Okay. Whatever.' I lift my flat palm to stop her speaking and hold the pose, like my friend Adesua does. Talk to the hand 'cos the face ain't listening.

Sarah's lying on the grass, making her eyes like slits, wondering who I am. Why I'm coming straight for her.

'She doesn't know about being our perfect timing,' Ellie murmurs. 'It'll work this time round. Sarah's a safe bet.' She starts singing next to Sarah's ear. Teasing her. 'How's the sad little scene, with the clean-living queen?'

Sarah can't hear her, but when I speak, she listens.

'Jo says I can have a lolly now.'

I know exactly what Sarah's thinking: Is this kid acting like she knows us for a joke? Or is she a smaller than average con artist? Her smile is all crooked. I definitely remember this – déjà vu – Sarah told me the translation once. Around again. No, not that. Seen before. It's pretty smart she can speak French, because that's where we are. Trespassing in a private health club. She doesn't know what to say to me. Strange seeing Sarah go dumb. She lifts her hand to scratch behind her ear. I do the same, like a mirror. Her right hand, my left.

'Are you all right? What's the matter with your head?' She sounds as if she's really bothered.

Say something. Make it up as you go along. 'Think I've got nits again.' I screw up my face to make it real and carry on scrubbing behind my ear. 'Did you bring the nit comb with us?'

I see the pink inside of her mouth as it opens with surprise. Then I hunt around for new inspiration.

'I saw a clitoris over there.' I fling my arm towards some flowery bush by the pool.

'What?'

'An' it quivered when I touched it.'

'What did it look like?'

'You *know*,' I tell her, pausing for a moment before my punch line, 'One of those things caterpillars turn into.' Then I wander away, leaving them both staring after me.

I take off, back into free fall and I hear them fading out behind me. At least Jo thinks it's funny. Her voice is smiling.

'She means a chrysalis.'

Sarah's in shock. 'She thinks she's ours.'

'Well... They're only lent to us, an' that!'

'Be serious, Jo. What do you really think?'

'Maybe she's checking us out before she's born.'

I spin and smile. Sucked up higher into the thinnest air.

'I thought that was before conception. Anyway, I can't believe a butch like you could fall for... How can you be so *bloody* calm, if you really think that's what just happened? You're kidding me, aren't you? Souls *choosing* their parents –'

'You're the only one who goes round promoting how tough I'm supposed to be. An' as for her, who knows about any of it? You don't.'

Sarah's answer slides through a sneer, 'There are more things in heaven and earth than are dreamt of in –'

'Maybe. And don't quote at me. I'm not one of your students.'

Sarah goes quiet for a while. 'Where's she gone?'

'Dunno.'

Slipping through. Permeating. Another word I got from Sarah. She tells me millions.

'Permeating like gas through muslin.' Ellie salutes goodbye to me with two fingers to her forehead.

In the next room, I can hear them trying not to wake me up.

'Wouldn't do them any harm, seeing their teacher enjoying herself.'

Sarah hisses. 'So I'm coming with you, then?'

I roll over, trying to find the covers. Frosty wind made moan... coming round. Slipping in... slipping out of sleep...

They're still puzzling by the pool.

'So, you reckon our unborn daughter just turns up to monitor our lolly-buying potential and our de-lousing abilities?'

'You don't have to be sarcastic. Anyway, we'll find out, won't we?'

'How?'

'We'll recognise her.'

Eight

Through the frosted glass door of the toilet, Jo could see Andi's out-line. Jo watched as the short figure unzipped her trousers and sat down. Under the soft lighting, Andi's hair resembled an orange aura. The shopping channel blared from a TV monitor inside the cubicle.

'How sad is that?' Jo called to her. 'The queue can spy on you watching telly, while you're trying to go.'

'Nah. I think it's a laugh, man. Performance art.' Andi's rising Geordie vowels sounded as sweet as chocolate. 'The other tape's miles better. They've got a video of the goings-on in the men's toilet up-stairs.' She stood up and smoothed her silk trousers into place, then shouldered the weight of the glass door, struggling with the effort of pushing it open.

'You got a weird sense of humour, you. They'd better not be taping us now. If Sarah was here, she'd complain to the manager about ram-pant commercialism and invasion of privacy.'

'More than likely.' Under the tap, steamy water trickled over the tips of Andi's fingers. 'She'd probably decide to shoot a docu-soap about it. "True toilet stories." Where is she anyway? I thought she was coming with you.'

Jo evaded her eyes. 'Too tired.'

'It's *you* that's done in, honey.' She felt Andi steer her by the shoulders, back to face the mirror. She was right. Exhaustion sagged in loose folds below her eyes. Jo rubbed her cheeks, trying to summon up some blood. But her tan stayed yellow. Sallow. Poisoned.

Jo pointed to the parallel lines cutting into the bridge of her nose. '*This* is what you've got to look forward to when you hit forty.'

With a small smile, Andi plucked at the tight design across her chest, realigning the printed pears into place over her plump breasts.

'Give over. There's more to it than that. You'll let us know what's up when you're ready.'

For one mad moment, Jo was tempted to tell her. Andi pulled a handful of boiled sweets from her pocket. A choice of traffic-light colours.

'Want one?'

The corners of Jo's mouth turned down. 'No. Won't go with me beer. That's if I ever get one.'

Andi unwrapped two of the sweets and pushed them both into her mouth, one inside each cheek.

'Mmm... Hamster,' she murmured, approving of the pouches they made as she inspected herself in the mirror. 'Anyway, happy birthday, you daft clown.' She pulled a khaki top from her bag and had to lift onto tiptoes to hold it against Jo. 'I got you something. You need dressing up.'

'Since when did punk come back?'

'Don't speak to us while I'm doing this. I've not got to grips with multi-tasking.'

Jo stood dead still while Andi pulled the worn black T-shirt over her head and deftly replaced it with the new one. Soft cotton brushed the down on Jo's arms to attention. Then one by one, Andi opened the zips along the sleeves and chest to reveal Jo's skin underneath.

Staring at her reflection, Jo looked uncertain. She fingered the intentionally visible label. 'Hope this thing didn't cost much.'

'A king's bloody ransom.' With a dressmaker's touch, Andi admired the details stitched into the cloth. Jo felt her stroke each perfectly fitted pleat down the length of her back. 'Don't be such an ungrateful bugger. It's a hell of a lot better than that scabby rag.' She hauled the washed out T-shirt from Jo's tight grip and dropped it into the bin.

Jo stooped to retrieve it. 'Hey! I like that.'

'Aye, well, if you want to dress from a dustbin.'

'You can't just chuck it away.'

'I can an' all.' Taking Jo's worried face between her hands, Andi spoke to her as if she was a child. 'Sometimes you've got to learn what's best for you.' Colouring a stubborn puce, Jo tried to straighten up. 'Do as you're told, or I'll tan your backside.' She squeezed Jo's still cupped cheeks. 'As soon as I find a stepladder.' Relinquishing her, Andi pushed her in the direction of the door. A Day-Glo poster swung towards Jo at eye level when she wrenched the handle. 'Lola's 80's nite,' loomed like a warning, in sixties bubble lettering.

As they climbed down the industrial metal steps, they could hardly make out their footing in the smoke haze. Dry ice obscured the edges of the open brickwork, the bobbing heads dancing below them and the stack of amplifiers, blasting out New Romantic tunes, which sounded simplistic with age.

'Just look at that lot.' Jo jabbed her thumb at the crowd. 'Baby dykes. They weren't even *born* when this music came out.'

'Does it make you feel old, our lass? Odds on they think they'll be dead before they make it to forty.'

'It's just weird. This is no big deal for any of them.' She targeted two girls, their faces bland with adolescence and their flat, exposed stomachs touching in a slow grind, destined to end up in a locked toilet within half an hour. 'When I was their age, I knew what I wanted too, funnily enough,' a brief smile touched the corners of her lips. 'As a matter of fact, by the time I was nine I'd had me hands down the knickers of half the girls on our estate. But no one ever talked about it. Nowadays...' God, that word made her sound like an auld antwacky mare. 'What I mean is, we never had anywhere to go. Now these kids think they own the clubs.'

Andi adjusted her tone to an ancient quaver and with trembling hands simulated advanced Parkinson's. 'Aye, and they don't realise how *lucky* they are, do they, pet?' She giggled and poked around with her fingers, searching for ticklish crevices between Jo's ribs. 'You're being a right old misery lately. A couple of months ago, you were telling us how brilliant it was, them having different chances.' Above the music, Jo heard her crunch the last glassy shards of her sweets. 'It's looking like I might have to find a new playmate.'

Jo's stomach clenched. She turned back towards the girls on the dance floor. Rainbows of refracted light bounced off the matching crystals in their navels.

'You should've brought your camera, shouldn't you? Those two would make a nice photo. You could've sold it for a feature on Manchester's club scene.'

Screwing up her nose, Andi wound a copper curl around her index finger and tugged. When she let it go, it sprung back into place like a component in a pretty mechanical toy and Jo caught the scent of spun sugar.

'I'm playing out tonight. Not working.' Andi adjusted the fine gold watch threaded around her wrist. 'It's your birthday in an hour and I'm going to see to it that you bloody *enjoy* it.' She slipped through the bodies at the bar reaching the two long clear glasses she'd signalled the barmaid for. As Andi handed the drinks over, Jo wondered how she always got served before everyone else.

'About this birthday business,' Jo started hesitantly. 'I know Sarah's planning something. But she keeps denying it. Please tell me she hasn't organised a surprise party.'

'She hasn't organised a surprise party.'

'Don't piss about. The truth. Swear on your cat's life. No, your camera's life.'

Before Andi could answer, Jo spotted a woman bulldozing the crowd, her eyes trained on them, as she swept a hand over her shaved head. The convex flesh of her stomach threatened to tear the buttonholes down the front of her shirt. Jo had seen this nutter in action before. Sensing what was about to happen, she drew Andi in close.

'All right?' the woman asked Andi. The whining Salford accent confirmed Jo's opinion, even before the woman insinuated her bulk between them.

'Fine, thanks,' Andi replied.

'Didn't you take them pictures of that hypnotist last week?'

'Butt in, why don't you? You know what they say about familiarity.' Easing her arm round Andi's shoulders, Jo honed her tone, ready to slice. 'That the fella you told me about, Andi? The famous Salford hypnotist who makes all the girls get pregnant by the time they're thirteen and turns all the lads into scumbags.'

Andi's pastel skin flushed pink as she shrugged Jo's arm away. 'I never said –'

Taking advantage of Andi's outrage, the woman swerved in. The gaping stretch of her shirt revealed rolls of midriff unfolding. 'Are you with her?'

'Nah.'

Jo wondered how the hell to make Andi listen, before the woman got out of hand.

'Let me buy you a drink. What's your name? Andi? ' The woman swaggered with the overconfidence of the inadequate. 'I'm celebrating.' She refused to elaborate, stage-managing the silence, for maximum attention.

Andi picked up the cue. 'Celebrating what?'

What're you doing Andi? Jo thought. Don't go getting into this.

'Just got me pilot's licence.' Beer slurred her speech and slopped over the brim of her pint glass as she tilted it, oblivious. Unexpectedly, she swung round to the D.J. box and bellowed. 'Play *fuckin'* "I Will Survive," I've asked yer *three* times.' Without missing a beat, she returned to her conversation with Andi. 'Been my ambition since I was a kid in the ATC. Flew a jump jet today. You know. Like in *Top Gun*.

Top speed of Mach three.' Her chest expanded visibly. 'That's a thousand miles an hour.'

Through her vodka, Jo spluttered a deliberate challenge. 'Oh, aye. How long did it take you to get your licence then?'

'Nine hours.'

Jo stepped back out of the woman's range. 'You haven't got a clue.'

'What you trying to say?'

'You're a sad case.' Jo winked at Andi. 'Next thing she'll be telling you is she's an alien abductee with a probe up her arse.'

The woman rolled her shoulders, preparing for trouble. Jo felt her fists tighten.

'Let's go.' Andi linked her arm through Jo's. 'I'm hungry, anyway.'

With her jaws stretched and a dog-fight stare fixed on the woman, Jo refused to move. 'Why should we?'

'If you don't stop acting like an arsehole, I'm going without you. It's like you came out tonight itching for a scrap.'

Andi marched away with her chin high, so indignant that her five-foot frame appeared tall. As she followed her to the stairs, Jo heard someone calling Andi's name. Checking over her shoulder, she saw a tall woman making slow progress towards them. Walking wounded. All bony angles, topped with wispy, black, baby hair, clutching something to her chest.

'Andi! I'll see you tomorrow then?' the tall woman asked. Her eyes shone, welling up, dreading the answer.

Another bloody bee to honey, Jo thought.

'Yeah. See you.' Andi flushed.

The woman's arms clamped around the cushion she was holding like a security blanket. Her chalky complexion made her resemble a black and white photo from another era. Cupping Andi's elbow, Jo steered her away.

At the top of the steps, Jo stopped her with a tense hand. 'Who was that?'

'Her name's Charlotte.' Andi walked into the cool air of Canal Street.

'Where d'you know her from?'

'Here actually. Tonight. While I was hanging about waiting for you.' She glanced up pensively at the converted warehouse opposite, as if she might be considering a late-night visit to one of the loft apartments inside. 'I saw her sitting on her own, looking... scared.'

'Sarah's right about you and lame dogs.' Jo ignored Andi's hurt frown. 'What are you seeing her tomorrow for?'

'Why are you so interested?'

'I said, what's happening tomorrow?'

Tapping the side of her nose, Andi stifled a slight smile.

'Keep your neb out of it, Pinocchio.'

'You got to be kidding! You'd break four years of celibacy for *that*?' Jo scratched at the scarlet patches forming around her throat.

Andi stared as if she didn't recognise her. 'Sometimes I dunno why I bother with you.'

'Because I'm so –'

'Because you're so vile, you make us look good in comparison. Come on. I need fried chicken.'

Every bar lining the canal heaved with skimpily dressed drinkers. They crushed against the plate glass and chrome interiors and spilled out onto the narrow street. Jo's attention was caught by the clatter of an aluminum can being kicked. The small boy strolling after it looked wasted. Despite his bleary vision, he managed to hook his toe under the beer can and chip it over the low stone wall. It landed softly in the sludge of the dredged canal. At the last moment, Jo swerved to avoid a flutter of pigeons around a meaty pile of vomit.

Her mouth twisted. 'Disgusting.'

'Mm...' Andi smacked her lips in childish exaggeration. 'Reheated leftovers. Funny how food's always more tasty the second time round.'

Jo squinted, as if contemplating someone insane. 'By the way, I was wondering, have you... er... seen your other mini-mate recently?' Andi's attempt to make her enquiry sound casual headlined it in bold.

'Who?' Jo shut off immediately.

'Don't jump down my throat. I meant Somoya.'

'No. She's probably too busy getting beaten up.'

Rage hardened Andi's voice. 'You're not amusing, you know.'

Jo considered telling her she wasn't the first one to say that tonight, then decided against it when she saw Andi massaging the bridge of her nose.

'I thought she was your mate,' Andi said. 'You sound as if you don't even like her.'

'She's sound. But there's a limit to how often you can be sympathetic when –'

'You reckon she brings it on herself?'

'No. But she's taking a hell of a time to do something about it. If Jaz was a man, she'd have been locked up by now.'

A neon chicken burned yellow above Andi, outlining her curls. 'Want something?'

Jo shook her head.

'OK, you can share mine.'

Jo leant against the wall of the takeaway and tracked the progress of a rat bounding along the cobbles, hugging the canal wall before making a leisurely dash for the cover of Sackville Park. Among the trees, the AIDS memorial spiralled into the sky like a metallic candle. Lit from inside, it shone with hearts, which looked as if they had been stamped out with a pastry cutter.

'Mmm... I love the spices they put on this stuff.' Grease glossed Andi's lips and fingers as she offered the red and green carton to Jo.

'Not hungry.'

'What's *up* with you, man?' Andi stopped on the corner and the concrete weight of a multi-storey car park overshadowed them. 'Not eating? Not dancing?'

Jo met her eyes for long seconds. She'd got to tell her soon. Might as well be now. A screech of brakes interrupted the pause between them. Ahead, she could see a large crowd gathered around a taxi rank on Bloom Street. Through the straining bodies, Jo caught a glimpse of a red BMW executing a bumpy reverse manoeuvre. Then it accelerated forward again, to the accompaniment of a shocked moan from the on-lookers. As they herded each other back, the heap in the road twitched. A body. Pumping adrenaline urged Jo to fling herself in front, hammering the bonnet, in case there was a remote chance he was still breathing. But before she could move, the car climbed its ob-stacle course for a third time and sped off round the corner. Disbelief rang round the crowd.

'Hit him, then reversed back over him –'

'... not a hit and run. Knocked him down, then ran over him again.'

Chicken grease she had only inhaled rose in Jo's throat. Swallowing the sick, helpless taste, she faced Andi.

'See? If you had your camera, you could've sold the exclusive and helped the police with their enquiries.'

Ash white, Andi's copper freckles stood out in stark relief. '*Listen* to yourself.'

'Well, what do you want me to do?'

'Phone an ambulance?'

'I think that's taken care of, don't you?' Jo indicated the mobile phones all around them singing electronic numbers in unison.

'Don't try an' make out you're a hard knock, it's us you're talking to. Don't forget I know you're soft as shite.'

'He'll be dead, anyway.'

Andi's head drooped, unable to meet her eyes anymore.

'*What?*' Jo demanded. 'One less piece of scum in the world. So what?'

'There speaks the voice of a social worker.'

'No need to spare any tears for *him*.' Jo cleared her full, salty throat. 'He's bound to be part of some drugs gang.'

'You're kidding no one. I'm away home.' Over her shoulder, Andi waved her fingers sarcastically. 'Thanks for a cracking evening.'

Jo sagged against the wall, covering her face with her hands and wondered what the hell she was doing.

When she looked up again, she noticed someone with his back to the crowd. The tall man stood opposite her. Unnaturally still. No one else could take their eyes off the dead body, but this one just seemed to have a particular problem with her. Deciding he was one headcase too many for one night, she set off for the car park.

'Excuse me.' It was him. 'Did you see what happened?' He targeted her more closely.

Jo shrugged. 'Some fella reversed over someone.'

Doubt cleared from his eyes. He gave himself a slight nod, as if he'd confirmed something about her. Jo tried to remember if she'd seen him before. Those rimless glasses, the thinning dark hair. Or maybe he was planning on robbing her.

'OK. Thanks.' He waited as she walked into the dim light of the multi-storey.

On the first floor, Jo located her Xsara in seconds. As she unlocked it, she glanced back to check there was no brick aimed at her head. She got in quickly and slammed the car door, hearing the echo bounce around the dark space. The key slipped in her fingers and when she tried to turn it, the ignition locked.

'Come on,' Jo yanked at the resistant steering lock and finally managed to start the engine.

As she reached the barrier and leaned out of the window to feed her ticket into the machine, she warned herself to get a grip.

Turning right and then right again, onto Bloom Street, she saw a white Fiesta pull away from the pavement behind her. At the end of the road, Jo braked for the oncoming traffic, indicated and veered onto Princess Street. The white car did the same, then followed her as she branched off to the right. For a second, Jo debated doing a U-turn, but she knew that was taking paranoia too far. The lights at the crossroads would sort it out. When they stopped, she'd be able to see the driver. The instant Jo braked, the Fiesta slowed to a crawl to let a Saab cut in. But even with that in between, Jo could make out the glare of his glasses. Stupid bald fucker. Did he really think she wouldn't spot him?

Who the hell was he anyway? Mentally, Jo filed through the clients she'd had over the years who'd been particularly pissed off. Changing into fifth, she slammed her foot to the floor, swerving off Oxford Road past the BBC. If the lights hadn't been against her, she'd have lost him already. Jo didn't want to think about what he wanted. None of her mates at work were immune to the reports from the child protection team that featured distraught fathers and sawn-off shotguns. Her tongue dried to the roof of her mouth. She had to calm down. Breathe. Had to stop letting everything get to her. He was probably just on his way home.

As the Hulme Arch curved overhead, Jo watched him let two more cars overtake him on the bridge. He had to be an even bigger moron than he looked, if he thought tailing her that badly in a frigging white car, she wouldn't see his every move.

'Come on then, you tosser,' she spat. 'Put your foot down. Let's see what that crappy Fiesta can do.'

Heading over the crossroads at The Whalley pub, she jumped the amber. He tore through on red. Soft shite. Jo couldn't believe he was trying to race her in a J-reg. She took her right hand off the wheel to wipe her palm along her jeans. What in fuck's name was going on? Just as she hit sixty, Jo registered the flash of a speed camera. She hoped there was no film in the thing. She couldn't afford to get any more points on her licence. Without thinking, she swung left on to College Road. She'd get rid of him round these small roads. Use the cover of the trees. Executing a series of erratic turns, she knew she'd lost him. She drove on automatic pilot the last couple of streets to home.

Pulling into the drive, she pressed her sore chest, trying to force some air in. It felt as if concrete had set in her lungs. Shakily, she secured the handbrake and let her wet forehead drop to the steering wheel.

'What have I done?' she asked. 'What the hell have I done?'

SATURDAY

Nine

Carrying a blanket to the car, Sarah steered Derrie around a sludgy coiled pile on the pavement. 'Watch the dog poo!'

'Why? Does it do tricks?' Comic timing perfected, Derrie's slight smile betrayed her pride at this new addition to her repertoire. 'Andi says, "Mind you don't stamp in that cacky."'

'It's terrible.' Sarah's mouth dipped with nausea at the idea of the stinking mess spread under Derrie's shoes.

Hands on hips, Derrie paused and transformed into the sixty-year-old member of Neighbourhood Watch who lived two doors away from them. 'I'm going to get them prosecuted. As soon as I see whose dog it is, they're in for the full fine.'

At any minute Sarah hoped Jo would have a brilliant surprise, but she needed to get her outside to appreciate it.

'Please can you run and ask Jo if she'll help us load up?'

Derrie skidded back inside.

While she waited, Sarah inspected the house for any windows beckoning in open invitation. Overnight, a burgundy flush had rushed through the veins of the Virginia creeper. It clung to their Edwardian semi announcing the end of the summer holidays. The exquisite shade filled Sarah with apprehension. She tore with her teeth at the ragged skin around her thumb at the thought of autumn term at college, minus thirty of her redundant colleagues. She still didn't know whether to count herself lucky that she was one of those who would be going back.

'What's the face for?' Jo asked, hefting a cardboard box full of food into the boot.

'Just steeling myself for going back next Monday. Not sure if I'll cope.'

Holding the car door open for Derrie, Jo raised one eyebrow at Sarah.

'You always say that. Until all your students decide they want to cultivate you as their replacement mother, or something even more dodgy.'

'What d'you mean?' Derrie piped up from the back seat. 'Do they still all think they're Steven Spielberg?'

Jo slid into the driver's seat and began fiddling with the crook lock. Sarah glanced up and down their street. She'd have to stall.

'It's not them.' Sarah pretended to be looking for something in the boot. 'It's the new ranks of agency staff I'll have to work with.'

'Time you left that dump anyway.' Sarah heard Jo's strangled irritation with a worn-out subject and registered the way she stabbed the key into the ignition. 'You'll give yourself a heart attack before *you're* forty. It's only work, Sarah. At this rate, you'll be on your deathbed, rattling on,' her voice dropped to a toothless lisp, while her face crumpled into the wrinkles of an octogenarian. 'My... *deepest* regret...is not... working longer hours.' Then she smiled. 'Come on. Get in. Forget it, you gorgeous creature. It's my birthday. We're supposed to be enjoying –' Her hand paused on the key as she saw the car driving towards them. 'Derrie! Just get a load of this. A Porsche Carrera 911. Arctic silver. Three-point-three turbo-charged. Top of the range. Customised. You're talking seventy-two grand. "A legend never dies, it's simply reborn." Wait... Wha' the? That's Somoya driving. What's she doing with...?'

Somoya pulled in alongside and stuck her head out of the window.

A childlike grin played on her face as she waited for Jo to speak.

'Whose is that?'

The grin got younger. 'Yours.'

'What d'you mean?'

'For the day, any road. Sarah hired it for you.'

'To match your distinguished streaks.' Sarah leaned down and raked her nails through the hair over Jo's ears.

'Oh my God! Oh my *God*!' Jo jumped out of the Xsara and squeezed Sarah into a vice forged from her arms. Sarah imagined deep blue bruises forming.

Resting her mouth on Jo's ear, she whispered, 'Thank goodness she hasn't brought Jaz,' and felt Jo flinch.

Derrie poked her head in between them. 'Why?'

'Someone's earwigging.'

'You weren't supposed to hear that,' Sarah added.

Dropping Sarah abruptly, Jo sprinted into the road, shouting at Somoya. 'Move over.' Stopping to lay her hand possessively on the roof of the car, her eyes probed the quiet, early morning to see if any of their neighbours were paying attention. None of the curtains moved.

But, at that moment, Sarah saw, thirty paces along the double-parked street, a man slump forward in the front of a white car, cleaning his glasses. She jumped. Even from behind she recognised him. Same sparse hair. Same curve to his spine. Colin. How on earth had he found them? She checked whether Jo had spotted him, but she was too busy admiring herself inside the Porsche. How come she hadn't seen him? She had the nerve to call Sarah unobservant. Still, Jo had only glimpsed him once, at a distance. And he'd lost even more of his hair since Sarah last met him. Nine and a half years ago. She felt certain that faded clips of Colin didn't replay like a looped repeat in Jo's mind. Colin handing over drops of himself, swilling inside a clear plastic container. No one would ever give Sarah anything more precious. And now he was here. As pale as Derrie. How the hell had he tracked Sarah down? What did he want with *her* anyway? She'd made it clear to him that the sperm was for someone else, not for her. Sarah knew she must've been mad. How could she have used it? From a complete stranger? She'd been desperate, far too desperate. She wondered how often he had watched them. A sharp spasm hit her stomach.

'You're all right, Sarah,' Jo called. 'No rush. We're only blocking the road.'

Stumbling towards their house, Sarah shouted over her shoulder. 'Just got to... lock up.'

In the white car, he placed a mobile phone to his ear. Sarah ran an imagined conversation through her head:

'Hello?'

'Colin, where are you? You've got Mrs Redmond here, waiting to view 82, Woodhead Road.'

'Morris, I'm sorry. I was going to call, but... I must've had something that disagreed with me last night. I've not slept for running to the toilet.'

'Right. Suppose I'll have to manage without you. Try a hair of the dog.'

'You know I don't drink. Look, I'll have to go. It's urgent –' He cut the connection.

In the hall, Sarah programmed the code into the alarm with skittering fingers. As she turned the key she realised that they weren't going to drive past him, so she wouldn't be able to see his face. She had to be careful. Maybe paranoia was playing games with her. Until she knew for sure it was him, she couldn't talk about this to anyone.

In the back of the Porsche, Somoya had flung herself across the graphite-grey leather and wrapped her arms round Derrie.

Clicking into her seatbelt, Sarah leaned over to kiss Jo's cheek. 'It's even got back seats, this model.'

A glint of mild sarcasm showed in Jo's eyes. 'Right. Let's buy a couple, then.' She revved the engine, 'Listen to that, six cylinders.'

Reverently, she stroked the steering wheel, making the leather speak in a dragging whisper. As she shifted into gear and released the handbrake, the tips of her fingers followed the swirling grain of the light burr maple. When she accelerated gently, they shot forward. 'Feel that *rush*... That power.'

'What's that computer screen thing?' Derrie asked.

'A computer,' Jo answered. 'Look and tell me what the outside temperature is.'

'Twenty-one degrees C.'

Sarah saw the intensity and didn't understand. But she allowed herself to relax slightly into the supple leather seat, knowing she'd got something right for once.

Jo touched the black gloss control panel and the sunroof slid open silently. On the empty main road, she eased her foot down. 'What speed d'you think we're doing?'

'Well over the limit,' Sarah warned.

'Go faster!' Derrie sang from behind.

'Cruising at sixty-five and you can't even feel it.'

'Slow *down*, Jo,' Sarah ordered. 'Wait till we get to the motorway.'

Still speeding, they streaked past acres of Southern Cemetery in seconds, the gravestones flickering lichen green under the trees.

Chipmunk giggles erupted from behind Sarah. She pulled down the sunscreen to find out from the mirror what the pair of them were doing. Derrie reached up and looped one of Somoya's dark curls round her finger as she listened to her. The sight made the fluff on the back of Sarah's neck stiffen, setting off a tingle along her shoulders. She wished she were the one near enough to breathe in Derrie's apple scent and nose the silkiest skin at her temples. She'd do *anything* to protect her from him. Anything. Sarah chewed at the skin around her thumbnail until she tasted blood.

'Go on.' Somoya nudged Derrie. 'Ask Jo, she might know 'cos she's from Liverpool.'

'Okay, Jo, how can you tell it's cold in Liverpool?'

'Don't be starting with that again, you scallies.'

Derrie spluttered into Somoya's neck making the punch line practically unintelligible. 'The Scousers have all got their hands in their own pockets.' The rising delight in her voice peaked in a series of squeaks.

Unzipping her make-up bag, Sarah smiled. 'It's like having two kids in the back.' Even to her own ears, her tone sounded too old. In the mirror her eyes were an intolerant green. But the soft warmth of the rest of her features surprised her. She would have expected some evidence of the past week's grief. Nothing... except her hair had gone crazy again. Far too long. She ought to cut it off, so she looked exactly how she felt. Shaved. She drew a quick layer of lipstick over her mouth and tasted Parma Violets.

'See these?' Derrie scraped the elastic band off a towering well-thumbed pack of cards and shuffled through them next to Somoya's nose. 'That one's so rare I could sell it for thirty pounds.'

'Just for one of them ones?'

The volume of cards proved unmanageable in Derrie's small hands so Somoya took them from her.

'That one's called Ghastly,' Derrie continued. 'It's got sleeping gas powers and it's Haunter evolved. That's Dugtrio and –'

'It's Diglet evolved,' Sarah interrupted.

Derrie clicked her fingers. 'Correct!'

Hazel-coloured curiosity filled Somoya's eyes. 'How d'you know that, you?'

'I test her every night.' Derrie sounded proud of her mother's achievement.

Somoya thumbed seriously through the images of strange creatures. 'Test *me*.'

'If we win the treasure hunt, yeah, I'm gonna to buy some Fossil and Rocket ones. With ten pounds you can get four packets.'

'What treasure hunt?' Jo asked.

Reaching back, Sarah plucked at Derrie's red Pokémon T-shirt and

Pikachu tracksuit bottoms. 'You're a marketing team's dream, aren't you?'

'No. I'm not affected by adverts. Only Pokémon stuff. Soon I'll have them all.'

'What treasure hunt?'

In one swift flourish, Sarah slipped a gold envelope out of her bag and circled it in the air. 'This one. First car to finish wins a surprise holiday.' Then she smiled sadly at Derrie. 'I'm sorry, love, but this Pokémon business is a con. It's not possible to collect them all.'

'Yes, you can, if you buy –'

'Just listen a minute. It said in the paper that in America packs containing certain cards were only on sale in particular states, so you'd have to spend a fortune trying to find –'

'They wouldn't hide them like that.'

'Believe me, Derrie,' Sarah caught herself sounding weighty and pompous again. 'Companies will do anything to make massive profits.' She saw Jo glancing at the shiny envelope, wondering whether to ask again.

Derrie grew still, concentrating with her whole body, until relief melted through her. 'Anyway, right, that's in America. They wouldn't do that in England.'

A blue sign blurred by, indicating the motorway a short distance ahead. 'Right,' Sarah pointed towards it. 'Head onto the M60 towards Stockport.'

'Do I get to know where we're going?'

The envelope gleamed in the sun as Sarah opened it. 'See if you can guess the first clue. I think I've worked it out. "Start at ten-thirty, in this village south of Manchester... Cinnamon babe. Is she, **or** isn't she? Or should the tabloid reporters go back to school?"'

The pages of a map book crackled in the back seat as Somoya flipped to the index.

'They used to be your favourite band, Derrie,' Sarah prompted.

'Who?'

'*Think*. What's cinnamon?'

'Spice. Spice Girls.' She puckered her top lip in a dismissive sneer. 'They never were my best band.'

'Mel C,' Jo chipped in. 'And she swears blind she's not.'

'Keep thinking,' Sarah instructed, thrusting the card towards her. 'There's a clue in the bold type.'

'I'm *driving*.'

'Mel or...' Somoya leaned forward, poking her head between the front seats. 'Mellor. It's not far from Marple. Too clever for you lot, I am.'

'You've got it!' Sarah said, studying the sheet she had printed out the day before. 'Says here that there are two clues planted in each of four different locations.'

A low-flying jet, coming in to land at Manchester Airport, dipped towards the distant layers of the Pennines. Jo ducked her head under the sunscreen to follow the progress of something hovering over the central reservation.

'It's a kestrel! Fan-bloody-tastic!' She slapped the steering wheel. 'Got its eye on breakfast.'

Derrie craned her neck violently. 'I just saw a horse with green skin.'

Jo scanned the flickers of grass against the concrete. 'Where?'

'Must've been a mouldy horse,' Derrie decided, happily.

'Maybe,' Sarah began warily. 'It was wearing one of those coat things.' Even as she spoke, Sarah wished that sometimes she could prevent herself offering the voice of adult reason.

'No. It was definitely mouldy.'

It was one thing to encourage Derrie's fertile imagination, Sarah decided, quite another dealing with the children at school calling her odd every day.

'You know that's not possible.'

Ignoring Sarah again, Derrie tilted her head high and pursed her lips, affecting nonchalance. 'Anyway, I'm nine in twelve weeks.'

Nearly nine. Sarah sighed. A sheltered naive nine. 'What's that got to do with anything?' She continued to push, even though she was used to not being able to follow Derrie's conversational leaps. That kind of communication came straight from Jo. Definitely. As well as the predilection for anything physical. The shed climbing, the desperation to be outside on her bike, the shaking impatience with anything resembling schoolwork. Proved that biology didn't always count for much, Sarah thought. It didn't matter how long she'd lugged her around in an iron-weight belly, Derrie still seemed determined to become a little clone of Jo. Gazing out the window, Sarah saw the smoky blue glass pyramid of the Co-operative Bank sail past, reflecting the sky.

Derrie launched into song. 'Suck a fanny, suck a fanny –'

Sarah tensed. 'Where's that from?'

'Dunno.'

Jo and Somoya stayed quiet, both concentrating on the road.

'Did you make it up?'

'I guess so.'

'Or did you hear it at school?'

'Yes. At school. Suck a fanny.'

Leaning backwards in her seat, Sarah continued. 'Oh, really?' A brief shadow crossed them as the car darted under the looping Victorian archways of Stockport Railway Bridge. 'Who were they talking about?'

'Dunno. Maybe you and Jo.'

'Well,' she heard her own overly breezy intonation and cringed, 'That's one way of making love. You can tell them they're right if you want.'

Derrie screwed her face up into unrecognisable folds. 'Er! Crusty! Nasty.'

'You're not...' Sarah paused. 'You're not being bullied, are you?'

'No.'

'Sure?'

Derrie nodded, leaving Sarah far from certain. She knew she'd have to broach this conversation again later, when Derrie was off-guard. Come at it indirectly to prise free a few more scraps of detail that she might be able to jigsaw together. Her mind leapt, linking to her own terror. Derrie had no way of knowing yet that bullying didn't stop in the playground.

Now that guy knew where they lived, Sarah realised, he could find out their names. Start proceedings against them for visiting rights. Or worse.

Ten

Somoya stared out at the massive detached houses nearly hidden behind densely planted trees. Old trees, she reflected, as they sped by. Ash interwoven with beech, weeping willows and oaks. It looked quiet. If she could get just one day's peace out here, maybe she'd be able to work out what to do. She sighed, filtering a controlled stream of air through virtually sealed lips.

'It's a right relief to be getting out of Manchester.'

'Yes,' Sarah agreed. 'I'd avoid getting into that subject with Andi though. Apparently, she's got an allergy to the great outdoors.'

'Andi's coming?' Jo snapped.

'Who's she?' Somoya asked.

'Jo's new friend,' Derrie informed her. 'She's got hair like orange candyfloss. You don't know her,' she concluded authoritatively.

'Andi's definition of the countryside is, "Too green. Not enough shops."' Sarah explained.

Somoya felt herself grimace. 'I'll not be keen on her, then.'

Jo twisted her neck to catch her eye. 'The strange thing is, you *will* be. Everyone is.'

Cynicism emanated from Somoya, as she made up her mind even more firmly not to go along with the views of the rest of the world.

'She's like that line from the Christmas carol,' Sarah's smile strained even more. 'Joyful and triumphant.'

Derrie reached for Somoya's hand, making her wince as she transmitted her excitement through a series of squeezes. 'Jo and me call her the bikini queen.'

'I've a feeling I don't want to know this, but go on, then. Why?'

Sarah slid into an exaggerated professorial tone. 'Probably her preferred mode of attire.'

Derrie pinched more strenuously. 'No. It's 'cos she's got so *many*. Special ones with labels.'

'*Well*,' Sarah paused for dramatic effect. 'You might be interested to know, she's bringing someone with her.'

'Who?'

Somoya noticed that Jo seemed disturbed by this new information, as if she'd been entitled to know before Sarah. Pausing deliberately, Sarah waited to see if Jo would incriminate herself further.

There were more trees than houses now and, as the car cut through a dark overhang of branches, Somoya glimpsed the blue promise of hills.

'She wouldn't say. Just went all mysterious on me. Anyway, it's about time. Never mind dry spell, from what Jo tells me, that girl's been suffering a drought. I don't understand it. I've met her. She's pretty and funny –' Sarah directed her next comment straight at Somoya. 'I've told her how nice *you* are.'

'You had to lie a bit, then?' Somoya replied.

Derrie began bouncing off the upholstery in anticipation. 'Are we nearly there yet? I'm gonna find the first clue before anyone else.'

'How have you managed to keep this a secret, you little minx?' Jo asked. 'You usually can't keep your gob shut for love nor money.' Her expression hardened. 'I don't believe this joker.' She jutted her chin at a petrol tanker hurtling past. 'Snidy little trucker. I'm doing fifty and he's *overtaking* me. Get in the way of one of them and you'd be very dead, I tell you.'

Ahead, at the bottom of the steep hill, Somoya saw the stone bridge over the River Goyt, then noticed fuchsia flushing Jo's throat.

'Well, why are you accelerating?' Sarah asked. 'How clever is it to race *that*?'

Jo's jaw set cold. 'There's no point having a Porsche, if you have to sit behind things.'

All Somoya's muscles ached from avoiding a string of imaginary pile-ups.

'Stop being *ridiculous*,' Sarah reached a patronising crescendo. 'You've gone crimson. *For Christ's sake*, you idiot, slow down.'

Trying to diffuse the tension, Somoya adopted a full-mouthed, tobacco-chewing, Texan accent. 'Now, hold on there, red neck. I said, hold on. Ain't no chasing going on 'til I say so, I said, 'til I say so.'

Jo lifted her right foot slightly and the car responded. 'Here you are. Marple Bridge.' She checked the dashboard. 'Ten-thirteen. Excellent timing.'

'Hey.' Derrie pointed at a new black Mini parked near the bridge. 'Who's that with Andi?'

Jo strained to get a better view of the person in the passenger seat.

Sarah aimed a wide smile at Jo. 'Maybe Andi's finally found a soul-mate.'

From a distance, Somoya watched two women emerge from the Mini. The small one strolled towards them, past a row of cottage shops and black Victorian street lamps, hung with huge globes of Busy Lizzies.

As she reached them, Sarah touched Andi's shoulder, which radiated pink under orange freckles. 'What the hell happened to you?'

'I went an' fell asleep in the sun, didn't I?' Andi's smile mixed self-deprecation with pride. 'It's awful sore.'

The flood of dropped consonants caught Somoya, making her listen more attentively.

Quickly, Sarah took a tube of Derrie's sunblock out of her bag and smeared thick white patches into Andi's skin. 'You won't do that again, will you?'

'I can't promise anything.' Andi basked in the special treatment as if it was well deserved. 'I'm a slow learner.'

'Somoya, come here.' Sarah beckoned to her. 'This is Andi.'

Somoya noted the way Andi's hair corkscrewed to her shoulders, like melting copper wire, perfectly colour co-ordinated with her freckles. She managed to mumble, 'Hi,' but unable to hold Andi's amused gaze, her focus drifted down. Slung over her shoulder, a Pentax hung on a worn leather strap like an expensive accessory. Andi's azure T-shirt, printed with creamy cumulus designs, stretched tightly over her breasts. The cotton wool clouds looked plump as fruit. An invitation to test for ripeness. Heat rushed to Somoya's cheeks as her eyes retreated even lower. The muslin shorts showed Andi's skin and traces of lace beneath. The whole ensemble had probably cost a fortune. She wanted to dismiss it as a ridiculous waste of money, but next to her Somoya felt faded. Faded and irritable. Hunting for an escape, she lifted her eyes to the sloping horizon and her chest expanded as she realised she might be able to breathe properly in the open air.

'It's magic out here, in't it?'

Right on cue, Andi sneezed. 'Too much green. Not enough shops.'

'Yeah,' Somoya said tartly. 'I've heard.'

'I'm allergic to countryside.' Wrinkling her nose, Andi tried to resist the tickling pollen. 'In the city, I can pretend I'm a big tough dyke. But places like this just make us disintegrate into a sniveller.' As if to illustrate her point, she snuffled into an already shredded tissue.

'Tough dyke? At five foot one?' Against her will, Somoya's lips curved up slightly. 'With that hair?'

Andi pouted like an indignant infant. 'I'm as tall as *you*, man!'

Jo towered over them. 'That's not saying a lot.'

In unison, they both jerked their chins up to object. 'Cheek!'

At the toss of Andi's hair, a hint of some kind of confectionery reached Somoya. Candyfloss, to match the clouds her curls made around her face. Derrie had been right. Somoya wondered how Andi kept away wasps. But even if they swarmed round her, she felt sure, Andi would never get stung. Fine, coiled insect tongues would just flick at her and come away sweet.

Sarah turned to include the dark-haired woman sitting on a bench beside the parked cars, on the approach to the bridge.

'Andi. Aren't you going to introduce us to your mystery guest?'

Pressed against the shade of a privet hedge, Somoya saw the tall pale woman look up. Pink guilt flushed Andi's sunburn even deeper.

Eleven

'Sorry, Sarah,' Andi indicated with an open smile and both palms upright in surrender. 'This is Charlotte.'

The woman stood up unsteadily and made her way towards them with studied care, as if sudden movement might cause her limbs to unhinge. Sarah took in the stooped shoulders, concave body and china doll make-up and her hackles rose. What on earth was Andi doing with this cling-on? Feigning polite interest, she leaned forward and something musky came off Charlotte.

'Hi, nice to meet you,' Sarah lied, holding out her hand. Charlotte's bone fingers clung together before flapping into an ineffectual shake. Sarah waited for her to speak, but only heard an indifferent silence. 'Have you known Andi a while?'

Before another silence could lengthen, Andi answered for her. 'Nah. We met up in town last night. She fancied coming along.'

Sarah widened her eyes with sarcasm. Fabulous. And you land us with her.

Andi had stopped listening. Sarah followed her eyes to the bridge where Derrie and Somoya faced each other, threading their fingers together. Steadying herself, Derrie climbed on to Somoya's feet and managed several robot steps, before they stumbled apart. The breeze carried another layer of Charlotte's smell towards her. Something cloying from Avon. Beautiful day for gatecrashing a friend's party, Sarah thought. Then feeling somehow in the wrong, she gave Charlotte another chance.

'So. Do you work in Manchester?'

'Charlotte designs web sites. Freelance.'

For Christ's sake, Andi. Can't the woman speak? 'Really? According to my students, our college web site is desperate. They keep complaining it needs sound bites and visual hits or something. Maybe you could give us some advice?'

Charlotte struggled self-consciously. 'Maybe.'

So much for trying to engage her in conversation. Sarah decided she shouldn't have bothered. 'Have you met Jo yet? It's her birthday.' That'll be a nice treat for her.

Charlotte managed a small shake of her head, then raised her watery eyes. Something haunted filled them, as Sarah guided her towards Jo without touching her. She noticed she could see Charlotte's scalp through her fluff-thin hair and it made Sarah visualise bloody tufts of it under her nails.

Charlotte's shoulders raised in a slight shrug as she faced Jo. 'Er... Happy birthday.'

'Is that a hint of a tint of a Scouse accent I hear?' Jo asked.

'The Wirral,' Charlotte answered.

'Thought so.'

While Jo stood awkwardly with Charlotte, Sarah mouthed at Andi, 'What have you brought her for?'

Andi drew her out of earshot of the others. 'She was all on her own in this bar and –'

'Don't tell me.'

'I felt sorry for her, like.'

'What is it with you and lame dogs?'

Andi caught her bottom lip between her teeth, lending her a five-year-old's unwitting cuteness.

Sarah tested the spring in one of Andi's copper curls between her thumb and forefinger. 'But why did you have to bring her *today*?'

'I dunno.' The sweet rising intonation and shy smile melted Sarah for a moment. 'She sort of invited herself.'

'*What?*'

'Told us she was good at working out clues an' I didn't know what... She doesn't say much, mind, but when she does, she's clear what she wants.'

'That's commonly known as emotional blackmail.'

'Okay, smarty pants.' Andi's consonants dissolved like marshmallow. 'Maybe I've just a... Atishoo... kinder heart than you.'

'What is it *you* call that? Ah, yes! Soft as shite.'

Stepping in front of Sarah, Jo's eyes issued a barbed command. 'Are we off, then?'

Sarah clapped everyone to attention. 'Over Marple Bridge, then turn right.'

The car doors slamming sounded far away to Sarah, as she registered Jo fastening her seatbelt beside her. Dimly, she heard Derrie asking questions.

'... far is it? Will you promise to help me?'

Draping her arm round Derrie, Somoya whispered in her ear, but Sarah had already tuned out. The scene in the car had the poor definition of a pirate video, while the film location in her head pulsed with 3D edges...

A hand-held camera tailed Colin jerkily through a warren of corridors and stone archways. Sarah recognised the Town Hall. He stopped in front of one of the doors and read the dull brass plate. Electoral Services Unit. His hand gripped the handle in extreme close-up. Locked. When he saw the sign said Monday to Friday, he swivelled and strode towards an oak-panelled reception box in the entrance hall. Inside, a doorman hunched over his crossword.

'*Excuse me.*'

The doorman barely lifted his eyes from his newspaper.

'*Mm?*'

'You just sent me down there to the Electoral Services Unit and it's closed.'

The man blinked behind the glass hatch.

Colin waited. 'Well?' What do you suggest?'

He unhooked his clipboard from the wall. 'You could try the Local Studies department.'

Colin's fingers flexed into a fist. 'Where's that?'

'The Library. Out of the Town Hall and turn right. First floor.'

Without thanking him, Colin walked away. Fade...

He'd nail her. Sarah knew. Nearly ten years on, this was her due payment for the interrogations masquerading as friendly conversations and her clipped instructions edited by nerves.

As she visualised him hurrying past the men's toilet, Sarah realised Colin would feel like he'd slipped back in time. Strange place to start a life. A library toilet. Sarah wondered if the reality of Derrie's blonde head made his palm itch. Whether he could already feel the warm dome under his hand.

At the top of the wide stone steps, the corridor steered him round in a circle. Sarah knew no one could stop him seeing a public document. When she saw him approaching the counter, the threat of diarrhoea cramped her stomach.

'I'd like to see the electoral register for Whalley Range, please.'

'Which polling district?' The woman's eyes bulged. Sarah diagnosed an over-active thyroid.

'Er, well, this is the address.' Colin shrank under her scrutiny.

'Hold on a minute.' She disappeared behind a door. There was the sound of a filing cabinet opening.

'Here you go.'

'Thanks.' He read the names. Jo McAvoy and Sarah Palmer. No child.

Of course, Sarah remembered. Not old enough to vote. He cleared his throat.

'Excuse me?' Sorry... I wonder if...'

'Did you find what you were after?'

'Yes, thanks. Now I need some... census information on... Do they hold more in-depth information about younger residents?'

Sarah willed the woman to suspect him.

'What do you mean?'

'Well... the electoral role only lists those over eighteen at each address. But I need –'

'Oh, no. We don't give out details like that.' Her eyes seemed to protrude further.

'What exactly do you want this for?'

'Never mind. I was just interested. His dialogue slipped out of lip sync.

'Never mind.'

Sarah had to keep Colin quiet. She felt worn out already, even before she'd spoken to him. Anyway, it might still have been a mistake. It might not have been him at all. She needed to concentrate on where she was. Not let anyone poison such a beautiful place. Not him. Not Jo. Not anyone.

Twelve

The village could have been coloured with paints from a child's palette. Sky blue. Grass green. It made Sarah imagine that Covent Garden flower market had been transported to this place and dropped in a frenzied arrangement. Her greedy eyes didn't know where to rest. To her left, nasturtiums spilled down York stone steps, vibrating orange in the mid-morning sun.

'Which way?' Jo shouted, racing ahead.

Along the other side of the path, rose hips, polished to a high shine, nudged at sour blackberries.

'She's not listening,' Derrie complained, her features set in collusion with Jo, as she reached for her hand. At least one of her parents could be trusted to take the hunt seriously.

A breeze teased Sarah with a sudden scent of wallflowers, kissing her nose then disappearing in an adulterous change of direction. 'I'm coming.'

'Which path do we take?' Jo asked again, indicating the two alternatives.

'What?'

'You got the map. Where's the school?'

Sarah tried to orientate it. But however she revolved and unfolded the brittle mass of paper, she couldn't make sense of the direction. 'Right?'

'Give it here.'

The jutting arrogance of Jo's chin and her long-suffering tone incensed Sarah. 'It *is*. Up this lane on the right.'

'If you say so.' Jo held out her hand, still expecting her to comply.

Glancing at the map again, Sarah felt no wiser, but refused to hand it over. She let them all charge off in front and doubt began a threadworm journey through her. As she hung back, not wanting to admit she might have made a mistake, pale petals stroked her cheek. A turquoise flower opened, as if it had been filmed in animation and beckoned her in, Wonderland style. Drink me. Essence of apricot flooded her mouth. As the fragrance filled her head, her heart swelled simultaneously. Falling in love with a flower. It happened to her all the time. Especially with ones she didn't recognise. Even though the voices of the others sounded impatient, she took her time to memorise the leaf shape and shade, so she could categorise it later. Still caught, she couldn't move. Flowers waited for her every place she went. Picked her. As she leaned forward, the shrub's leaves fingered through her hair, making her shiver.

'*Come on*, Sarah,' Derrie shouted. 'We want the map.'

The flower held her even while she wandered away. But new distractions lined the lane and she inhaled the Mexican orange blossom, like lifting the lid on a jar of honey. Balloons flew from distant gateposts all the way up the hill, marking hand-written signs. Gathered around each one, she could see small clusters of grey-haired women adjusting their spectacles, to consult identical buff-coloured booklets. The others waited edgily for her by a stall selling homemade jam.

'What's going on here?' Sarah asked when she caught them up.

Jo pulled the map from her hand. 'Dunno.'

'It's Mellor's open garden day.'

They all swung round to locate the wavering voice. A man grown small with age peered over his fence. 'In aid of Cancer Research.'

'Not boring gardens again,' Derrie pushed her head into Sarah's side. 'We're not going round them, are we?'

Wistfully, Sarah patted Derrie's hair, wishing she could abandon this whole thing and just drift around all morning, talking plants. Four-foot-tall seeding grass, interwoven with buttercups, framed the shrunken man. The effect of this wilderness was like a deliberate insult to its manicured neighbours.

Sarah stood on tiptoes to get a better view of his patch of land. 'Very Chelsea Flower Show, your garden.'

'Isn't it?' His words sagged round ill-fitting teeth. 'Try telling that to this lot round here.'

'You're not in the National Garden Scheme, I take it?' Sarah smiled sympathetically at him.

The man's chin drooped as he worked up to a grunting giggle. 'They've organised a hate campaign against my garden.' Straightening to his full tiny height, he delivered the rest of his speech at the top of his flabby voice, aiming it over the fence towards anyone who might be listening. 'They think they're going to get me out.'

'They obviously don't realise this is the height of horticultural couture.'

'Excuse me,' Derrie interrupted, snatching the map from Jo's hand and homing in on the man. 'Where's the Primary School?'

'You've come at it a bit of a long way round.'

Jo sighed as he gave them in-depth directions, while Andi and Somoya ran off, swinging Derrie between them – an oddly matching trio.

Banks of flowering herbs made the air medicinal as they brushed past. Fresh spearmint and coriander. Soon the lane tailed off into a Victorian illustration. Set against sloping hills, a cul de sac of stone cottages were dressed as debutantes in climbing roses. Rampant vanilla Kiftsgate, reaching their roofs. The whole vain scene cried out to be admired, Sarah thought. But for all its pretentions, there was no escaping how pretty it was. She wouldn't say no to a house and garden here. But it was ridiculous even thinking about it. If Jo was leaving, they'd have to sell up. They could finish up split between two shitty flats in Salford.

Buy one, get one free. With all the negative equity around there, that was probably all they'd be able to afford. Sarah could see Jo storming towards her and knew it would take more than a twee view to wipe away her grim preoccupation.

'You shouldn't have asked me to find it, then,' Sarah began defensively. 'You know I'm dyslexic when it comes to maps.'

'*And* cash machines, *and* cookers. You just don't *look*, that's all. You prefer making me wander round like a daft mare.'

Their progress down the stony footpath, through woodland, was mottled with welcome shade. Jo glanced back at Charlotte, trailing way behind them, negotiating the uneven surface with difficulty in her stiletto heels. 'Look at the state of *her*,' Jo continued to harangue Sarah. 'You could've chosen a better route. Schools do have *roads* leading up to them these days.'

Making sure that Derrie was still far in front, Sarah took a breath deep enough to fortify her for a confrontation.

'I want you to tell me what I've done to make you speak to me in such a vile way.'

'Sorry.' Jo resembled a resentful toddler pressed into insincere apology.

'That doesn't answer my question.'

'It's nothing.' A burst of trapped air croaked up into her throat.

'I need to know. You've had a face like thunder on and off for weeks.' She paused. 'You don't seem... happy.'

'What d'you want me to do? Clap my hands?' Two slow handclaps punctuated the sarcastic silence. 'If you're happy and you know it.' She stamped her feet.

Sickened, Sarah speeded up. 'I don't know why I bother.'

Catching snatches of their rising tension, Somoya doubled back. 'Less of the domestics, you two.' She aimed her thumb at the fields. 'Yer scaring bloody horses.' Then she jogged back down the path to where Andi was showing Derrie something on the map.

The peacemaker strikes again, Sarah sneered inwardly. Pouring oil on troubled waters. Pity she can't make it work for herself.

Chastened, Jo stood still. 'You've got yellow powder on your nose.'

'Pollen.'

Jo smoothed it off with her fingertips. 'It's nothing. Honestly. There's nothing wrong.' They both knew it wasn't true. But when Jo leaned in and kissed her, Sarah felt some kind of truth in the brief touch of their lips. Jo nudged her cheek against hers and Sarah breathed in an infusion of citrus. A clean, male shave scent.

'So much for the scenic route,' Sarah said.

'At least someone's found the clue for us.' Jo raised her eyes in the direction of a modern low-rise school building. A car full of women pulled up outside, jumped out, prised the envelope from the door and then replaced it before slamming back into their car, all within thirty seconds.

'The hiding place wasn't exactly taxing.'

Derrie motioned to them frantically. 'Hurry up. Those other women are beating us!'

Strains of a brass band playing a strangely syncopated version of 'Perfect Day' made Sarah happy for a moment, as if the song's sentiments could heal just by being heard. The red, white and blue bunting strung from the school entrance performed a limp dance over the heads of the band. Slouched with her back against the wall, Somoya angled her face towards the sun. Across the car park, Andi lifted her camera and adjusted the lens to catch her.

Jo wriggled uncomfortably. 'My bra's come undone. Can you do it up for me?'

Sarah raised her voice enough to be heard by the small crowd in front of the band. 'Do I have to? Everyone will think I'm a lesbian...'

Jo wrenched away from her. 'Stop making a show of me.'

'What's wrong with you, Derrie?' asked Sarah.

'*Shame.*' Derrie tilted her chin at Sarah in an attitude of disdain, as she reached for the clue. 'Don't talk to me, right? You're so embarrassing.'

'That's my job. Obligatory part of my parental duties.' Derrie tried to study the writing on the card through her hair and Sarah stroked the gold tangles out of the way, behind her ears. 'Whoever you love when you're big will be lucky.'

'I know,' Derrie agreed absently as she read. '"She painted flowers like women."'

'Georgia O'Keeffe,' Charlotte answered quietly from behind them. Regarding her with surprise, Sarah saw Charlotte flattening herself against the shaded side of the school entrance.

'So, the clue could be inside a flower.' Derrie moved off towards the orderly beds at the school entrance.

'It could, Derrie, but there's so many here. We need to narrow it down.' Sarah caught her hand. 'What about a flower shop?'

'Or a gallery?' Andi asked, scrubbing at her nose in irritation.

Derrie raced up to a group of pensioners seated in front of the band and asked anyone who would listen, where she could find the painting shop. A collection of old voices deliberated.

'There's no DIY store here, love. You'll have to head back to Marple.'

Remembering the exhibition poster in the antique shop they'd passed, Sarah motioned the others to follow her. 'Come on, I know where it is.' And she also knew that Jo had better damn well talk. As soon as they were on their own, Sarah would make her. Then she'd decide.

Sarah narrowed her eyes as Charlotte tried to disengage her heel from between two stone flags.

'She's a royal pain. She's slowing us down.'

'Nah, she's not,' Andi replied. 'She was quicker at working that clue out than you were. She does look shattered though and the sun seems to be getting to her. I'll ask if she fancies waiting by the car while we do the next bit.'

Sarah sighed in Charlotte's direction. That one could do with getting a bit of sun, she thought. She's beyond white. It's not healthy.

'What is the matter with her? What's with the pained expression and what's that bloody cushion in aid of?' Way in front of them, Jo held Derrie's hand, helping her balance as she scrabbled dangerously up a high stone wall.

'Go easy, Sarah. She's had an operation.'

'What kind?' She ground her teeth as she saw how much higher the wall got, further down the street.

'Don't broadcast it, all right?' Andi continued.

Mildly interested, Sarah nodded.

'Technically speaking, until a short while ago, she was a man.'

That explained it. Sarah had known there was something weird about her. A sudden pool of guilt seeped into her stomach. 'Christ. I've been a bitch to her.'

'When?'

'Well, I've not *said* anything exactly. But she'll have seen it in my face.' She stared at Charlotte, realigning her view. Gauging the size of her feet, measuring her height again and searching for shadows along her jaw. Sarah wondered what could have made her like that.

'Did she have a traumatic childhood or something?'

Andi laughed, 'You could intellectualise the fate of a plate of mushy peas.'

Sarah glanced away and caught sight of her daughter performing a tightrope act along the top of the wall. The smile soured on her lips.

'Jo, that's *way* above your reach. Derrie, that's *enough*. Get down now.'

'Take a chill pill, mate,' Derrie drawled before dropping from the wall into Jo's outstretched arms.

'Still,' Sarah tried to get Andi to understand. 'There must be something pretty dysfunctional lurking in the murky depths of Charlotte's family.'

Andi didn't need to speak. The quick, high arch of her eyebrow communicated eloquently and Sarah could guess at the diatribe she was being silently subjected to – some sardonic, wittily worded attack on Sarah's ignorance, or her overly deterministic view of gender.

Outside the antique shop, at the foot of the hill, Jo shouted as Derrie executed a stamping triumphal dance with the gold card. '"A place that asks you not to leave. It's a long way to go, to read this funny girl's second-hand words."'

Sarah tried to work out the answer before anyone else, to prove Andi wrong. A place that asks you not to leave. She ran through the thesaurus in her head. Remain, linger, reside.

Cupping her mouth, Andi called back, 'Stay. It's Stalybridge. Could be in the second-hand bookshop.'

'I don't get it,' Derrie complained, running back towards them.

'Tell you later, chicken nugget.'

Lowering her voice, Sarah made a last attempt to redeem herself. 'Hey, I didn't mean to sound like a bigot, but having bits of your body chopped off is so extreme.' Another raised eyebrow from Andi, forced her into embarrassed back-pedalling. 'If society accepted everyone, they wouldn't need to do it.'

Andi's ironic smile kept something from her. Something obvious, to do with what Sarah had just said.

'I dunno.' With each alternate syllable, Andi's tone swung wildly from high to low. 'I'd cack meself if I woke up tomorrow with an alien growth between me legs.'

'*Right.* Enough already.' Defensiveness dragged at the corners of Sarah's mouth. 'It's usually me up on a soapbox.'

Sarah scrutinised Charlotte again. She was still behind, now accompanied by Derrie, and Sarah's gaze locked on to where her daughter's fingers joined Charlotte's. No wonder Sarah had felt so uneasy with her. It was bloody weird, having bits of yourself sliced off. Where the hell did you draw the line? There were people who convinced surgeons to make them into double paraplegics because they felt their legs didn't belong to them. Surely that shouldn't be allowed? Christ. She'd better not say any of that to Andi. Sarah knew she'd get trashed. Still, maybe Charlotte had only been strange because Sarah had stressed her out.

Andi dropped back to flank Charlotte on the opposite side to Derrie and linked her arm. Overcompensating, Sarah decided. You shouldn't tell people's secrets if you can't take the consequences. Judging by Charlotte's sickly flush, they were heading for trouble with that one.

Breaking free, Derrie charged down the hill to the car. 'I'm going to beat you all.'

Charlotte tried to smooth down a light drift of flyaway hair as the breeze exposed her pink scalp.

As they reached the car, Derrie clutched Jo's arm. 'How did Andi know we have to go to Stalybridge?'

Jo waited till they were all in the car before she answered.

'She says it's got something to do with that song.' She pulled away from the kerb. '"It's a Long Way to Tipperary".'

Before Sarah could offer Derrie a few facts about the First World War, she sensed Jo stiffen. As she examined the cold set of her mouth, she knew that in her mind, Jo had already left her.

Derrie started to hum behind them. Sarah had no idea how she'd be able to keep their girl safe on her own.

Thirteen

Following the signs for Stalybridge town centre, Jo blocked out the chatter in the car, while a more insistent conversation replayed in her head...

'Get off the phone, Dave.' Tara leaned back and swung her computer chair in a half-circle, as she twined the telephone cord into a caterpillar around her finger. The hard light from the window showed her long black hair was several shades too dark to be natural. 'I've got work to do... Cheeky get.' Her fey giggles made a rash of raspberry hives break out at the base of Jo's neck. Desperate to scratch, she sat on her hands. She couldn't let Tara know just how easily she could reduce her to the response of a frigging clockwork toy. 'Tonight?' Tara's voice mellowed with her steamy smile. 'What makes you think I'd be seen out with you? All right then, I want Thai food and you're paying.' She slammed the receiver down, then resumed her chair-swivelling with an air of complete relaxation. Her cheeks shone. But their permanent rosy patches didn't look healthy any more. At close range, Jo had seen the broken veins stitched through the flesh.

Jo dug her nails into the base of her throat, making it even redder. A sick silence swelled in the office. To force away the slight curve at the corners of Tara's lips, Jo explored the photograph on the wall – a black and white Ansel Adams that Somoya had given her – and tried to take in the scene as if she was there.

Snowblindness glazed her eyes as they filled with the contours of the Himalayas. She could feel the imprint of each rock pressing up through her soles. Nothing to think about except moving forward, finding the steadiest position for each foot. Watching her boots pushing higher towards base camp, while exertion made her suck in ice clear air.

She breathed deeply, but the office clogged her lungs with something heavy. Air with virtually no oxygen content. The silence in the room hurt her ears and amplified the shuffling sounds of the administration staff in reception. Without moving her head, Jo chanced a brief glimpse at Tara from the corner of her eye. When she saw her leaning way back in her chair, eyelids closed, feigning serene sleep, Jo wanted to kill her. It's all because of you, she screamed at Tara with her eyes. This whole mess. The phone chirped on the coffee table between their desks. She glanced at Tara again and knew she wouldn't stir herself to answer it.

'Hello.' Jo pressed the phone to her shoulder, leaving both hands free to scratch. She hoped Tara's eyes were still shut, as she tried to listen to the new secretary telling her that two of her clients had arrived. 'Thanks.' Replacing the receiver, she rooted through the files on her desk. The Jackson file was missing. Jo had put it there just before dinner. She began at the bottom again, walking her fingers deliberately through the pile, feeling Tara's sneer begin to singe the back of her scalp. She's moved it. Hidden it just to... Jackson... the typed white label made Jo release the breath she'd been saving for accusations. This was ridiculous. She'd got to be more careful. In her mind, Jo practised nonchalance, framing sentences to see how they sounded. Her final choice leaked out weakly.

'I need... Mr and Mrs Jackson have come for their appointment with me.'

Tara opened one eye reluctantly. 'And?'

'You know what!' Don't let her. Just don't let her wind you round in stupid circles. 'I need the office for the interview.'

'I'm using it.' Tara's expression calcified, her sentiment clear. Go fuck yourself.

'But... But you're not.' Jo tried to stop herself spluttering. 'You don't need –'

'Use the broom cupboard.'

'Don't be pathetic. You can only get one in that office at a push. Come on, I'll only be a short –'

'Go fuck yourself.' Triumph lay under the surface of Tara's unmoving features.

Jo took in the ruddy cheeks, the geriatric black of her hair. What the hell had she been thinking of? How could she have... with her... with that? How did she get to be another one on Tara's long list of losers? Never mind the gender, cram in the quantity. Her neck flamed. Her nails raked at it. She knew she'd never move Tara out of the office, so she stood still, trying to decide what to do. What she wanted, like an ache, was to escape, get to the fire exit at the back of the building, jam the safety bar down, ignoring the alarm, and keep going. But where to? She couldn't go home. Sarah would wonder why she'd finished work so early. Jo knew she couldn't report any of this to her seniors. They'd only want to know how things had deteriorated so far. Feeling five years old, with the eyes of the whole school playground piercing her, Jo left the office. The downturned smile on Tara's lips followed her along the corridor.

In a state of shock, Jo observed herself chattering pleasantly to Mr and Mrs Jackson as she guided them into the office that everyone referred to as the broom cupboard.

'You *are* joking?' In the tiny space, Mr Jackson stood in uneasy proximity to the woman who would be his ex-wife within weeks. 'You don't really expect us all to fit in here?'

'I'm sorry.' Jo lowered her head as she manipulated two extra chairs like an impossible IQ puzzle past the door and desk. 'It's the only room available. Divorce is a busy business.' Christ Almighty. What did she go and say that for? Mr and Mrs Jackson compared notes with each other, as if, faced with such a crass lack of tact, for once they might consider being allies. 'Sorry,' Jo mumbled again, edging her seat a centimetre to the right so that her knees wouldn't touch theirs. 'I don't know what... Sorry. Now, before we start, my job is not to re-solve any disputes that may have occurred between you –'

'That's what you lot *keep* saying, but I'm being penalised for hav-ing a job.' He shifted uncomfortably, muscle turned to fat filling the chair. 'I love my kids. They should be with me. But just because I can't get back 'til late –'

Dry strands of nicotine-yellow hair sprung loose from behind Mrs. Jackson's ears, masking her eyes. 'He's got my kids calling his *slag* their "pretend mummy", *you* tell *me* if –'

'See what I mean?' Mr. Jackson leaned forward demanding Jo's full attention and his soft-boiled belly bulged over his belt. '*That's* how she talks in front of my children.'

Avoiding eye contact with him, Jo scanned the form on her lap, confirming names. 'You're here to make arrangements for Kirsty and Kevin. I suggest you use the mediation service to resolve these other disputes –'

'They don't like going to see him, anyway.' The voice had a weedy underdeveloped quality, prompting Jo to guess the woman's age. At least half her husband's. 'They've told me he won't let them watch telly.'

'Not up until *all hours*, watching rubbish to keep *you* company!'

Jo rubbed harshly at her eyelids and when she opened them again, a meteor shower burst across the desk.

'I appreciate this must be very difficult, but we do need to work out the schedule for visits. Can we just concentrate on what's in the chil-dren's best interests?'

Mr. Jackson's face twisted. His words were a malicious imitation of Jo's. 'Well, it's not "in their best interests" to be with *her*.'

Jo transferred her inspection from him to her and back again. You're lucky your children are still young enough to love you, she thought, however you treat them. It won't be long before they work out it's a wasted bleeding effort. If you could see that, you might have a chance with them. But you'd rather spend you energy on revenge. It's your call.

'As the children are just old enough to talk about what they think, I'll base a large part of my report on what they want.'

'Yes. After *she's* turned them against me.'

The start of a headache bit into Jo's temples. She took one hand off the steering wheel to locate the pain with her fingertips. If Tara said anything to Sarah, Jo might not be able to see Derrie again. The idea wrenched at her heart, making her check the rear-view mirror to make sure Derrie was still safe. Or they could be stuck with irregular access visits, acrimonious pockets of measured time. No. Sarah wouldn't go on like that... Would she? She had too much compassion. It didn't matter how weird Sarah had been acting lately... didn't matter how sharp she sometimes pretended to be, Jo had amassed twelve years of tenderness from her.

Without her and Derrie... Without those two, Jo knew she'd be entering a wasteland.

Fourteen

'There it is.' Andi depressed the brake, slowing the Mini to a halt so she could point down into the valley. 'Like a crater. A bubble of weird.'

A trapped quiet hung inside the car for a few moments, until Charlotte spoke.

'Stalybridge?'

The windscreen magnified the sun's heat and, with the car now stationary, Charlotte's peppery perspiration got even more difficult to breathe. It reminded Andi of something blocked. A sink. The thought came in a burst of guilty, uncharacteristic cruelty. She flicked the button to lower the electric window further on her side, then pulled the car away from the grass verge, picking up speed downhill. The fresh air caught her, making pain reverberate through her sinuses like horse-radish. She tried to ignore it, as she wondered how far ahead of them the Porsche was. A sign flew past announcing they were entering the town.

'Stalybridge... *Atishoo!*... Twinned with Armentières... A factory and five houses.' She hoped she could stir Charlotte up soon, because the woman's inability to hold any sort of conversation had started to unnerve her. That and her appearance. Everything so sadly outdated: the matching cream skirt and cardigan, the make-up – a confectionery of sugared almond shades tinting her lips, her cheeks, her eyelids. It was a shame, a waste, because she wasn't unattractive but her misguided choice of style detracted from her fading prettiness. She needed someone to dress her. Charlotte remained silent, her hands folded over her white handbag, in the same position she'd held them during the whole journey. Andi wondered what could be in there.

'D'you fancy one of these?' She showed Charlotte a half-finished packet of sweets. 'They're new. Rhubarb and mustard flavour.' Then eyed her with a sly smile, but Charlotte just shook her head. Andi unwrapped a couple of sweets and, for a second, she was lost to a sugar trance. 'On a Sunday this place is like a Clint Eastwood movie, complete with tumbleweed rolling down the high street in a bid for freedom.' Another long pause followed. Resigned to an indeterminate wait, Andi refused to fill it this time and caught Charlotte's lost look, as she tried to think of something to say. Finally, with an audible intake of breath, she geared up to reply.

'You don't... like it here, then?'

Hallelujah. A complete sentence. 'Nah, I do actually. It's funny.' Wait and give the poor lass a chance, Andi told herself. Come on, you can do it. Return the serve. No. It looked like she was on her own again. 'Makes us laugh. It's famous for three things. The Tripe and Sandwich shop,' Andi jabbed her thumb towards the town centre. 'It's the only specialist tripe vendor in the country, open for precisely three hours every Saturday. Then there's that miracle of town planning, the canal. Tore it out in the late nineteen-sixties, now they've rebuilt it in the same place, through the shopping precinct, as a tourist attraction.' In the absence of any encouraging noises from Charlotte, Andi heard herself gabbling. 'There's this gaggle of little old geese women who waddle to the building work at an appointed time every day to say, "It's coming on, the canal, in't it?" Same when the new bus station was being built, they were there bumping together, gawking. "It's coming on, the bus station, in't it?" They've only got the one line of dialogue, but they all have to repeat it at least twice each.'

Andi forced herself to shut up as she realised she'd be tempted by Charlotte's silence into even sillier exaggeration. What can you do, she thought, when you're playing to a dead audience? With anyone else she'd have raised a few laughs by now. Andi saw that they had caught up with the Porsche and accelerated to keep it in sight. Why had she brought Charlotte? Why did she automatically go into rescue mode as soon as someone was low? Pretty stupid. Now she'd have to see if she could palm her off on the others for a bit of riveting chat, otherwise she'd never get anywhere near Somoya. She couldn't waste the only time she'd ever seen Somoya without Jaz welded to her side. Elated bubbles inflated against each other like gum inside her chest, until they reached her rib cage. *This* is the day, she thought. Something is going to happen today. Andi didn't know how Somoya had never noticed her before, never caught her getting close enough to inhale the scent of coconut on her curls. Coconut weaving through the stale air of smoky clubs. Close enough to compare their arms leaning on the bar. Hers plump and pink, copper freckled. Somoya's crème caramel, chiselled by muscle.

A recent still shot stayed with her. One of Somoya unfolding the map in Mellor. Smoothing the tired paper with a silk sound, one slender forefinger had traced along the path she thought they should take. Too distracted to hear her words, Andi had only been able to zoom in on Somoya's hand. How could someone exude such casual elegance, just by pointing their finger at a map? As Somoya paused, keeping her place in the centre of the village, the sun had caught the loose silver band round the knuckle of her thumb, so it seemed to shimmy. How could anyone fall in love with a finger? A knuckle? But there was that arrogant, hurt look as well, coming at Andi full force when she stood too near. Somoya had shifted away, folding the map, and the memory built the pressure in her chest, until every one of her hope-filled bubbles burst.

It's dangerous to wish myself on her, mind. On *anybody*, Andi remembered. Only have to dump them before they trade us in for a refund. Part-exchange us for someone in full working order.

'You seem to... know the place well. Have you lived here?'

Charlotte's question took her by surprise.

'Comes from being sent to the arse end of nowhere on a regular basis to shoot photos for the paper.'

'That must be... interesting.'

Encouraged, Andi relaxed slightly. 'Interestin', aye. I take lots of shots of wheelie bins. Local people standing *by* wheelie bins, standing *on* wheelie bins, or of course that perennial favourite, standing *in* wheelie bins. The permutations are endless.' Hold on. Not so heavy on the sarcasm. Don't scare her off now she's getting going. 'Oh, and kebabs.'

Pause. 'Kebabs?'

The conversational gaps between them began to feel different. Thoughtful rather than gaping.

'Another one last week. Lad found a car valve in his kebab. Went to the police. I mean, what's that about? S'pose he was after a chance at compensation.'

Charlotte patted her upper lip with a folded cotton handkerchief. 'Is it... difficult?'

'What?'

'Getting people to be... natural?'

A recognition surfaced that Charlotte actually sounded interested. Instead of the raucous audience Andi usually commanded, Charlotte's quiet questioning felt kind.

'It can be. I only work in ten-second bursts, like, but to get those ten seconds I have to spend a while spouting any old flannel to get them smiling right. Sometimes, just sometimes, you catch something special... It's weird what sells, though. Best one I had was a toddler who poured lighter fluid all over his mam's new settee. Franchised all over the world, that one. See there?' Charlotte slid the hanky out of sight and lifted her gaze from her bag. A row of shops slurred past. 'That's the last thing this place is famous for.' Andi pointed at the Tipperary café. 'The fella who wrote "It's a Long Way to Tipperary" lived here, so you've got a Tipperary everything. That's how I got the clue so quick. It's a bit esoteric, I know. But most people will have guessed it from the *stay* part.'

'I'd like to move somewhere like this.'

Andi's eyes widened in disbelief. 'Really? No joke?'

'Yes. It's odd... like me. Like people think I am.'

This bald insight struck Andi as funny, but she felt unsure whether Charlotte was serious, so she pressed her lips together to stop herself laughing.

'But what about work?'

'I can design web sites anywhere.'

Andi was stumped for anything else to say. It wasn't the content of Charlotte's speech, more the final way she announced personal details. Her rare statements had huge full stops at the end of them, as a warning not to go any further. Andi decided to revert to the comfort of her comic routine.

'That's the place they call the bridge. It's just a ditch really, where the young ones go to copulate. You can see them on Friday and Saturday nights, climbing over with bottles of White Lightning. And you don't have to strain to hear them. He says to her, "Suck me off." She says, "Okay then." He says, "Only joking. I think you're an ugly cunt, but me friend fancies you." She says, "Okay then." Five minutes later his mate comes back and says, "She was shit."'

Charlotte gazed blankly ahead. Only a cagey movement of her eyelids revealed that she had no idea how to respond.

'There you are,' Andi edged the car into one of the only spaces left in the carpark. 'Tesco's megastore. Heart of Stalybridge.'

As Andi stepped out of the car, she felt cradled by the hills that surrounded the town. Already ahead, she saw Derrie jumping across the new red-brick canal bridge. The expanse of still water gave off a flat platinum glare. Set in an island of clipped grass, the freshly painted locks looked unused. While the others followed the mock cobbled pathway, Derrie swung herself along the quayside railings with the easy reach of a chimpanzee. Andi lifted her camera.

From across the street, she watched the sun swell against the lime-stone façade of Victoria Market, so that a honey light basted the swags of carved fruit. Even the iron fretwork, curling around the clock tower, glittered. She noticed her inner core warm slightly.

'Check *these* out!' Derrie nudged Charlotte, then pressed her nose against a shop window, exactly level with a pair of shoes. The ruby, platform sandals twinkled at them from behind plate glass. Andi could see both their chests expand. Infatuation at first sight.

'Sarah, these are so sick,' Derrie breathed. 'Please can I have them?'

Barely bothering to register, Sarah continued hunting in her bag for something. 'They're far too high, you'd break your neck.'

'Like I *would*!'

Sarah doubled back. 'Anyway, you've got enough shoes. I'm going to start calling you Imelda Marcos.' She unclenched Derrie's fist and wrapped it round a sandwich. 'Eat this. It's tuna.'

'I can't. I'm a vegetarian.'

Sarah huffed, 'Since when?' then carried on walking.

Andi wound a strand of Derrie's hair behind her ear and whispered into it, 'You can never have enough shoes.'

Charlotte cleared her throat, as if she might agree.

'Come on, you shoe fetishists!' Glancing back, Sarah took a few steps, then paused in front of a florist's display spilling out on to the pavement.

'Flower fetishist,' Contorting her face into a full-lipped monkey grin at Sarah's receding back, Andi took Derrie's hand and started walking. But her arm was yanked sharply as the little girl refused to move her feet. Twisting her body towards the sandals, Derrie placed the bread in her hand over her heart, as if she had a pain.

'I love them *so much*. I wish I could have them.'

'I'd buy them for you, pet, but I think the pair of us might get in a bit of bother with your mam.' Andi tried to guide Derrie away again, this time with a hand under her elbow.

Taking a last look over her shoulder, Derrie began a conversation with herself, too low for Andi to hear. But she guessed it was a continuation on the theme of shoes and the nature of justice. A yellow trail of sweetcorn and blobs of tuna followed her as she dug the offending filling from her sandwich. In the distance, Somoya tried to match Jo's casual strides.

Twin bronze figures floated at the entrance to the bridge ahead. Angels. Andi could just make out the wounded soldiers they were protecting. A sigh escaped from Charlotte. Andi hung back, waiting until she could frame Charlotte standing underneath them. Through the viewfinder, she caught the statues flying bare-breasted over Charlotte's head.

Still muttering, Derrie barged through the memorial garden, her feet whipping the municipal bedding plants.

As she caught up with them, Andi indicated with an outstretched arm, 'You lasses have come down the wrong road for the bookshop. We need to go left, then same again.'

Following her directions, they turned the corner. At the bottom of the long incline of Market Street, the river flowed under the road. On her right, Andi saw Charlotte focusing on the vista of bridge after bridge crossing the town's main artery, and stopped beside her, taking it all in. Spiny trees forced their way out of the stone walls and green damp rotted the wooden frames of the buildings that rose from the river. Joining them, Derrie hung over the bridge, dangling soggy bread from her fingers, but Andi could tell she was blind to the ducks bumping along the surface of the water. She wondered whether to ask if they could give the ducks a small piece of her sandwich, then noticed that it had already disappeared.

'Those shoes reminded me of Dorothy's magic slippers,' Derrie murmured.

Andi witnessed a string of fairy lights switch on inside Charlotte's head. This time she didn't hesitate.

'*I'm* in love with *The Wizard of Oz*, too. How many times have you seen it?'

'About a hundred and fifty-three. I've got it on video.'

'Which is your favourite bit?' Charlotte asked, as if she genuinely wanted to know.

'Where they kill the witch!' She clicked her fingers inexpertly. 'Nice one.' Then she waited for confirmation.

'I'm melting! I'm melting.' Charlotte's cheeks looked hot as she attempted the witch's scratchy death throes. She paused, her eyes fixed on the middle distance, as if she'd just remembered something. 'When I was in school in Liverpool –'

'That's where Jo's from.'

'I know. Anyway, there was this boy called Billy, who changed his name to Holly –'

'That's a girl's name.'

Andi laid her hand on Derrie's mouth. 'You're a bit too mouthy, kid. Let Charlotte speak.'

Derrie pressed her lips together and flattened her own fingers over Andi's to ensure she could keep quiet.

'Well, he changed his name later to Holly Johnson when he was with this band –'

'Frankie goes to Hollywood.'

Derrie poked Andi in the ribs. 'Now *you're* interrupting.'

'But when he was about fifteen, he came to school one day dressed up as Judy Garland. Pigtails, glossy lips, red high heels and a blue gingham dress.'

Andi saw an enquiry tickle along the surface of Charlotte's skin as Derrie touched the fluff on the arm of her cardigan.

'Didn't the other kids tease him?'

'Yes, but he went all dignified and acted like he couldn't hear them. So, it kind of, slid off.'

For a moment, Derrie was silent before responding. 'That's a good idea.'

'What d'you get teased about?' Charlotte asked so casually that Andi had to admire her sleight of hand.

Derrie's pupils enlarged, wide as hope. 'How did you know?'

'All kids get teased,' Charlotte's mouth sloped sadly.

'Innit? Some of them are so snide. They call me "Suck a fanny" an' I want to punch their faces in, but I have to feel sorry for them.'

Charlotte blinked rapidly to stop tears forming. 'You must be very strong if you can be that tolerant.'

'I have to feel sorry for them, yeah, because their brains aren't ready to understand yet.'

Andi took Derrie's hand and squeezed it. 'You're such a canny lass.'

'I'm going to do that thing Holly did. Pretend I can't hear them.'

A determined smile compressed the corners of Charlotte's lips. 'And think to yourself, I'm just as good as you. In fact I'm better.'

'*And* tell the teacher?'

Andi nodded. 'An' tell the teacher.'

Apparently satisfied, Derrie started skipping past the tiny shops that studded the length of the hill. Through the open door of an ironmonger's a glistening explosion of objects confused Andi. They overlapped like gems, from every inch of wall and uneven floor space. Deeper inside, more and more packets plastered several connecting rooms, the restricted height of each doorway recalling a time when people were smaller. It reminded her of one of those paintings within paintings that went on forever.

Andi cocked her chin at the boarded-up shop they were passing. The hurried aerosol scrawled across it proclaimed 'Faz is an ugly bitch'.

'I'm not keen on the softwood double-glazing. Someone ought to come down at the dead of night an' put their windows in.'

Once Charlotte had worked out the joke, it was too late to laugh. She shook her head wistfully and clung to the rapidly disappearing shade. Andi noticed that Charlotte's skin was spit-roasting. Threatening to blister.

'Maybe it wouldn't be such a good idea to move out here.'

Charlotte smiled to herself. 'I'd probably get woken in the middle of the night by crosses burning on my lawn.'

'Come on.' Derrie encouraged her. 'Here's the bookshop.'

Fifteen

Christ, my fucking leg itches. Cut's gone a weird grey colour. That's a new one. A new hue. The others never went like that. Can't scratch it. Can't move. They might spot me. Breathe, don't scratch. Mind over fucking matter.

Got viewfinder vision. Long way to Tipperary Bookshop. Find the right window. There. Last of three. Load. Take aim. Black cross dissecting your faces. Fire. Woah! I like the new interior design. Splattered. Serious red. Wish I did have a gun. One of those long fucking range efforts. Could flatten against that rooftop and... Still, there's better ways. More drawn out.

There she goes again. Andy fucking Pandy. Fat-arsed ginger bitch. Moving in all contagious with her sugary smile. So close you can taste her breath. For fuck's sake, the pair of you are so blind around each other, I needn't bother to hide. But I want to see just how far she'll go. Just how far you'll let her. So I know how much you'll have to answer for, when I shatter the whole cosy picture. She's going nowhere with you, fat arse. She's mine and you haven't got any idea who you're dealing with.

Sixteen

The air in the bookshop weighed heavy with the smell of old, mouldy cardboard. Twisted piles of shabby books rose from the stripped oak floorboards like architecture. It reminded Somoya of long ago. A time when shops didn't come linked together in chains and no one had heard of ergonomics.

Derrie barged straight up to the counter. 'Is this where the funny girl clue is?'

'Come in. Come in. You've found the right place. My... lovely shop.' The man's vocal pitch had the sweet awkwardness of an adolescent boy, but his face was older. Thirty something. A pretty pixie with neat shaved head and petitely packaged body. 'Or am I cheating, telling you that?'

'No,' Derrie pushed her face into his. 'How many are in front of us?'

'You're about the tenth lot of stampeding women in the last half hour.'

'See?' Derrie ran back to Sarah and pulled at her dress, ecstatically. 'We're nearly in the lead.'

Somoya saw Sarah grow serious as she stroked her daughter's hair. The tenderness of Sarah's expression made Somoya tune in to an unexpected piece of telepathy, about Derrie floating along on a stream of optimism. Like Sarah, Somoya hoped that life wouldn't capsize the girl.

Sarah cleared her throat. 'This treasure hunt thing is a bit of fun, Derrie. We might not win, you know.'

'We will.' Derrie sauntered back to the counter. 'Where's the clue?'

A teasing challenge lit the man's eyes. 'I won't spoil the thrill of the chase for you.' Then he posed a forefinger, sparkling with rings, over his shiny, shy smile. A gesture that clearly stated 'my lips are sealed'. For some reason, this pantomime made Somoya want to imprint both his cheeks with kisses. Today, affection seemed to seek her out, preventing her scurrying for refuge.

Sarah surveyed the shelves doubtfully. 'The books aren't in alphabetical order.'

'No.' His smile shone again.

'That's handy.' Sarah projected cool sarcasm.

'This is a second-hand bookshop. It's meant to be archaic chaos.'

'Part of its charm,' said Charlotte, as everyone spread out to work their way methodically through the shelves.

'It *must* at least be organised into sections,' Sarah said. 'Look for books on comedy.'

The man shook his head. 'Fiction,' he waved his hand to the right side of the shop, 'and non-fiction,' his fingers moved gracefully to the left.

Somoya saw Sarah roll her eyes in reply. Jo shuffled rapidly through the tattered, fluff-edged paperbacks on the top shelves, while Derrie struggled lower down, with a weight of bulky hardbacks.

A dust-filled sneeze made Somoya jump and when she spun round, her eyes were level with Andi's, noses almost touching, within breathing space. Andi's mouth parted, but she held still. Somoya held even stiller. As she scowled at Andi's lips, the circuit completed, triggering volts between her legs. Sensing something, Andi relaxed forward imperceptibly. Somoya could hear Andi's hair giving off the commentary of a pot plant as it's watered: 'Soak me. Do it now.' She had to get away, before she made an even bigger bloody idiot of herself. As she turned, her face burning, the replay of Andi's mouth next to hers wired new shocks through her. The uneven floorboards complained mildly when she stepped away.

'Hey, Charlotte, look!' Sarah shouted.

Everyone crowded in.

'A book for you about transgenderism.'

The owner stopped opening mail to reappraise Charlotte. Somoya couldn't believe what Sarah had just done. She hardly recognised her friend today. She even looked different. Hard. As if she was under attack, with every piece of armour up.

'That's right,' Jo snapped. 'Tell the whole shop, Foghorn Leghorn. You got a gob on you like the Mersey tunnel.'

Sarah's head drooped towards the floor. 'Sorry, Charlotte. I didn't mean –'

'It's okay,' Charlotte replied.

Derrie took the book from Sarah and flicked through it awkwardly. 'Have you found the clue?'

Charlotte held her hand out. 'Do you mind if I see that?' Derrie passed it over, still craning her neck to read the small print, while Charlotte skimmed the blurb on the back cover.

'Of *course*! This is it! A biography of Barbra Streisand.' Sarah looked pleased with herself as she waved a second book in the air. 'She was in that film, you know, *Funny Girl*, like it says in the clue.'

Jo lifted the paperback out of Sarah's hands and shook it. 'Nothing in here.'

'There *must* be,' Sarah insisted.

'I've found it!' Andi laughed. 'Ellen DeGeneres.'

Sarah's face fell. Waving the book and the gold card over her head, Andi targeted Derrie with teasing invitation. The child skidded up to her and executed a series of terrier jumps in the air.

'Gimme.'

'Say pretty please with icing sugar on.'

Clawing up Andi's T-shirt, Derrie produced a whimper, which built into a howl. 'Just gimme it... *Please.*'

Andi dropped the card hastily to rearrange the Lycra clouds in the correct location over her breasts. 'Hey. Not me clothes. They're sacrosanct. You're a proper little yep.'

Extending her arms into apelike limbs, Derrie scooped up the card and curled her lips as far back as they would go, into a monkey grin. 'Oo oo oo. That's me, smells of wee.'

From over Derrie's shoulder, Andi read. '"Americans might call her a vacation. Find her relaxing in a giant seat of learning."'

'These are a bit bloody cryptic,' Sarah complained.

'Billie Holiday,' called Charlotte from the counter, where she was rooting in her bag to pay for the book Sarah had given her. Somoya could see the tempo of Charlotte's flustered breathing increase as she piled the contents of her bag in front of the pixie man. 'I'm sure I brought...'

Sarah placed her hand gently over Charlotte's. 'Please let me get it for you.' She checked the price and gave the money to the man. 'Even though it won't make up for me being such a stupid, loud-mouthed git.'

Derrie took Charlotte's free hand and laid it on the counter. 'Play this.' She picked up the man's right hand and slammed it down on top. Somoya could see the blood pulsing in Charlotte's cheeks.

Derrie slapped her hand onto the sandwiched pair and observed with interest as the owner's face caught like wildfire, mirroring Charlotte's. 'Now your others,' she said. 'You've got to put your others down fast.' Both did as they were told, until their hands became indistinguishable in a skirmish of slapping stings.

Finally, Derrie patted the man's hand benevolently. 'Where's the giant chair?'

'Well, seeing as it's you,' he replied, disarmed. 'I'm pretty sure it's in the mock Tudor hall, second floor of the library.'

'We've already been past there,' Sarah said. 'We're going in ever-decreasing circles.'

'Like my life,' Somoya murmured to herself.

The man's fingers moved towards the blue stones half hidden in Charlotte's hair. 'I like your earrings.' Carefully, he cupped one in his palm. 'Lapis lazuli.' He paused to compare the exact match with her irises.

'My mother's,' said Charlotte.

Something about the tone between them made Somoya close in to watch. As if she was unable to stand the man's scrutiny, Charlotte's gaze drifted down to his mouth, his fox-sharp eye-teeth.

'Come on,' Derrie urged Charlotte, pulling her by the hand. 'We're in eleventh place.'

Andi was waiting at the door, with her back to the glare from outside. Her hair radiated gold heat, as if her head were the true source of the sun. A brawl kicked off inside Somoya – something she faintly recognised, a small atrophied thing, located in her chest, was scratching and punching. There had been no movement there for months and at first it was a relief to feel it, but then Andi smiled suddenly at her... Warning signals went off and the alien thing in her chest shrank away again.

Seventeen

'Look,' Sarah indicated the pub sign. '"Stop and Rest." Shall we?'

Andi noticed that Sarah didn't bother waiting for the others to answer before easing herself between the table and the wooden bench outside the pub.

'Aye, why not?' Andi perched on the opposite corner, scorching the back of her legs. 'Me throat's awful parched.'

'"Faith, something else and Charity will lead you to the third place."' Tapping insistently on Andi's back, Derrie tried to insinuate her tiny behind in beside her. 'What's it mean?'

'It's Hope, hinney, the name of the next place,' Andi told her, 'But we're not rushing off again, just yet.'

'"If you're an ace detective,"' Derrie continued to read the words she'd copied onto a crumpled scrap of paper. '"You'll find this woman flying above sleeping... souls."'

Sarah waved a five-pound note in Somoya's direction and addressed her as if she were speaking to a servant. 'Get us all a very cold drink, will you?'

Somoya took the money without comment and Charlotte followed her.

'I'll help.'

'Me too.' Derrie flung herself against Somoya's back, trying to climb her neat frame and Andi knew exactly how the bairn felt.

As they disappeared into the pub, Charlotte said, 'I think the answer to that clue is Mary Wings, you know, the crime writer.'

Sarah wrenched at the neck of her dress to bare as much flesh as she could to the sun. '"Raging like a bitch in heat,"' she announced inexplicably.

Andi tried to work out who she meant.

'"But we have *reason*", don't we?' Sarah continued, '"To cool our raging motions, our carnal stings."'

Jo snorted. 'She's off.'

Andi saw the curve of Sarah's cleavage outlined with lacy black. Quickly, she averted her eyes, focusing hard on the table. As she scored her thumbnail along the silver grain of the weathered wood, a waft of warm creosote reached her.

When she raised her eyes, she saw Sarah draw her legs up on to the bench, making multicoloured cotton violets gather and spill over her open thighs. Andi caught another glimpse of intricate black. What's she mucking about at? she wondered. She's acting like she's drunk.

Jo cleared her throat, staring at Sarah: 'You're not ovulating are you?'

'How... did... you... guess?' Sarah weighed each word with triumphant lethargy. 'Nature's last-ditch attempt to take advantage of my fertility and con me into going straight for a night, before the hot flushes commence.'

'Behave,' Jo sounded exasperated. 'You got years to go before all that starts.'

'And you're about as likely to touch a man, as Jo is to play for Everton,' Andi added.

Jo preened. 'Quite likely, then.'

Andi sensed that Sarah was leading up to something and initiated the first stages of an escape plan. Licking her lips, she contorted her face into an inane mask and clasped her throat, miming thirst.

'Where've those daft clowns got to with our juice? I'm so dry I could drink me own waste products.'

'D'you *have* to?' Jo screwed up her nose.

'What? Any amount of people swear by drinking their own urine.' Andi made a move to stand up, but Sarah placed a hand on her arm.

'I'm making a study of the effectiveness of all the electrical appliances in the house,' she said. 'Had sex with the shower and the washing machine before the world was awake today.'

Either she wasn't right in the head or she had somehow found out about Andi's secret and was taking the piss. Andi had to get her to shut her big gob before the others came back.

'Don't talk to us about sex. I've been celebrate for thirty years,' she said.

Sarah's eyes gleamed like she'd caught a mouse she'd been chasing forever. 'You mean *celibate*?'

'I'm *celebratin'* a lifestyle choice. Out and proud. Part of a growing number who know the truth. It's all hysterically overrated.'

'What is?'

'Have you not worked it out, pet? Orgasm is just a word used to sell women's magazines. Sprinkle liberally on a glossy front cover and watch the sales figures rocket. Why, they all know it doesn't exist, like, but this month's free gift is *guaranteed* to help you get one. They should get done by the Trading Standards.'

Embarrassed, Jo swiped her hands down her cheeks, forcing her mouth open. Good, Andi thought, now maybe she'll get her bloody girlfriend to leave me alone.

But Sarah rested sad eyes on Andi and patted her shoulder. 'You just haven't met the right woman yet.' She screeched with laughter. 'Still, with a line like that, they'll come flocking. Roll up! Roll up! Come and hear the truth about the non-existent orgasm. Fucking hell, it's genius. No woman would be able to resist the challenge.'

Andi poked her tongue out at Sarah through acid-green bubble gum before looking away.

'The connection's got to be right, that's the key,' Sarah persisted, oblivious to the way Andi had her eyes fixed on the pub, as if she wasn't with them. 'There's this woman at work who's making her way through all the blokes on the staff. After each new crap shag she waits till they're walking out of her front door, then shouts downstairs, "*I'll have the orgasm next time.*" There's got to be chemistry, but she still hasn't grasped that.' Sarah tuned in on Andi with clear calculation. 'You and Somoya make nice playmates. Why don't I have a word?'

Andi refused to answer. Why the hell Somoya liked this woman so much was way beyond her.

Finally, Jo intervened, slipping her arm under Sarah's and roughly coaxing her up. 'Come ahead. Let's go and see if they need any help with the drinks. Take no notice of her, Andi. She likes to spend her spare time spouting politics.' Jo slipped into a vaguely Russian accent. 'But deep down she's just a matchmaker from the old country. Very conventional about marriage. Can't bear not to see the entire gay community in couples.'

'I'm sorry. I didn't mean to upset you.' Sarah struggled up, standing on her tangled dress. 'Tell you what. I'll buy you a vibrator instead, then. A gold one.'

'Save your money.' Andi showed her teeth in place of a smile. 'Got one. It sounds like a helicopter. Makes next door's dog bark. I'm going to put an ad for it in *Loot*. Search and rescue equipment. One careful lady owner. As new.'

'But –' Sarah tried again.

Jo shook her head apologetically in Andi's direction and pulled Sarah away.

Alone, Andi thought it through and concluded that Sarah knew what she was planning. Why else had she made all those cracks and talked about Somoya like that? She'd obviously worked it out. Considering what they'd witnessed in the bookshop, about how well Sarah kept other people's secrets, it wouldn't be long before they all knew. That would be the end of the one thing Andi had left – her integrity. Well, she wanted to believe she still had it, but she knew no one would believe her if they saw the collection she had hidden at home. It was made up of years of chance shots: Somoya sitting, head tipped to the sun, weight balanced on her straight arms, her dark polished knees and cheeks as smooth as pebbles, and above her head, rainbows of balloons. Click. Somoya at the Show bar, chin propped in long fingers, elbow resting on the grand piano, musing over sheet music, deciding what to sing. Click. Candlelit vigil, cheek bones carved by film noir shadow and light... and more, many more.

She'd have to hide them. No, destroy them. Andi knew that if she ever saw stuff like that of herself, taken telephoto, without consent, she'd think she'd got someone bloody nuts following her. But she wasn't a stalker. She didn't sit outside Somoya's house for hours, waiting; didn't even know where she lived. There was no gallery of images ripped and plastered round Andi's walls. They were framed beautifully in an album – her gran's album that shimmered all its mother-of-pearl shades at once. It was covered up safe, layered over with lingerie that only Somoya would be allowed to see.

She's *the one*. Every time Andi looked at Somoya, she was plagued by that idea. She couldn't understand where it had come from – she'd never been all that fond of fairy tales. And even if there was such a thing as 'the one', what were the chances that she'd found her in a world population of six billion? With those odds, there could be at least, dunno, at least three thousand who'd be a perfect fit. But each time Andi ignored them, the words came back, sure of themselves: 'she's the one'.

Eighteen

'See?' Derrie explained authoritatively, 'Cows shagging. Doing the Lambada.'

'*Behave.*' Scanning the fields, Jo couldn't see anything. 'Where?'

Ignoring her, Derrie continued her lecture for Somoya's benefit. 'They can't get pregnant, though. They need a bull.'

'True,' Sarah agreed, seriously.

'Only one bull, though, for all those cows.' Jo grinned in the direction of the herd. 'They obviously prefer each other. Bet when they let him, he has a field day!'

'No. They don't do it like that, don't you *remember*?' Derrie's question held an edge of patient disappointment. It was the exact tone Derrie's teacher used at the end of most school days, when she collared Jo with the dreaded rhetorical line: 'We've not had a very good day again, have we, Derrie?'

'I'm not with you.' Somoya frowned. 'What you on about, little 'un?'

Derrie's voice deepened as she began quoting. 'They don't do it nature's way any more, yeah. It's all artificial 'semination.'

Jo sensed Sarah shuffling, as if she felt tempted to correct her pronunciation, but Somoya jumped in, her interest piqued.

'You're a right expert, aren't yer?'

'Ellie and Uncle Mark took her on a tour of his dad's cattle farm last summer,' Sarah explained.

Derrie carried on proudly. 'They make the calves that way so they're healthier and stronger.'

'Like you?' Somoya asked.

'Yeah, 'cept the sperm Jo and Sarah used for me wasn't frozen.' Jo glanced in the rear-view mirror for Somoya's reaction. 'Auntie Ellie said that, even though I'm built like a runt, I've got good genes.'

Jo mumbled aggressively, her mouth tense. 'Ellie's a cow, herself.'

Sarah turned on her with a cutting whisper. 'Why? Because she doesn't like *you*? Just for once it would be a relief if you'd lay off my sister. Especially in front of Derrie. She loves her.'

'That's half the trouble,' Jo hissed under her breath. 'I don't want Derrie thinking the sun shines out of her arse. It's dangerous.'

'Don't exaggerate.'

'*Fine*. If you want our daughter learning the finer points of getting banned from every supermarket chain in the country and lots, lots more.'

Derrie undid her seat belt and leaned forward between them. 'What're you saying about Ellie?'

Nobody answered.

Nineteen

Why's Jo going on about the supermarket? Does she know what happened, or is she just trying to find out and make me say? Ellie told me not to tell, but it's giving me cramps in my stomach now. Like with that policeman...

So massive. His uniform's blocking the sky with black. Even though I try smiling at him, his face stays stiff.

'The store has decided to press charges.' He says it low to try and stop me and Becka hearing. 'You're going to be prosecuted under the retail store initiative. Have you got somewhere you can leave your children?' He bows his head towards me and Becka, but Ellie doesn't tell him I'm not her girl. She's got a dead look in her eyes. Becka sort of slumps against her, sneaking snide glances at the stuff on the desk, as if she's trying to magic it invisible. But Ellie shrugs her off like she can't stand Becka hanging on her.

Ellie still won't speak, so I try to help. 'Jo and Sarah are in. They won't mind if –'

'*No!*' Ellie's scream stings my ear. Her face is all stretched. I've never seen that happen to her before. It makes my heart jump. Then she presses something hard in my hand – a pink bubbly out of its wrapper. I know she's trying to bribe me, so I don't put it in my mouth, just make a see-through basket for it out of my fingers.

'I don't want them involved.' Ellie looks like she's crying. Not sad. More like in a temper. 'They're the *last* –'

A bony bit pokes from the policeman's cheek when he grinds his teeth together. 'Is there a neighbour they could go to?'

'A neighbour.' Ellie talks as if her brains are in outer space.

In the police car, it's quiet. He doesn't put the siren on. Becka and me sit in the back and Ellie still won't speak to us. I think we must've done something wrong. The quiet gets more loud and I don't like it. Becka is acting like she can't see me as well, so first I look out the window. With my eyes nearly closed, the blocks of flats are all slurry. Then I stare at the two heads in front. His is bristly at the top of his neck and Ellie's zigzags like yellow lightning. Everyone says I've got her hair.

When we get to the neighbour's house, we have to wait ages while she fumbles the chain thing off the door. I don't think her hands work properly. Seeing the policeman makes her eyes go watery.

'Mrs Laverick? Sorry to bother you. We need to have a word with Ms Palmer and she wondered if you could take care of the children for a while?'

'Who?' Wavery tears.

'You know Becka and Derrie, Mrs Laverick.' Ellie's voice does all these high skips, like she's sorting out a treat for us.

'Yes, I do… I do…' She opens the door, wipes her eyes, then pulls Becka off the front step into the hall.

When we're on our own inside, we stand still until she shuffles back to find us.

'Come on, trouble.'

I wonder which one she means. I don't think it's me. She doesn't know me much.

'What's your naughty mum been doing now, then?'

Becka shouts, 'Nothing,' at the same time as I whisper, 'Nicking.'

I have to step back 'cos Becka swings round and stabs me with her eyes. It well gets on my nerves, the way she acts like she's the boss, pretending she's the oldest.

The room is full of dark stuff and shadows, like a cave. A flowery cave, with paper flopping off the walls. Floppy roses. Why are the curtains shut? Maybe she's got hiding places in here. Another old lady walks past the wall and I jump. Then I see it's a mirror in the carved black thing that reaches the ceiling. It smells of wee in here. I breathe through my mouth, but then I think I'm swallowing the wee, so I hold my breath.

'Sit here.' She points a curly finger at the wooden chairs pushed under the table. They're heavy to pull out. She waits for us to stay sitting still, then her squashy face comes close in. Her crinkly crêpe-paper skin is right in front of me. Nasty. She reminds me of ET. The bubbly in my hand has gone all slimy with sweaty sugar. I want to phone Sarah.

'Would you two like a cup of tea?'

Becka and me look at each other. Don't know what to say. We don't drink tea.

'Well, what about some juice?' We nod to make her move away. 'Sure I've got some squash somewhere.'

I can't take things from strangers. It might be poison. As soon as Mrs Laverick can't see, the budgie starts flicking seeds at us. I don't think the clock is working properly, the big hand isn't hardly moving. When she brings the squash, I make it look like I'm drinking it. But when the glass is next to my nose, I can taste toothpaste or something. Becka nudges me and then at the plate of custard creams, to see if I'll take one. They're probably soggy, but I don't want to make Mrs Laverick mad, so I nibble the corner off one with my front teeth. It's okay, but the old lady isn't eating any, so I stop.

Ask her. Ask her. I hold the plate up. 'Aren't you going to have one, Mrs Laverick?'

'Better not. I've already had too many today. I'd live off biscuits.' She sees us stop pretending to eat and her eyes go sad.

It makes me sorry – and angry. My fingers stick to the rest of my hand, then peel apart. My palm's bright pink. 'Have you got a telephone, please?'

Becka kicks my knee under the table and hisses. 'No. You're not allowed, Mum said.'

If we weren't in this house, I'd kick her back, till I made a blue and black mark. Mrs Laverick isn't listening. She has to pick the budgie's seeds off the carpet one at a time.

I try to think of another plan. Make up a lie. 'I've got fifty pence to spend. Can I go to the corner shop for you?'

'Sorry, lovey.' She does a sort of heavy stroking on my shoulder. It's quite nice. 'I promised to keep my eye on you.' Her hand stops as if she's thinking of something. My shoulder feels cold when she moves away. I listen to her scrape a drawer out of the big black furniture thing and hunt about inside for something hidden at the back.

She's so pleased when she lays the paper and biros on the table in front of us. 'Do me a nice picture.'

It's the wrong kind of paper. Lined. No good for drawing. And, anyway, you can't colour in with biros. But her face is still smiling, so I say, 'Okay.'

That stroking hand lands on my neck again and doesn't move until she can see I've started. Becka won't draw. She's waiting for Mrs Laverick to go away so she can stab my picture. Mine are always better than hers. If I do a picture for Ellie, sometimes Becka screws it up. Bet that's 'cos she thinks Ellie likes me more than her. It might be true. Ellie always calls Becka too tame, even in front of me.

'When I was young, like you,' Mrs Laverick sounds as if she's telling a fairy story, 'I thought old people were men and women from Mars and if you touched them, you'd catch their wrinkles. I never believed I'd be old like this.' She pinches the back of her hand and her skin does a slug crawl back into place. I cover her hand over with both mine, so she won't think I'm scared of getting a wrinkle disease from her. She starts to nod lots as if she's shaking and a picture comes into my head, of my own hand grown old with slow skin. Wonder how long I've got to stay here...

*

My stomach's doing that gripping, like I need the toilet. I'm not sup-posed to keep secrets, but they might not let me go round to Ellie's any more, if they know all that. Sarah says I have to tell her every-thing, even the bad things. But Jo keeps saying things about Auntie Ellie and I don't want to stop going to see her. She always gets me loads of stuff... I mean... It's not just the presents... It's not. Ellie says she's my special extra mum. Extra special.

I need the toilet. It hurts. Don't know whether I should ask them to stop the car again. We've already stopped loads. It might make us lose. No, I'll have to. I've got to go now.

Twenty

Way below, Jo saw what appeared to be huge grass sculptures looming over the valley. They took on animal forms as she steered the Porsche carefully, negotiating the steep hairpin bends.

'A frog,' Derrie decided, pointing at one of them. 'An' there's a horse's head.'

'Gargoyles,' Sarah joined in.

Somoya consulted the map. 'The Winnats. They're only about twelve hundred feet. You could climb them easy, Derrie.'

When they reached the foot of the hills, Sarah leaned back to stroke Derrie's legs, indicating the low, hut-like building on their right.

'There's Speedwell Cavern. I'll take you down there one day when we've got more time.' Her tone lifted, swinging into forced enthusiasm, 'You'd enjoy it. You sail along this pitch-dark lead mine in a little boat.'

Sarah was trying too hard, Jo thought. She sounded manic. Queasy, caustic detonations fired off in Jo's windpipe. She had to tell her. It wasn't going to stay down. She'd got to get it out, so she could stop feeling sick.

'Couldn't you take me into the devil's arse instead?' Derrie asked as they approached Castleton and she saw the large sign in front of them. She read it with deliberate, legitimate pleasure. '"Welcome to Peak Cavern, the *Devil's Arse*."'

Not waiting for an answer to her question, she slid her headphones over her ears and began to drone a vague approximation of the music playing on the tape. The lyrics were her own, providing a running commentary to the view through the window. 'Café... gift shop... café... pub... café... gift shop,' she sang while the car cruised past an array of china pigs, china clowns, lacy dolls and sponge cakes.

Old food scraped the back of Jo's throat.

The village gave way to open fields scattered with grazing sheep and a thin, pale chimney rising up from the horizon.

'What's that?' Sarah's nose crinkled as if she could smell something rotting.

Picking up the Ordnance Survey map again, Somoya located their exact position.

'Cement works. It sticks out like a sore thumb.'

Sarah checked Derrie's headphones were still in place. 'Or a skinny prick.'

Sarah was getting worse. Starting to get frigging hysterical. Trying to provoke a reaction. When they stopped, Jo made herself promise, she was going to tell her everything.

A long row of nineteen-thirties semi-detached houses flanked the road leading into Hope but, as they approached the village centre, the architecture slipped further back through the centuries.

'Wicked!' Derrie screeched. 'That pub's got a swing. Can I go on it?'

'Not if I get there first, mate,' Somoya teased.

'How about parking down by the church?' Sarah directed Jo.

The instant the car door opened, Derrie squeezed through the gap between the two front seats and scrambled over Sarah. Then she sprinted to join Charlotte, wandering towards the country lane next to the cemetery.

'Wait up, mate,' Derrie shouted. 'Have you found something?'

Hearing her, Charlotte beckoned. At the same time, Jo saw Somoya heading off in the opposite direction, up the high street, with Andi following a few steps behind.

Self-congratulation crept across Sarah's face. 'Apparently those two have abandoned the literal treasure hunt.'

Now Jo was on her own with Sarah, the village, the peace, sounded too quiet. Beneath the sporadic birdcalls, she heard an ancient silence. Leaning against the roof of the car, Jo pulled a letter from her pocket and handed it over the bonnet to Sarah.

'What's this?'

Jo shook her head, so Sarah skimmed the first few lines. Knowing its contents off by heart, Jo could hear silent, snatched phrases above the pulsing inside her skull. 'Dear Jo, After several discussions with you... sickness record... request you attend... medical examination... Tuesday 2 September 10.00am...'

Sarah lowered the sheet of paper, 'You haven't been ill. What do they mean?'

'You're the intellectual. Work it out.' Jo saw her sarcasm stun Sarah. 'I'm sorry.' Scraping trails through her hair, she tried again, more tentatively. 'Don't know... what to say.'

'Well, say *something*. Say anything.' Sarah's rising volume forced an acid flow of fear through Jo. 'How about a multiple choice? You've killed someone? You've gambled our house away? You're leaving? All of the above? For God's sake, speak.'

'You never let me.'

'*What*?'

Searching for something to fix on, away from Sarah's critical stare, Jo saw that the point of the church spire looked sharp enough to puncture the full-bellied clouds. She willed them to spill their slate-grey liquid.

'Everything I say is... wrong. So I don't bother.'

'Right. It's *my* fault. Okay. I won't say a thing. Just tell me why you haven't been going to work. Go on. Speak.'

Words stumbled about in Jo's mouth, emerging half-formed as if trying to disguise themselves. 'Can't... if you... pressure...'

She sensed that Sarah felt sorely tempted to stalk away, spitting an end to the conversation behind her. Something searing with conde-scension: come back when you've learned to communicate. At that moment, Jo knew that attack felt like the strongest means of defence for both of them. Anything to stem the tide swelling against their joint centre of gravity, threatening to swill them away. But instead of turning to run, Jo forced her feet to stay put. Anchored. Silver cherubs and pastel horseshoes from a recent wedding papered the pavement.

'Whatever it is, we'll cope with it.' The certainty in Sarah's voice was a cover. Jo could tell. Just now, wheedling out the truth was Sarah's only motivation.

'It's so...' Long pause. 'Whatever I... for years...you never let me...' Each gap in Jo's speech was choked with even more resentful words than the ones she squeezed out: '... say what I... let me decide any-thing.'

'Hang on. It works the other way too, you know. I try all the time. I never stop asking you, where do you want to go out? What should we do about Derrie playing up at school? Which bloody curtains should we buy?'

Across the road, the empty cattle market looked pristine. Jo couldn't detect a single strand of straw left on the ground. Attached to the corrugated roof, a bright red notice jarred with all the living colours growing around it. 'Keep Britain farming.'

'I hate them.'

'*What*?'

'Those new curtains.'

She saw Sarah curb the compulsion to screech in her face, 'Fuck the curtains', unwilling to supply Jo with a flippant punchline.

'All you ever say is, "I don't mind. I don't *mind*," 'til we're both sick of the sound of it.'

Jo drew in a tight lungful of air. 'Usually I don't mind. But –'

'No, because it's so much easier to let me sort everything out. You make out you're so tough –'

'I never –'

'The truth is, you wet your knickers with pleasure when strong women boss you about. You want someone to be articulate and confident for you, because you can't be either.'

'See what I mean?' Jo pleaded with an invisible jury. Raw cerise patterns began to burst out across her chest. 'I try to explain and she just twists –'

'Christ, this is turning into a helluva day. I shouldn't have wasted my money.' Sarah released her breath in a series of pained sighs while Jo edged away. 'Where are you going?'

'I've had it.' Cutting a palm over her head, Jo continued to walk.

Twenty-one

What's Charlotte looking at by that little chapel place? I can't see anything. That hedgerow's hanging right over her head. Maybe she's found it. All the diamond-shaped windowpanes are winking at once. Gotta catch up, see what that notice is pinned to the wooden door. Ceilidh this Saturday. Proceeds to Hope Nursery School Fund. No, that's nothing to do with treasure. Charlotte's got something. It's in that purple bush.

'Let me see.' My hair's all tangled in the way, so Charlotte squats down and brushes it behind my ears. Clinging underneath a leaf, a papery thing is quivering as it cracks open.

'Cool!' My shadow colours it dark brown. 'It's trying to be born.' Something feels trapped, fluttering inside my stomach. 'It can't get out.' My giant fingers reach out to help it.

'No, *don't*.' Charlotte's voice goes sharp. My fist freezes.

'Why? It's stuck. I can get it out, so we can see it fly.'

'You'll hurt it if –'

'Like I *would*. I'll be careful.'

Charlotte catches my hands between hers to stop me. 'It won't be able to fly if you –'

I pull my fingers free. She can't tell me what to do.

'*Listen.*'

She sounds like she's going to tell me something important, then her arms drop and her eyelids shut as if she's gone very tired. I try to lift her hand up again, sliding my fingers through hers. Twining round them.

'Tell me.'

I watch her eyelashes get blacker, sticking together as she starts whispering.

'I opened one once when I was about your age. My grandad had lots of buddleia bushes like these, growing in his garden, especially to attract the butterflies. Anyway, I took its body out so gently, trying not to touch it, so I didn't damage the wings.'

I puff a bit of air onto Charlotte's nose, to make her look at me, so she knows I'm listening. Her eyes open but they're staring over my head, far away. 'Then I waited. I waited for ages, but it didn't fly.'

'Why not?'

'I even pulled the wings wide to make it easier.'

'Did you kill it?'

'No. It was alive... so I took it inside to show my grandad.'

'Come on, you two,' Sarah's shouting at us from the top of the lane. 'We're going this way.'

'Did he fix it?'

'He told me that butterflies have to be left to fight their way out, because the struggle makes their wings strong enough to fly. I felt sick when he pushed the pin through it and told me I could start my own collection with it.' While Charlotte carries on talking, I can see all the pulpy yellow stuff oozing out of its body. '*Vanessa atalanta*, that's the Latin name for Red Admiral. Whenever he saw one, he used to salute and say, "Aye aye, sir."'

I can't stand it, thinking about the silky insect spiked inside a glass coffin.

'Where is it now?'

'In a museum. He left all his display cases to me. But they gave me the shivers.'

'Didn't any of your brothers or sisters want them?'

'I'm an only one, like you. When I was little, my mum and dad always told the world they broke the mould when they made me.'

I squeeze her fingers and stare straight, deep into her eyes, the way Auntie Ellie showed me, and I see Charlotte's dad standing in front of me. I wait to see what he'll say...

His throat makes a chuckling noise. 'What's that you've got on, Charles?' I feel the pink lacy stuff on the end of the blouse touching my knees. Long enough to be a dress. 'That your mother's, you little monkey?'

Mum lifts her head up from her book when he says her name. 'My *best* blouse. Come here. You haven't ripped it have you?'

I lean into her lap, touching the fluffy pattern that stands out on her skirt while she checks.

'No. I was very careful.'

'Let me look at you.' She spins me round by the shoulders. Her lenses split each of her eyes into two glass halves behind her spectacles. 'Beautiful. *You* are a little beauty.' Holding my chin in her hand, she stares as if she's searching for something inside my brain. One of her earrings gives me a blue blink. Then she taps my cheek every time she calls me a new name; 'My sweet... heart, precious... treasure,' and leaves a lipstick kiss on my nose.

My heart feels funny, inflating like a balloon that'll float away if I don't keep hold of it tight. Helium. My toes point – right foot first, right heel second, left toes, left heel. My arms push out, under the spreading chestnut tree and I twirl, making lace ripples around me. I can't see their faces, but I can hear them both laughing. Not laughing at me. Laughing as if they're pleased. They're saying, 'Look at that... Will you look at that dancing!' Talking about me. They sound nice, those words. Will you look at that dancing. Feel a bit dizzy sick, but I have to spin faster.

'Look at me dancing. I'm a girl.' The chest balloon lifts me off the rug. No, it's Dad floating me, along the wall. More and more glass cases spin past. Grandad's collection.

'Careful, son, you were about to smash your head on the table. Don't want to knock your block off, do you?'

He flies me round the ceiling, then brings me in to land on Mum's knee. Her neck's got a minty leaf smell.

'Let's take this off before it's ruined.'

When she stands me up and shakes me, a roll of flesh falls out of my pants. For a second, I wonder what it is. She pulls the shivery pink blouse over my shoulders and smoothes the creases out of it against her chest. Then she pinches the material exactly together, folds it in half and smoothes it again. 'Put this on to keep warm.' Her cream woolly cardi makes my arms feel small.

'I want a dress like that,' I tell her.

'Well, we could have a sort through for some old stuff. Make a dressing-up box.'

'No. I mean a new dress for me, like one of yours.'

She's quiet. I've said something wrong. The skin sausage wrinkles upwards and I tuck it back between my legs again to hide it.

'Can't be going to school dressed like that, son,' my dad says. 'What would the other boys say?'

Stinging starts to wet my eyes.

Mum pats my cheek twice. 'Hungry?'

My tummy twists, wringing at nothing.

'What do you want to eat?'

I can't decide.

'Come on,' she arches one eyebrow at Dad. 'There's not just you to pander to, you know.'

I tap my forehead. Decide.

Dad rubs his hands together so they whisper like paper. 'What's your favourite thing that Mum makes you?'

I know this. 'Sandwiches.'

'Yes, love,' Mum sounds relieved. 'What kind?'

'Bread and marg.'

They both laugh. I've said something funny and I'm glad again.

'Right, you,' Mum gets up and I hang on her neck. 'Go to your dad while I work on your difficult dinner. I may be gone sometime.' She bends down and I fall into his lap. His trousers are a bit rough under my legs.

'Isn't it your turn to tell me a story?' he asks me.

'No. Yours.'

'Take it in turns?'

I nod. He closes his eyes to think. He thinks for a long time and I can't tell if he's fallen asleep.

'There once was a little magic boy,' he whispers.

'Who could turn into anything he liked,' I say and then hold my breath.

'Animals, trees, streams –'

'Or sometimes a girl.'

'Yes. Sometimes...'

'Or bread and marg,' my mum says, balancing the plate on my head. 'You are what you eat...'

I patter my fingers like a moth on Charlotte's hand to bring her back. She blinks and smiles then leads me away from the bush.

'Let's get going, flutterby. Don't want to be left behind.'

'Can't we wait and see?'

'That one's going to take a while before it's finished fighting. Anyway, I thought you wanted to win some treasure.'

I scan round, 'D'you know where they've gone?'

'Not exactly, but I've got a fair idea where the "flying above sleeping souls" clue might be.' I follow her hand waving in the direction of the churchyard. 'Trouble is, I can't climb trees.'

'It's well easy. I'll show you. I've done it pure times.'

Twenty-two

Sarah rushed after Jo, pulling at her T-shirt. 'Come back and talk to me.'

Jo aimed an ironic, 'Ha,' her way as she strode across the road, towards a small row of shops.

Falling into step alongside her, Sarah tried to judge what might calm Jo down. She searched around for something that sounded genuine. She could decide later whether it had been worth the effort.

'Listen, I'm sorry. It's just that you're frightening me.'

'I'm... frightening myself.'

Once, Sarah remembered, she had found Jo's diffidence appealing. She studied Jo as she leaned against the plate glass of an outdoor shop, feigning interest in a pair of hiking boots.

'I'm such a bossy cow, I know. Such a bloody big mouth. But I can change.' Sarah realised the salt water in her mouth must be tears. Cool sweat started a trickling journey, armpit to elbow. Even in the middle of her performance, mind and body were playing to different audiences. While her psyche insisted that intellect was in control, the rest of her leaked the truth. 'I could save up for a personality transplant.' Jo laced her smile with a grimace. 'But don't make me do all the work here.' Sarah indicated the space between them. 'It's like blood from a stone with you. That letter... you not going in to work... it's not about you and me, is it?'

This time Jo didn't pause. 'No.'

Sarah almost asked. Almost delivered another multiple choice. But she knew she had to learn quickly to keep quiet.

'I haven't been going to work...'

Covering her frustration, Sarah nodded.

Jo took a strangled breath. 'I'm not speakin' to Tara from my office –'

Sarah couldn't resist. 'Is that all? Of all the *petty*...' Then she understood. 'You're having an affair with her, aren't you?' In the paved courtyard to the right, two elderly women lost interest in their cream teas. Blinking into their gold rims, they waited for the answer.

'Was.'

Red cells rushed her vision, while crass questions fought to be first out of her mouth. She wondered which one to choose. Then she remembered. Questions could wait. Her incisors itched for the jugular.

'You *lied* to me. I couldn't give a shit about you dancing to the attention of that pathetic piece of work. It was inevitable.' Sarah caught the two women still staring. She waited until they redirected their open-mouthed interest towards a ceramics display in the art gallery opposite. 'I told you last summer at your work barbecue, when she was pissed and going round telling everyone she'd just got your boss's dick out in the garden. I told you then you'd be on her list, just like everybody else. She'd shag *anything*.' Vitriol surged up Sarah's throat. As Jo lowered her head, Sarah noticed that her hair no longer looked silver, just a sad grey. Not special enough. 'I knew there was *something*... I *asked* you if that was what was going on and you *lied*.' Sarah's relentless emphasis on every other word tired even her own ears. 'Made me feel like I was going *mad*. That's what makes me ill. You piece of *shit*.' She left Jo standing alone.

'I know,' Jo whispered to herself.

Sarah stopped dead. She could smell herself. A fishy sweat seeping up her body. 'Don't think you'll get to see Derrie, after *this*,' she screeched, then turned around in time to see Jo bend at the waist. Witnessing her words impact like a stab wound, Sarah congratulated herself on her aptitude with a rhetorical blade.

In front of her, Derrie was shouting and punching the air.

'Me and Charlotte found it without you,' she crowed. 'In the graveyard, up in a tree. Check it, Charlotte, you were right, "Planted in a garden on wheels."' Her thin arm flexed into an arrow aimed at a wooden fruit and vegetable cart in front of the greengrocers. 'There's the next one.'

'I wanted to show you something in the church.' Pulling a weathered guidebook from her bag, Sarah examined it, searching for the page she'd folded back. 'Here it is. "The parish of Hope was mentioned in the *Doomsday Book* of 1086."'

Derrie continued to gloat at Sarah as she picked up speed towards the cart. 'We got Rita Sack Vest without you.'

'Vita Sackville West,' Charlotte corrected her and smiled apologetically to include Sarah. '"A woman with blue blood and green fingers."'

'"Although the present church building is mainly fourteenth century,"' Sarah carried on reading from the guide book, '"Traces of earlier beliefs exist, such as Celtic horned Gods and a phallic symbol."'

Derrie stopped, slid her arm through her mother's and pulled. 'We're not going back.'

While Derrie scoured the cart from all angles, Sarah stood silently, trapped by the future.

Christ. It was laughable to think that only three months ago Jo was suggesting Sarah should have a break from work. There was no chance of dumping her fucking job now. She was going to need every penny she could get.

Derrie felt behind the spokes of the wooden wheels and decorative panels, which blossomed with floral Victoriana. Then she poked through the fruit and flowers packed firmly together on top.

'Here it is!' Derrie pulled the gold card from a bunch of chrysanthemums.

'"Make this while the sun shines."'

'Back full circle to Hayfield,' Charlotte mumbled.

'"A place fit for Mall... Mall..."' As Derrie struggled, Charlotte read over her shoulder.

'Mallika.'

'"... fit for Mallika and her mistress to bathe al... fr..."'

'Al fresco,' Sarah inserted, without looking. 'It means outside, the literal translation from the Italian is cool.'

'What can I get you, ducks?' Beaming at Derrie, a sturdy woman materialised from inside the greengrocer's, with a paper bag plumped up, ready to fill.

'Nothing, thanks,' Sarah dismissed her.

'Not even for you, ducks?' The woman's fat grin grew warmer as she cupped Derrie's chin.

Derrie eyed Sarah for a reply.

'No, thanks,' Sarah repeated.

'Everyone's handling, but no one's buying today.' The woman puckered her lips up at Derrie in a prune kiss, before retreating out of the migraine-bright light.

'Weird,' Derrie's gaze followed her back into the shop, then she opened her palm to reveal a plum. 'Just before, the girl in the Post Office laughed at something and gave me a bubbly.' She pulled her pocket open to show the evidence. 'Everyone here keeps smiling at me.'

'That's because they live in Hope,' Sarah said, screwing up her eyes expectantly at Derrie. 'You can groan now.'

'Why?'

'Because that's what people do when you make a pun.'

'A bun?'

'Are you going deaf?'

'Pardon?'

'Behave!' Sarah pushed Derrie along with a palm between her shoulder blades. 'You've definitely got Jo's sense of humour.' As she re-alised she couldn't see Jo anywhere, her forehead pinched with worry.

'I think Mallika's mistress was called Lakmé, you know, from the opera by Delibes.' Charlotte slid the card back into the cellophane wrapping round the bouquet.

Sarah shot her a bitter look. 'Aren't you going to let anyone else solve any of the clues? Anyway, Lakmé isn't a dyke. She poisons herself over some bloke who decides to bugger off back to his regiment.'

'Well, she should have been one,' Derrie decided, 'then she'd have saved herself a lot of trouble.'

Sarah felt cynicism twist her mouth.

'She might not be a lesbian,' Charlotte said quietly to herself, 'But that flower duet is one of the gayest things I've ever seen.'

'Come on, then,' Sarah held her hand out to Derrie. 'Now we've found the thing, we better hurry up and fetch the others.'

When the little fingers found hers, Sarah shut her eyes for a moment. Instantly, a reel of squirming, slow-motion footage of Jo and Tara began to play in the dark. Sarah tried to force her mind to clear, but her paranoia had already taken on a celluloid intensity of its own. A new location...

The agonisingly slow pan along the houses on her side of the street, reached Colin, shading his eyes against her neighbour's window, cold calling.

She watched him ring the bell.

The woman's face looked blank but not hostile, busy concentrating on swallowing a mouthful of food.

'Hello. Sorry to interrupt your lunch.' He wrung his hands together. 'I wonder if you can help me? Sarah and Jo next door asked me to bring this round for their little girl. Uh... sorry, her name's slipped my mind.'

She brightened. 'Derrie.'

'Yes. Of course. Derrie.' Strange name, Sarah heard him think. Still it suited her, he decided. Rhymed with merry.

Sarah's thumb set up a radioactive throb where she'd bitten it again, to bleeding point.

'That's fine.' The woman held her hands out. When he didn't move, she lifted the silver package away from him. 'I'll give it to her later.'

The contents crackled. Sarah knew exactly what was in there. Four packets of cards, printed with mythical monsters and a collector's file full of plastic wallets.

The neighbour eyed him strangely, curious as to why he was lingering about.

'It wouldn't fit through the letterbox,' Colin explained.

'I'll make sure she gets it. Is it her birthday?'

'What?'

'Derrie's.'

'Er… I'm not sure. Better be making tracks.' He turned and walked quickly down the path. 'Thank you. Give them my regards.'

'Who shall I say called?'

Pretending he hadn't heard her, he opened the gate and kept going.

'Press pause, rewind, edit, delete,' Sarah chanted.

'What you on about?' Derrie demanded.

As they carried on walking towards the car, Sarah tried to work out what she'd said out loud.

Twenty-three

'So, what d'you do as an antidote to hiring out cars all day?' Andi asked, with a honeyed smile.

Somoya kept her eyes on the cemetery. 'Um... Well... I sometimes go climbing.'

'Naked, without ropes, like Catherine Destivelle?'

Somoya's forehead flickered with surprise. 'But I've not had much time for it lately.'

'Why not?'

'I... um... was doing this access course thing, for university, to get me, you know... into being able to write.'

'Did they learn you how to do your letters joined up?'

In answer, Andi heard a crack of bone as Somoya laced her fingers together and flexed the joints. She smiled to herself as she saw Somoya's defensive scowl, which made her look as vulnerable as a cub. Andi could've jumped her right then and clipped on for decades. She knew she'd have to do something soon, make it happen. Without pausing long enough to talk herself out of it, she scooped suntan lotion from her thickly coated shoulders and smeared it over the bridge of Somoya's nose. The stripe stood out in milky contrast to Somoya's dark complexion. For a moment, she was too surprised to wipe it off.

Andi grinned. 'Sarah says someone should try and talk some sense into you. Something about you throwing away the chance to do a Sports Sciences degree. What's that all about?'

Somoya bristled. 'It's complicated.'

Ahead of them, two young men lay in the grass, each with their elbows propped against crumpled motorbike leathers. From a distance, their shaved heads and scorched chests made them indistinguishable. One of them waved in Somoya's direction with a can of Kestrel, making the block of metal on his knuckles flash, MUFC.

'Hey. You with the hair...' he began drunkenly.

Andi could hear him ready to narrow his choice down in case she turned instead. She didn't need to be telepathic to know it would be something along the lines of 'Not the fat ginger minge. The decent one.'

'Come and sit on this.' He indicated the erection prodding a tent in his loose shorts and his head relaxed back, towards the sun.

Seeing Somoya's expression, Andi moved fast, linking their fingers and pressing Somoya's hand to her lips. Sex clenched at her stomach.

The man nudged his friend. 'What a *waste*.'

Andi couldn't resist. 'Why?' She smiled sweetly. 'Are *you* the alternative, Nobby?'

The men paused between fight and flight. Touch and go. The silent one snorted with laughter. Uncertain how his joke had been turned on him, the first man swiped briefly at the movement in his crotch, then grinned as he decided to add his own punchline.

'Nice one... In my next life I'm coming back as a lesbian.'

As soon as they were safely past, Somoya dropped Andi's hand and glared at her in disbelief. Andi tried to think of something to diffuse things.

'Wonder how many GCSEs those two have got between them? They're the kind Jo calls thick as dog shit. D'you want a Smartie?' She shook the tube of sweets, rattling it in rhythm with the percussion section in her head. 'You can have any colour you fancy as long as it's not orange. Well, seeing as it's you, I'll let you have one.'

Waving the tube away, Somoya gave Andi a flinty look. 'What made you so sure they weren't gonna kick off?'

'Don't make out you don't know. My charm is irresistible on full power. So's yours. But you only use it on women.' As Somoya's dark cheeks darkened, Andi realised how much she'd infuriated her. Hearing a struggle behind them, they both checked over their shoulders. The mouthy one had his disloyal friend in a headlock, pushing his shaved head down towards the bulge in his shorts.

Punching ineffectually, his captive whined, 'Fuck off, you queer.'

Andi saw the stronger one brace himself as he heard his cue to mount and ride. Applying more pressure to his throat, he rolled his new enemy on to his stomach. 'Who you calling queer? You fucking shit-stabber.' He sounded sober. With his free fist he punched repeatedly, as his hips ground the other man into the grass. Andi noticed he paused to adjust himself surreptitiously between the buttocks beneath him.

Hearing the smaller youth begin to retaliate, Somoya glowered. 'There you are. They could've give us a right battering 'cos of you starting, winding 'em up.' Two livid points emerged on her cheekbones like mosquito bites.

'No chance.' Andi's double-take formed part of her renewed comedy routine. '*Who* did you say started it, again? Anyway, there was no way they'd bother us,' she shook her head with certainty at the wrestling bodies behind them. 'There was enough homoerotic tension there, to keep 'em busy, flat out, for at least... two minutes.'

Somoya sucked her teeth. 'Where d'yer get your kicks, *Casualty*? It takes sod all to make that sort lose it.' She carried on muttering into the distance, her accent broadening. 'There were no need for it.' Striding away, she yelled her final words. 'Even if you've got no sense of self-preservation, you can leave me out of your *pathetic* games.'

Andi's heart heaved with nausea. Her huge heart, which only this morning had filled her chest, now compressed with industrial pressure into a mould half its natural size. Ready to cry, she berated herself – and there was she thinking they were getting on so well.

She wanted to scream after Somoya, to make her understand. But she would sound too desperate, too similar to that mad-head girl-friend of hers. So she mumbled, 'Sorry,' and started off in the opposite direction. Four years had been too long to wait, hovering to cash in on their inevitable break-up, like a vulture picking the bones before the corpse was dead.

Through tears, Andi could vaguely make out Sarah's bleary outline heading up the main street towards her. Some people definitely looked better in soft focus. Hiding her eyes, as if she needed to shade them from the sun, Andi pushed past her, managing a muffled 'Toilet'. Then she broke into a run towards the nearest pub, before Sarah could tell her what a moron she'd been. Andi knew they'd all seen wild hope shine from her, every time she'd shoved herself too far into Somoya's space. Ridiculous... insensitive... fool.

'You look terrible.'

The proximity of the voice made Andi flinch, stopping her hand forcing open the heavy oak door. Sarah again. 'Just... need to... go to the toilet.'

'I'll come with you.'

'Nah. Leave us. I'm not feeling... over clever. Can't go when I'm not on me own.'

Sarah moved her mouth into a smile, which left her eyes blank. 'I didn't have you down as an anal retentive.'

'I'm not,' Andi directed her attention at the stone step, using her sandal to cover the splash marks from her face. 'Only about pooing.' Instantly she regretted the childish word.

Sarah laughed and placed a hand on Andi's pink arm. 'Have you heard yourself? Contradictions, kindergarten vocabulary and all.'

'Stop giving us a *fucking* lecture.'

Sarah backed off.

Charging through the dark bar, Andi scrubbed her fists over her eyes. She opened the toilet door and slammed the bolt so fiercely that skin scraped from her forefinger. Resting her forehead against the wall, she thrust the finger in her mouth. This is too much. All too much. What a fucking cretin I am. No wonder Somoya shouted at us. Andi had never seen her like that before, never. The memory of Somoya's face twisted in anger made her cunt tug sharply. She sucked on her torn finger. It slipped out steadily, then pressed back into her mouth as if it didn't belong to her. Not her own, but Somoya's finger sliding over her lips and deep into soft warm. Her cunt tugged some more. No, please, she begged herself, not this, not this. The others would be wondering where she was, but she couldn't stop. A wet finger jumped in flurried haste through the zip in her shorts. Not her finger, but Somoya's jabbing at her with ragged threats. Tears hung on heavily, dragging at her lashes. Waiting. Too weak to stand, she fell back against the seat, legs spread taut in front of her, head flung back against the cistern. She barely registered the familiar voices outside in the corridor. She was all cunt. All cunt and Somoya's hand thrashing between her legs. Even though she knew it would go nowhere, would lead nowhere, leaving her high and dry, fierce with frustration.

Stupid bitch, you should know better by now. Thrashing, all cunt and legs tensing, trying too hard for some non-existent spasm. All jerking, panting, crying cunt. She opened her legs wider, begging her in. I've ruined everything, she realised. Somoya won't even look at us again. The idea left her homesick with loss and blocked shuddering. As she strained against her own, not Somoya's hand, tears spilled down her neck and hot piss trickled over her knuckles, making her pulse inside. Still squirming at the edge of an orgasm that would never come, she watched hope careening off into the distance, leaving her no way to get down. Trapped against a ledge with reeling vertigo. Stupid. Stupid. She'd got to stop putting herself through this. Somehow, she knew it *had* worked at least once before. A time when she'd been in working order. A five-year-old time when floating had been followed by stinging, slapping hands and her mother's demented face. I'm not totally empty then, Andi remembered. Still got the familiar sickness of shame to keep us company. Hurt haemorrhaged over her cheeks, her mouth and her already wet fingers as she tried to wipe it away.

'Andi? Are you sure you're okay?' Sarah's voice rang out, far too near again, on the other side of the door. 'We're heading off now.'

Andi held her breath until she could let out measured speech. 'Yeah, fine.' Then she stood up shakily, zipping her shorts and trying to smooth down her hair. 'I'll just be a second. Tell Charlotte to wait for us in the car.'

When Sarah had gone, she let herself out and steadied her body against the basin to wash her hands. Something moved in front of her. Glancing up, she met her red eyes in the mirror and knew she wouldn't be able to disguise them. Her only consolation was the certain knowledge that Charlotte wouldn't ask her to explain.

The walk to the car felt uncomfortably clammy with her pants alternating between clinging and hanging between her thighs, her limbs weighted with too many layers of flesh and her heart performing a final contraction, so that it could fit into a walnut shell.

Twenty-four

There she is now. Andi. Sweet as sugar candy. I need to get hold of her, before she reaches her car. Yes! Gotcha. It's piss easy to spin her. She's so off-guard. Weird. She's not even giving me any grief about being pinned against the wall. Got to press 'til my torso spikes her. She's bloated. Heavy but weak. No match. Disappointing. But it's cool the way she bites her mouth when I scrape her arm down the bricks. It's only fair to let her know who she's dealing with. Just in case there's the remotest chance she hasn't worked out who's in charge. Strange how blood-red a face can go. Now where's your Tate and Lyle smile?

'Jaz? What are you...?' She squeaks. I've caught a fat mouse.

This time is just a warning. There's no way you're having what's mine. Inhale. Mouth a smoke ring. A wavy halo over her crown. Make her wait. Inhale. Stream hot plumes through my nostrils. Drop the cig between her feet. There... now... speak.

'Somoya told me to tell you, she's not interested. Said, you're to leave her alone.' The bone in my groin grinds into hers. There's a spark of disgust in her eyes. Nice. Maybe I could work up to something if I keep pushing. There's not even an itch. Every nerve-ending is well dead and buried by the tranx. What if I go at it harder? Faster? Still nothing. I contemplate a handful of her orange curls wound round my fist. That might do the trick. 'She says, the way's clear for me. If I fancy it.'

Her plump mouth opens and closes again. Doesn't know what to say. It's nice. I lean in to force her lips against the ring in mine. Hold her still with my elbow against her throat. Ugh! God... filthy bitch. Spit's stinging my eyes. I try to pull her back, but she twists away, racing off to her car. Moves fast for a fat girl. Right. You're finished now, lady. That's a promise. I'll have you...

Twenty-five

'Where to now, then?' Jo asked as they approached the Porsche where Sarah and Derrie were already waiting.

'Hayfield,' Somoya answered, then yawned, rubbing her eyes in gritty circles.

'You look frigging knackered, girl.' Jo play-punched mildly at her arm in sympathetic bullying, which would precipitate tears if Somoya gave them half a chance. 'What have you been up to?'

'Nowt.'

'*And* the rest.'

Somoya tried to make her move away unobtrusive. As she climbed into the back seat with Derrie she set her tone for neutral: 'You don't want to know.'

For once, Sarah stayed silent.

'*I do,*' Derrie said.

As if she hadn't heard, Somoya simulated sleep. Even she didn't want to know any more. No wonder she was shattered after last night...

'Get up, Somoya.'

The light's too bright. Too white. I try to cover my eyes, stuff the pillow over my head, but Jaz pulls it away and sheet lightning strikes.

I dive under the duvet, waiting till the imprints on my retinas aren't so blinding, then reach for the alarm clock.

'It's three o'clock in mornin'.' From somewhere I remember this is the best time for optimum disorientation. 'What's up?'

'I can't find your purse.' The bleached lacquered points in Jaz's hair have collapsed under the strain of disturbed sleep.

'You don't need it now. Come back to bed.'

She pulls at the duvet sharply, managing to get it half off. But I catch it and wrap myself around, curled into a shell, covers fisted.

'Get. Up. And. Look.' Her words stab the cold air. 'It's not in your bag.'

Say it. Go on. Say it. 'I'm not givin' you any more money.'

'What?'

Deep inside the padded cell of the duvet, my anger's muffled. 'I'm not payin' for you to kill yourself.'

'I'm not. I've told you. *Everyone* does a bit, now and then.' Through the cloth I can see the light flicking on and off. 'You just don't understand. I can handle it.'

'Not on my money.'

The tugging at the duvet starts again, much more doggedly.

'Oh, Yeah. Miss fucking *superior*. Just 'cos you've got a job.'

It's impossible to hold on. My nails bend back, so I lose my grip. My skin's iced now the covers are off and the electric glare is way too much. I grab my dressing gown and try to get out of the bedroom, but she pulls me back by my hair. I'm not going to react, not going to give her any excuse to blame me. I extricate her fist from my hair and face her, making my solid stare say: I won't be your victim. I've planned my escape route.

The whining begins. 'You know I can't just stop. It's not possible.' The grasping hand feels freezing against my neck. 'It's the only thing that makes me feel normal.'

'Get on a programme, then.'

'You said you'd come with me. You promised.' The piercing in Jaz's lip is red-ringed with infection and exhaustion has drawn with a bloody eyeliner inside her lower lids. 'I can't go on my own.'

'Name the day.' How many times can she play out this scene?

Jaz stills. 'Please don't say I've killed it.' Her pale fingers curl into claws. 'I've killed us. Haven't I?'

My throat blocks, too sorry to speak.

Twenty-six

In the other car, the sun's rays seared through the windscreen, smudging Andi's view of the hump-backed hills. The graze down her arm stung like a bastard. Why the hell had she frozen? She'd just stood there like a lobotomised rabbit. But that was *assault*. There was no way she could let Jaz get away with it.

'Are you all right?' Charlotte sounded concerned. She obviously wasn't going to ignore the swelling around Andi's eyes.

Andi jammed the car into top gear and floored the accelerator.

'I'm champion, me.'

Embarrassed, Charlotte continued flicking through the book Sarah had bought her, until one paragraph made her pause and mark it with a pink acrylic nail.

Andi tilted her head towards the book. 'That bit good?'

'I wouldn't say good, exactly.' Charlotte pressed her lips together so severely that they disappeared. When she started to read, the words were flat and matter-of-fact. 'It's about this woman who demanded to see her medical records, because she couldn't function sexually and she knew she'd been in hospital for some sort of surgery, when she was one and a half.' She stopped for a moment to let out a sigh that caught in her throat like a sob. 'Turns out, they thought she was a boy when she was born, but the parents were ashamed of his small penis, so then this doctor decided she was a girl with a huge clitoris, which had to be removed.'

Andi swallowed. 'Christ, that's sick.'

'The doctor seemed to think that congratulations were in order, for rescuing her with his amazing cosmetic surgery.'

'Cosmetic? More like mutilation. When did this go on?'

Charlotte peered at the page. 'It's not ancient history. Still happening, as far as I can tell.'

'How very bloody enlightened... The mighty intellect of western medicine. Does that bunch not read at all? Some cultures have accepted for ages there's a third gender.' As Andi ground her teeth, she felt her jaw protrude below her cheekbones. ''Bout time some people worked out we've all got something special to contribute, like, to being human.'

'I don't think Sarah would agree with you. A couple of times today, I'm pretty sure I've caught her thinking once a man, always a man.'

'Aye, well, she wouldn't say, once a straight, always a straight, would she nah? That lass'll not use her brain in case she wears it out. At the risk of sounding like an auld hippy, someone needs to get it through to her that looking after each other is the real rebellion.'

Andi watched Charlotte's chest fill to capacity. A mountain-top expansion of spirit.

'I can see why she's scared. I know how ambiguous I am... six foot... gawky. I'm not going to blend in and pass for a woman. I don't even want to try to pass any more. I'm not a man or a woman. This is just me.'

'Dead right, hinney. It's hiding that's ganna have us all loopy.'

'Yes, but walking round being a bridge between the two makes you a –' Charlotte paused, 'a target.'

'Aye, must be grim having to be a warrior all the time.' Andi hoped she was throwing a lifeline. 'But it must be better than being –'

'... a victim?' Charlotte sealed something between them with a nod.

Twenty-seven

'Phew! Derrie.' Somoya waved her hand in front of her nose, as Sarah swivelled to investigate the goings-on in the back seat.

'What does it smell like?' Derrie asked, delighted.

'Terrible!' Sarah and Jo objected in unison.

'No,' Derrie corrected, sniffing the air like a connoisseur. 'Beef and onion crisps.'

Somoya pushed Derrie away from her. 'Get away from me, you stinker from Treblinka.'

Derrie's eyes creased shut with a grin.

'That's a rather unfortunate description,' Sarah objected. 'Given its association with concentration camps.'

'I didn't mean –'

Jo stabbed the switch to open her window. 'God Almighty. Open the one behind me, Somoya.'

'Why? Have you done one, too?' Derrie's spiralling giggle triggered a general splutter of laughter, saving her from any further censure. Sarah folded down the mirror over the windscreen and saw Somoya lifting her long-sleeved T-shirt at the wrist to check her watch. Usually she kept her sleeves rolled up to show the watch off, saying 'Peter Storm' in reply to anyone who noticed it.

'It were at least fifteen minutes since we stopped for a toilet break,'

Somoya squeezed Derrie to her chest. 'Think it's about that time again, no danger.'

'Turn at the crossroads up there. Can you see the sign?' Sarah demonstrated with an air steward's signal to the left. 'Family pub. Quarter of a mile.'

'But that's the opposite direction to where we're headed.' The complaint in Jo's voice catapulted Sarah back to being a child on one of the interminable journeys she'd endured with her father. The car invariably made her nauseous or desperate for the toilet and each time she asked him to stop, he'd hiss, 'Ye... s, ye... ss.' Her hope fermented with every approaching pub, as she tried to sound reasonable, 'There... we could stop there.' But he'd accelerate past so many, that she couldn't help crying. Tears always prompted his inevitable protestations of innocence. '*What*? What's the *matter*?' Sarah gritted her teeth as she studied Jo's profile, wondering if she'd drive past the turn-off.

'Yes, there,' Derrie demanded. 'It says it's got a fun factory.'

Jo indicated to pull into the left-hand lane.

'I bet they have them height restrictions.'

Sarah smiled at Somoya's tone of regret.

Poker-faced, Jo swung them into the crowded car park. 'You'll be all right then, Somoya.'

Derrie smacked the palm of her hand against the back of the driver's seat. 'Leave her alone, you.'

Somoya preened, her chest swelling. 'It's getting beyond a joke, is this. Snack size is gorgeous. We're midget gems, us two.'

Sarah got out to let Somoya pull Derrie from the back seat.

'Yeah, *see*,' Derrie jeered at Jo just before she slammed the car door.

They watched Derrie and Somoya race each other to be the first to the indoor playground, ignoring the families blocking their way. 'You two,' Sarah shouted after them, 'We're only stopping for the toilet.'

The queue outside the door marked Mums and Girls stretched two deep down the mock Victorian staircase. Children leaned and climbed on the dark, shelved walls, threatening to topple reproduction cottage teapots and worn hardbacks.

Just as Sarah reached the head of the line, Derrie wound an anaconda grip around her waist, tangling them both together with strings of helium balloons.

'Can I have two pounds to go in the Fun Factory?'

'I thought you said you were going to win the treasure hunt?'

'I am but –'

'Toilet.' Sarah took hold of Derrie by the neck, like a skittering puppy, and steered her towards a vacant cubicle. 'You go in there. I'll be in the next one.'

As Sarah tried to lock the door behind her, Derrie slipped past and jammed the bolt across, her eyes almost closed in a triumphant grin.

Feigning impatience, Sarah hitched up her dress. 'Can't I even wee in peace?'

'No.' Derrie laid a hand on her mother's chest, and applied an even pressure until she over-balanced.

'Hang on,' Sarah struggled to pull down her pants from a sitting position. 'Give me a chance.'

'Hurry up,' Derrie scolded. 'I need to go and there's a loads of people waiting.'

Sarah strained. Nothing happened. 'I can't now.'

'*Concentrate.*' Derrie bent her knees into a standing squat, and forced her lips forward to hiss, 'Go on. Pisssss.' The balloons squeaked between Derrie's back and the wall and an irresistible cackle rose from Sarah. Delight creased Derrie's eyes into slits. She exaggerated her crouch, riding the joke like a miniature jockey and increased the hissing to full volume. Doubled over, helpless and high-pitched, Sarah giggled as her pants danced round her ankles. Even while everything else was falling apart, she realised that her girl could still raise her up, save her from oblivion.

A sharp voice followed an even sharper knock on the door. 'Are you kids quite finished in there?'

Kneeling down, Derrie slid a hand under the gap in the door to give the woman outside a royal wave. Sarah gathered her dress rapidly into a ball and forced it against her mouth to muffle her spluttering. In the momentary quiet, Sarah heard the outside door whine open.

'This is the *ladies*,' the same indignant woman told the newcomer.

'I *know*,' Jo's bitter tone made Sarah break out in an empathetic rash of humiliation. 'Sarah, are you in there?'

'No, we're not,' Derrie piped up.

'Have you nearly done? I thought you must've fallen down the plumbing.'

'We're coming now,' Sarah tried to placate her.

The door screeched again as Jo left.

When they tried to get out, the balloon strings caught in the cubicle door, tugging them back. Sarah kept her face to the floor, afraid to meet the eyes of the women waiting.

'Somoya!' Derrie's volume turned heads as she charged up to the bar. 'Show me that trick now with the balloons.'

'Not in here, pal.' Somoya flashed her chunky silver watch. 'Time to get back on trail. We've lost eight minutes. The others will be long gone.'

Pushing back through the pub, Sarah noticed Derrie's head bent over two muscular figures in her hands, crashing plastic fists against each other, inside a tiny boxing ring. She remembered her daughter's developing talent for acquiring things that didn't belong to her and brought Derrie to a halt by squeezing her shoulder.

'Where did you get that?'

The sparrow bones under her fingers jerked away as Derrie shielded the battling bodies with her palms. 'Somoya got it for me.'

Leave her in peace. Learn to trust her, Sarah told herself. But she couldn't.

'Did you?'

Jutting her chin at Sarah, Derrie draped her arm around Somoya, her new favourite.

'Yeah. They're giving 'em away with the kid's meals.'

'She didn't have anything to eat.'

A modest smile played hide and seek around Somoya's lips.

'You can even prise plastic boxers out of barmaids.' Sarah slapped Somoya's back. 'Is there no end to your charm?'

Staring straight ahead, in the driving seat, Jo's fists were locked around the top of the steering wheel, as if to stop her falling.

'I'll have you another game, muscles.' Squashing into the back seat of the car, accompanied by the rubber screeching of balloons, Somoya lifted the toy out of Derrie's hands. 'Are yer going to give us a go, or what?'

Derrie leaned in, her nose not quite touching the plastic figures. 'I'll be the blue one this time.'

'Make it best of three. I'm not letting you hammer me this match.' She flipped a lever and they both followed the movements intensely, willing the outcome. It took the blue fighter only four punches to knock his opponent out. Somoya tossed the toy back to Derrie in disgust. 'See that? She's only gone and done it again!'

'Yes. Yes. *Yes*.' Fists outstretched, Derrie punched the roof. 'I'm the *winner*.'

'Put your seat belt on, champion.' Intrigued by the toy's action, Sarah leaned back to reach for it. 'Made in Korea. Some kid will have got paid ninety pence a week for packing these.'

'What kid?' Derrie asked.

'A lot of children. Millions of kids aren't lucky like you.' Sarah couldn't believe she'd said that. But it didn't stop her slamming it home with the subtlety of a sledgehammer. 'They can't go out to play, they have to work all day.'

Jo winced. 'You sound just like me auld fella.'

'And mine,' Sarah agreed, realising her words were an exact repeat of her father's, but at the same time gratified by the pain on her daughter's face.

'Can we send them some money, so they don't have to work?'

'It's not as simple as that.' Go on, you bitch. Cultivate her helpless middle-class guilt. 'We can't stop people being poor on our own. It takes real political change... It takes governments...' She felt herself wading through cynicism too thick to go on.

'But we could sell the holiday prize. All the treasure.'

'What makes you so sure we're gonna win?' Jo fed the wheel through her fingers with smooth control.

I still love her hands, Sarah realised sadly, as she glanced away out of the window. Under acute sunlight, the hills were a washed-out patchwork of muted shades.

'I just know. Give us them men back, Sarah. We want another fight... fight... fight.' Derrie savoured the word, as it scrambled higher into a playground chant.

'If you like this,' Somoya waved the toy. 'You'll go mad for me new Lara Croft. She's got all different weapons and moves, I tell yer.'

Sarah saw her little girl's curiosity pique to such a point that she lost concentration on the game in Somoya's hands.

'What like?'

'Jo likes those little grunts she makes when she jumps and lands from a great height. Gets her all excited.' Sarah dropped into an un-mistakable sensual whisper. 'Huh... Huh... Huh... Pathetic, eh? Grown woman getting off on a computer image.'

'Not really. Them are my favourite bits an' all.'

Sarah tutted loudly. 'Too sad for words.'

'What new weapons?' Derrie persevered.

'You'll have to wait and see, won't yer?'

Desperate for Somoya's approval, Derrie boasted, 'She looks like my Auntie Ellie.'

'Who?' Somoya asked.

Sarah translated, 'She means Lara Croft.'

'Only Ellie's got blonde hair,' Derrie continued.

'Look at Somoya's face,' Jo teased. 'All flushed. She wishes she knew her.'

'Who?' Sarah aimed a mean glint at Jo. 'Lara?'

Jo rolled her eyes. '*No*. Your *sister*.'

'Hah!' Sarah snorted. 'You're so easy to wind up.'

Sighing heavily, Jo jerked the steering wheel round the tight bends. 'And *I know* which of the two I'd rather spend time with.'

Sarah noticed Derrie listening intently, so she gave Jo's leg a warning pat. 'That's enough now.' Jo swiped at her hand, on the pretext of changing gear. The car's lurch downhill sent Sarah's stomach into freefall.

While Somoya battled with the toy, Derrie squeezed a red balloon to the brink of bursting and back. Jo flinched.

'Get that *off* her, will you, Sarah? I'm trying to *drive* here.'

Sarah made a snatch at it. 'Give it to me now.'

Calculation flecked Derrie's features as she seized the invitation to a well-loved game. Holding the balloon a precisely judged inch out of Sarah's reach, she dug her nails into the rubber.

'Stop it *now*, or –'

Somoya sat up. 'D'you want me to show yer that belting trick with the balloon I told you about?'

Derrie handed it over. Untying the knot, Somoya said, 'Imagine what the android would make of this.'

'Who's that?' Derrie asked.

'Me boss.' Somoya dropped her voice an octave. '"You may or may not know, luv, that we've a stack of applicants that'd snap up your job, given half a chance. Think on." He's Bolton born and bred, so he sounds human, but scratch his plastic surface an' yer can spot the android a mile off.'

'Really?'

'She's kidding you, Derrie,' Sarah explained. 'You want to be careful what you tell her. She's got a bad case of heroine worship. She'll believe everything you say.'

Making her eyeballs bulge, Derrie shouted back. 'No, I *won't*.'

Somoya sucked the gas from the balloon and with tightened vocal chords, began a fast burble. 'Carlton Car Hire. How can I help you?

Giggling frantically, Derrie grasped Somoya's upper arm. 'You sound just like Alvin from the chipmunks.'

'How can I help you, modam?'

Derrie didn't need any more prompting. 'Um... I want a car, please.'

Somoya took another gulp and tried not to laugh as she let out the squeaky words.

'Yes, modam. What model would you like?'

Sarah felt pleased to see Somoya so carefree for the moment, but at the same time worried about the consequences of this new party trick. Derrie would want to add it to her repertoire any second and might too much of the gas be harmful?

Derrie tried to grab the balloon, 'Gimme it. I want a go,' but Somoya whipped it out of her way.

Sarah shook her head slightly in Somoya's direction. 'I don't think it's a good idea, Derrie. You might hurt your –'

'You never let me do *anything*.'

Copying the downward pull of Derrie's mouth, Somoya whined, 'You're not bothered about *me* damaging myself, only *her*.'

Unsure whether this was another game, Derrie watched as Somoya let go of the balloon through the open window. Its rude, rubbery departure and the speed at which it collided with the dry-stone wall made Derrie's mouth drop open. The distraction complete, Somoya carefully fitted headphones over Derrie's knotted hair and pressed the play button on her mini-disc player.

'You remembered!' Derrie yelled over the tinny, insistent rap music. Sarah resisted the temptation to tell her to turn it down. Being an ogre twice in two minutes was too much. Instead, she studied the valley, noticing farms the colour of hay, camouflaged by scrubby trees.

'That's 'cos I'm brilliant, aren't I?' Somoya crowed.

Derrie's eyes glazed seriously, as she bobbed her head in a self-conscious pre-teen copy she'd committed to memory.

Listening to the tinny beat, Sarah sighed gratefully. 'Thanks. *Now*, first peaceful moment we've had to find out how *you* are.'

Somoya paused, 'I'm all right.'

Jo took her eyes off the road to glare at Sarah, but she affected a fascination with the small stone cottages lining the steep slope into Hayfield.

'No, I mean how are you *really*?'

'Sarah, if she doesn't want –'

'I'm allowed to be concerned about our friend, aren't I?'

'At the risk of causing another domestic... I'll talk.' All traces of the girlish face vanished. Worry cut parallel lines into the bridge of Somoya's nose and her weary tone made her sound like a stranger. 'What d'you want to know?'

'Well, how are things with you and...' In her mind, Sarah inserted 'that bitch,' and in answer, she thought she heard Jaz spit a laconic reply in italics. Sarah had always found Jaz's jumpy delivery annoying... no, more than annoying... unnerving.

'Oh, you know...' Somoya replied finally. 'She's graduated to carving knives.'

Sarah dug at Jo's thigh asking for help, but got a silent refusal. A crowd sprawled on the cobbles outside The Packhorse, drinking and staring as the car passed.

Without removing her blaring headphones, Derrie flattened her nose against the glass. 'Everyone keeps nosying at us.'

Jo nodded. 'Goes with the territory when you're in a car like this.'

'I've been wondering...' Somoya whispered, 'Does Derrie know the bloke?'

'Who?' Sarah asked, recognising Somoya's attempt to change the subject.

'Er... you know... the donor.'

Disgust shrivelled Sarah's features as she recoiled. '*No!* He's *nothing* to do with her.' She knotted her arms. '*Nothing* at all.' The guttural clearing of her throat closed the matter. 'Anyway, you were going to tell us about last weekend. Did you two go over to stay with Jaz's mother?'

'Mmm.'

They slowed through the centre of the village, crawling past an old-fashioned red telephone box, a pet shop and a post office, as Jo searched for somewhere to park.

'And?' Sarah decided to keep pushing, despite Jo's rolling heaven-ward glance.

'When we got there, Jaz's Mam were trying to shave the back of her own head. She said she had to do it because the long ends were spik-ing right back into her neck, like an in-growing toenail, or something.' The strain showing around Somoya's eyes negated her sudden bright smile. 'But she's got a nervous twitch, so as she was shaving she –'

'Is this a joke?' Sarah demanded.

'... took a huge chunk out.'

Jo snorted with laughter. 'Pity she didn't slice her head off.'

'Then me and Jaz had to sit and watch, while she drew the missing hair back in with a black felt pen.'

'I don't believe you,' Sarah said.

'You can't go wrong with proper drawn-on hair, can yer?'

'No wonder Jaz is a maniac,' Jo observed. 'Tough fighting an in-heritance like that.'

On a roll, Somoya spilled the rest in rapid bursts. 'So then Jaz's brother phones, all tanked up, making demands. "Where's our Jaz?" he says, "Put the little get on." Likes to use the free call time on his mobile to have a go at her. Says he's having a trauma. Actually,' she paused for breath, 'it were just another tantrum. Loves throwing his teddies out of his pram.' Sarah visualised a massive male version of Jaz. A bleach-headed blur flinging soft toys. 'Meanwhile, we're sittin' there starving, wondering if dinner's ever gonna materialise.'

'No worse than usual then?' Jo asked.

'Never mind those retards,' Sarah said. 'What about you and Jaz?'

As they pulled into a queue of cars waiting to park outside the

Royal Hotel, Somoya made sure Derrie's gaze was still directed out of the window before she lifted up the long sleeve of her T-shirt. An extensive line of haphazard black stitches emerged, woven through the yellow bruising on her forearm.

'What the...?' Sarah couldn't finish.

'The weekend just got better and better.' Sarcasm made Somoya sound jaunty. 'Jaz stuck a bread knife in me an' I ended up waitin' half the night in Casualty. Beats watchin' *Match o' the Day*.'

'I'm hungry.' Derrie snatched the headphones from her ears.

'Me too.' Somoya slipped her sleeve back in place.

Sarah leaned back to pat Derrie's knee. 'We're stopping now for a special picnic tea for Jo's birthday. See? There's the park where we told Andi to meet us.'

Jo sniffed with derision. 'That's a cricket pitch, Sarah. Where, in case you haven't noticed, they're having a match.' Sweating, she manoeuvred the car into a cramped space, then switched off the engine and relaxed her neck back against the headrest.

'Can't we just have a sandwich now, in the car?' Derrie pleaded. 'Charlotte said we have to search by the river.'

'No. We're going to sit down for a proper –'

'We'll end up last!'

A mobile phone chirped. In a synchronised move, Somoya felt for her pocket as Sarah picked up her bag.

'That'll be Andi now, wanting directions,' Sarah said. 'I told her she should stay close behind us.'

'Andi can read a map.' Jo's tone implied 'even if you can't'.

'It's mine,' Somoya said punching buttons. The line buzzed with static and Sarah noticed the warmth drain from her cheeks when Somoya heard the voice on the other end of the line. The phone bleeped as she cut the connection.

'Who was that?' Sarah asked.

'No one.'

Twenty-eight

'Little shits.'

Andi turned to see who Jo meant and saw her grasping the corners of a broadsheet from a rack screwed to the newsagent's door.

'Snidy little no marks.'

Somoya was leaning against the wall but Andi avoided looking at her although she knew she'd have to get her on her own and warn her that Jaz had followed them. But there was no way she could bring herself to speak. Logic lost out, strangled by fury. She was even madder at Somoya than at her maniac girlfriend.

'See that?' Jo slapped the headline with the back of her hand. '"Women deserve to be hit, say boys."'

'Let me see,' Derrie said, pulling at the pile.

'Listen to this.' Bringing the newspaper down to Derrie's eye level, Jo carried on reading. '"A study revealed that half of all young men aged sixteen to twenty-one think rape is acceptable in certain circumstances and one in four of them believe it is okay to hit a woman."'

Andi put three weighty carrier bags of food down on the pavement and rubbed her stretched biceps. 'These are a ton weight.' She handed one of the bags to Jo. 'Where are you parked?'

'Right next to the *picnic* grounds Sarah found for us on the map.'

Ignoring her, Sarah asked, 'Where have you left Charlotte?'

'Still in the car, she'll be down in a bit.'

Andi leaned over Derrie's shoulder to skim the article.

'But why?' Derrie asked. 'Why's it say that stuff?'

With a rigid jaw, Jo answered. 'Because they're little wasters. What we need is another war to clear them out. At the end of the day –'

'Here begins the sermon,' Sarah slowed to a leaden delivery, 'Of that renowned social commentator and humanitarian wit –'

'Half-wit.' A self-mocking smile edged Jo's mouth. 'Sarah's trying to teach me some more big words.'

Andi poked her tongue into her cheek to cut off her first instinct for sarcasm, but she couldn't keep quiet.

'Give over, man. Convenient pinning it all on the lads, isn't it? I don't know why I'm bothering to argue the toss with you, mind.' Hoisting her bags, she took off towards the gates of the cricket club. 'If you read on, you'll see it says, "Surprisingly, twenty per cent of girls between eleven and fourteen also thought some women deserve to be struck."' Andi tilted her chin harshly in Somoya's direction. 'There's a lass not too far from here who'd agree with those sentiments.'

Andi picked up speed along the street, making the bags slam into her legs. As she'd planned, Somoya caught up in seconds.

'Who d'yer mean?' Her face drained to grey.

Andi refused to answer. You know fine well. Don't pretend you don't.

'*Please*, Andi.'

'Your girlfriend just tried to strangle me.' She dumped the bags on the pavement and covered the contaminated part of her neck. 'Poor soul's a bit touched.'

'Where is she?'

'Ask if I give a bugger.'

'I need to get a hold of her before she does some real damage.'

Andi held up her grazed forearm. 'As opposed to the imaginary injuries she inflicted on me?'

'I'm sorry.' Somoya's blush resembled a scald, then a sudden change of mind flared in her eyes. 'Bollocks to this. I'm not her bloody keeper.' She crossed the road to escape.

I'm done with this, Andi decided. Strange how it takes no time to fall in love and even less to fall out. Jaz had gone and done her a favour by making her realise that anyone who could pass the time of day with that nowt, let alone live with her for years like Somoya had, must have something seriously wrong with her.

She waited for the others to reach her.

'Have you got those special things you said you'd made me?' Derrie's voice climbed high-pitched with hope.

Andi slapped her forehead too severely. 'You catch up with Somoya, hinney. I'll go back to the car for them.'

Twenty-nine

As she searched for the perfect place to spread their blanket, the sun-dried grass stabbed Sarah's bare feet like harvest stubble. The day had reached a deep-fried August heat.

'Watch me, Derrie. Can you do this?' Finally free of the driver's seat, with enough green space to spread out, Jo performed a string of leggy cartwheels. Hurriedly, Sarah dropped the blanket and unzipped the video camera from its melting plastic case. The hollow crack of a ball being hit echoed round the grounds.

Seeing Sarah trailing her through the viewfinder, Jo delivered a cool warning. 'Don't point that thing at me.'

The navigation of her cartwheels became erratic and they all saw the long loops of blackberry thorns well before Jo landed upside down in them.

'Ow. Shit!'

'You want me to do that?' Derrie heckled, mischief creasing her face. 'Including the last bit with the bush?'

'Professional foul,' screeched from the roots of the shrub. In the background, the late afternoon light made the players in the distance vibrate white against the lime green pitch.

The camera jerked in her hands as Sarah attempted to suppress her laughter. But the voice in her head told her that this was going to turn out like any other crappy home movie, worse than her students' work. She didn't know why she was filming Jo anyway... it was pointless. She ejected the battery roughly, slotted it into a pouch alongside the camera and zipped the case back up. She regretted bringing it. No one liked it in their face and she couldn't be part of what was happening if she kept trying to record everything. The end results weren't even worth it. Never perfect.

Jo jumped up, freeing herself from the brambles. 'Oh, by the way, there's no permanent injury, thanks for asking.'

Against her will, the amiable slovenliness of Jo's speech held her and she watched as Jo clamped her arms under Derrie's, swirling them both into a wash of colour. Trees and T-shirts ran into a sick spin picture. The instant they hit the ground, Derrie dived full length against Jo, pinning her down with ferocity.

'Get out of *that* without moving, you mongrel.'

From experience, Sarah knew that the pressure Derrie could exert far outweighed the suggestion of her slight frame.

'Right rough, you're getting,' Somoya shouted across to Derrie.

'Uh... I'm rock hard, me.' Jo's groans sounded real.

Sarah couldn't believe she'd said that stuff about stopping Jo seeing Derrie. There was no way she would hurt her daughter like that... but Colin might. Where was he now? Sarah strained to pinpoint him. For some reason, he'd dissolved from her internal radar screen. She chewed a piece of rubbery skin from her forefinger. Perversely, she wanted him back, so she could keep track of his movements.

From nowhere, a tortoiseshell cat padded in a circle around Jo and Derrie.

'She's a magnet for children and animals, that woman,' Sarah told Somoya out of habit, as they prised open plastic sandwich boxes. Then she raised her voice in a panicked command. 'Don't touch it, Derrie. You might catch something.' But the pair of them were already taking turns to drag lines down the cat's spine.

'I don't *think* so,' Derrie pronounced, with premature adolescent petulance.

'Leave her, Sarah,' Jo murmured, mesmerised by the fur under her fingers. 'She's all right.'

Sarah waved a packet of baby wipes at Derrie. 'Let me clean your hands before you eat.'

Derrie turned several shaky cartwheels around the cat, as if she hadn't heard.

'Come on,' Sarah beckoned again.

Pausing briefly to inspect her hands, Derrie wiped them on the seat of her shorts.

'They're not dirty.'

'There's germs on the grass *and* the cat.'

Jo ambled over, shaking her head. 'You'll give her a complex.'

Derrie followed, screwing her nose up at her from behind Jo's back. 'I'll wash them in the river, now, if we go and look for the next clue.'

Sarah seized her hands and scrubbed at them with a wet tissue. Each pearl nail had fine grime lines drawn under the surface. 'Have you been sticking your fingers in the chocolate spread?'

'No.'

'Sure?'

Derrie wound her arms round Sarah's neck. 'Well, maybe.'

Jo leaned back, legs sprawled wide, claiming the grass, and Sarah marvelled at the way her long limbs belonged everywhere. Even the silver threading through Jo's hair did nothing to dispel the image of casual energy. Casual enough to betray me. That, Sarah knew, would have to be stored till later. Otherwise, she would never get through the rest of the day. Raising her gaze to the opposite side of the pitch, where the grounds were bordered by three-storey terraced houses, she spotted Andi traipsing towards them.

Charlotte minced several steps behind, clasping a cushion to her insubstantial chest. She picked across the clipped grass, trying to withhold her weight from her sinking heels. When she made it to the blanket, she hovered at the periphery, as far away from them as possible. They all watched her plump up the paisley print cushion and arrange it on the ground. Her mouth strained during her painful descent and just then a smattering of applause rose from the crowd around them, accompanied by mild murmurs of 'Well done'. Charlotte spun round to make sure the approval was for the game, just as the umpire raised his arms. Then she stretched the knitted filigree material of her twinset over her giraffe bones. Sarah tried not to stare. It must feel like a furnace in those things. What could she be thinking of? Charlotte's fashion sense struck Sarah as having less to do with retro than with reproducing a copy of a favourite aunt in some coveted seventies snapshot. She didn't offer to help them unpacking the picnic, so Sarah left her alone to gaze around with watery eyes.

The play fight on the fringe of the pitch entered round two. 'Here you go, you little smartarse. Let's try this for size. Grievous bodily harm with a cheese an' tomato sarnie.' Jo straddled Derrie and dabbed her nose and forehead with the sandwich.

'That's puny,' Derrie taunted back.

Andi walked in a wide circle, avoiding Somoya, and arranged herself on the last available corner of the blanket. As Andi held out a faded tin, covered in pink tea roses, Sarah saw the hay-dry scent of the grass nettling her nose.

'Here. I made some biscuits.'

Andi lifted the lid and Sarah smelled spice. She picked out a crumpled chunk and took a bite. Instantly, her mouth shrank from sugar overload and pain probed into her root canals.

'Gorgeous, aren't they?' Andi exclaimed, selecting a large piece for herself. 'I can't stop eating them.' Cheeks bulging, she offered the tin to Charlotte, then vaguely in Somoya's direction. When they both shook their heads, Andi's smile slipped. She peeled her sticky fingers apart and sucked them. 'They're awful claggy.'

Dropping her biscuit back on the pile, Sarah tried to swallow her laughter along with the syrupy mixture clinging to her palate. 'Those things will give you diabetes.'

'What?' Andi bit her lip. 'You can't get it like that... Can you?'

Sarah's head reeled drunkenly. 'I'm floating. You're all so small down there... going into... a coma.'

'Oh, aye, hilarious.' Andi forced the lid back on. 'More for us.'

'Glad to see you're not on a diet,' Sarah said.

'Nah. I *love* my big bum.' Andi broadened her Geordie vowels for emphasis and Somoya glanced up briefly, resentfully, to check her over.

'Half the world on a diet,' Sarah's soapbox delivery gathered momentum. 'The other half starving. All those skeletal American sitcom stars, desperate to be a size nought. Aching to disappear up their own arseholes.' The sight of Charlotte nibbling miserably at the corner of a sandwich stopped her.

'I know who *will* appreciate these.' Andi swiped up the tin and marched over to where Jo and Derrie were still wound in a tumbling bundle on the grass.

Without conviction Sarah tried to stop her. 'She hasn't eaten any salad yet.' But she knew it would be pointless trying to force-feed Derrie. She'd end up eating even less. Years of subdued fights about food had taught Sarah something. Still, she'd never understand how anyone could be so uninterested in eating. In compensation, she bit a chunk of bread and cheese in half and without swallowing, crushed in the rest.

'Slow down, girl,' Jo called to her. 'You'll choke yourself.'

The bread burned, sand-papering the back of her throat as it resisted peristalsis.

Absentmindedly, Somoya scratched at the stitches in her arm.

'So. What brought *that* on?' Sarah croaked through dry crumbs.

Somoya frowned, unsure what she meant until she saw Sarah's eyes trained on her forearm.

'Told her I'd had enough... for the millionth time.'

'But I thought she'd calmed down since she started taking –'

Abruptly, Somoya cut into Sarah's speech. 'It's gonna take more than Prozac to sort her head out. Especially now she's on this new drug-combining therapy.'

'What new –?'

'It's called neck everything you can get your hands on.'

'Fruitcake,' Jo interjected, heading towards the picnic.

'Er! *I'm* not eating it.' Derrie's lips curled to her nose as she jogged to keep up. 'The raisins are like rabbit poos.'

'I just thought...' Sarah continued more carefully, clutching for code as Derrie closed in to listen. 'The last time I saw you...'

'Oh, aye, in her more lucid moments she knows she needs help. But next minute she's convinced there's nowt wrong. I swear, it's getting worse, if that's possible.'

'Who you talking about?' Derrie flung herself down on the blanket.

'Just someone Somoya knows,' Sarah answered quickly.

'It's Jaz, isn't it?' They all turned, captured by Derrie. 'Nutty as a fruitcake.'

Right on cue, as if they were all limping through a bad B-movie, they heard a familiar voice.

'Talking about *me*?'

A cheer went up from the crowd. Sarah felt her face blank with shock. Jaz's bleached blonde twists of hair pointed accusing spikes in everyone's direction. With the exception of the hair, Sarah decided she resembled a refugee from the nineteenth century, a Barnardo's child – fragile undernourished bones, skin the colour of pastry, cuffs fraying over bloodless knuckles. Her tongue worried at the ring piercing her lower lip. Complete with accessories, the ensemble named itself Amphetamine-chic... begging to be saved... costing an unreasonable amount. Only the eyes were hard, shining and dilated with a chemical concoction. How long was it that Sarah had managed to avoid her? Five? Six months? In that time, deterioration had pared Jaz down more brutally than Sarah had expected. She noticed Andi disappearing, already half way across the cricket pitch.

'What are you doing here?' Sarah heard her own undisguised hostility.

Thirty

'I was *invited*. Wasn't I, *Sarah*?' Jaz's face is all scary and sicky grey.

'Yes but... I didn't think you could come.'

Behind Jaz's back I can see Jo frowning questions about something at Somoya.

'That what *she* told you?' Jaz is doing this jabbing thing with her thumb at Somoya. She won't answer. Just fiddles with the grass for ages. Her ringlets are bobbing up and down like slinkies. I want her hair. I mean I wish mine was like hers. It keeps springing up and down. She might be crying. I want her to stop. If I climbed on her knee... But I can't, Jaz is staring at her too fierce.

After a long time, Somoya lowers her head down more, then kind of whispers, 'How did you find me?'

Jaz snorts. 'Had to follow you. Seeing as you neglected to fill me in on the arrangements.'

Everyone's passing these funny looks round and I try to hear what Somoya says back, but Sarah blocks in front of me and points to the other side of the pitch.

'Derrie, I'll count and see how long it takes you to run to that oak tree and back. See? Where Andi is. But don't go across the pitch. Ready... Steady –'

I could run it easy in... twenty-five seconds, but I know she doesn't want me to listen, so I push my way round to see. Jaz is holding her hand out to give Jo something.

'I made you a card. Have to find you a present later.'

Jo does this weird smile. I don't like it. 'No need to bother.'

'I said I *will*. And I *will*.'

Sounds like Jaz wants a fight. I wait to see if she will and try to work out how she gets her hair in white spikes like that. Sun's shining on the silver ring in her lip. It makes me touch my mouth to see what it would feel like. Metal and cold. Jo opens the envelope and there's all these sparkly bits stuck on the birthday card. I have to pull it out of Jo's hand. I can't help it.

'Don't *snatch*.' Sarah's so sharp I can feel my face hurt. So then she starts chatting rubbish to make up to me. 'It's like one of your collages, Derrie. See? Hologram patterns.'

It is a *bit* like mine, but not as good. Jaz hasn't even cut the pieces out properly. Some of them are just ripped. Inside, the writing's all scratchy, just scribbles. If I did writing like that, Miss Lester's face would go well red. Probably put my name on the board for being silly.

I point to the words. 'What does this say?'

'Don't even bother trying to decipher it,' Sarah smiles, like she's telling a joke.

Jaz takes her card back. 'Yeah. I know. My handwriting's chronic.'

I still want to know. 'Is it proper writing?

'No. It's code.'

'Read it to me.'

Jaz comes too near. She smells. Nasty. Kind of gone off, mouldy, smoky clothes. Have to hold my breath.

'They could have used me as a secret weapon in the war,' Jaz says.

All the people sitting on the grass do this big groan and Jo slaps her forehead at the pitch.

'This guy's useless.' Jo's staring at the cricket, so she can ignore Jaz. ''Bout as exciting as watching a fish piss.'

Jaz takes off her shirt. Her arms are all stiff like sticks painted white.

'My handwriting would've made a cracking code. No one can read it, except me.'

She's got that wrong. I know she has. 'What about when they need to work out the message at the other end?'

'I'd fly over and decode it for them.'

I *know* that's not right and I'm trying to say but Sarah is shaking her head at me. Well, I'm not going to let Jaz think she can trick me with daft stuff. So I tell her.

'You've got no common sense.'

Jaz swerves in like a snake. No, what's it called? Strikes. And her eyes go like glass, as if she's going to eat my head. It makes a fart come out. I grab Sarah's leg and she steps in front of me, covering my face with her dress. When I pull it away, I can see millions of silver scar marks on Jaz's arms. All the same length, like patterns. Have to remember to ask Sarah what they are later, 'cos I'm never going to say anything to Jaz again. It's no wonder Somoya doesn't want to talk to her. In my head, the words and tune from my best programme start playing: 'Do you ever... do you ever find, weird stuff happens? Are you going out your mind?' I want to sing it out loud, but they might get angry with me. Might guess who it's about. What's Jaz messing with in our bag? Taking a packet of Wotsits out... didn't even ask. She's sitting down and eating them all in... I count... five mouthfuls. Then she gets another packet out and opens them. They're mine. I know the first ones were Sarah's, so now Jaz is eating mine. I pull Sarah's dress.

'Can I have my Wotsits now?'

'Have you eaten your rice and salad?'

It's a waste of time. Have to go fast or Jaz'll finish them all. Greedy smelly git. I speed round to Jo and push my head into her chest and kiss her T-shirt three times.

'Jo. Can I have my Wotsits now?'

'Howzat! Did you see that? Bowler's caught him out.' I force my head further in. 'Yeah, all right. I think they're in Sarah's bag.'

I race back fast and open the bag, even though I know they

won't be in there, only cheese and onion crisps. I hold them up.

'I don't like this flavour.'

Sarah takes them away from me. 'Derrie, I haven't seen you eat anything healthy yet.'

Jaz is hooking the last few Wotsits out of her mouth with her yellow finger. I want to kick her smelly teeth in. I push against Sarah, but I can only talk quiet 'cos my throat's gone all sore.

'She's eaten my... She's eaten my –'

'Don't whine, Derrie.' Sarah smoothes my hair. 'We'll buy you some more.'

There's a shop over the road. 'Can I have some money?' Jaz picks up Somoya's jacket, and feels in the pockets. She's going to give me some.

'Got any cigs?'

No, she's not.

Somoya pulls her jacket away. 'I've given up.'

Jaz makes a grotting noise in her throat. 'No, you *haven't*.'

I try again. 'Sarah, can I go to that shop?'

'I'll come with you in a minute. That road... The cars come round there pretty fast.'

I move back. Jaz has found a cigarette and she leans forward as she lights it so the smoke is all in my face. 'She's old enough to cross a road, surely? How old are you now? Seven?'

I don't say anything.

Sarah's screwing her eyes up like she's got a headache. 'She's nearly nine. Derrie, can you wait a minute? Just till I've finished my food?'

'I can go on my own. You fuss too much.'

'Yeah,' Jaz says. 'You fuss too much. Hey, what's up with Somoya? She's got a face like a *smacked arse*. Cheer up. Here,' she slides a see-through plastic packet out of her shorts pocket. 'I got that Viagra you wanted.'

I try to see what's in the packet, but it's hidden in her hand, so I nudge Sarah. 'What's Viagra?'

'I... never... asked... you... for... that.' Every word Somoya whispers is tired.

Jaz spikes me, poking with her finger. 'Antidote to Prozac, little girl.'

Sarah picks up her purse and puts a coin in my hand. It's a pound. A *pound*. 'All right. You can go to the shop.'

Jaz waves the plastic packet in front of Somoya's nose. 'It'll be a laugh.'

'What will?' I pull Sarah's dress. 'Why won't you tell me?'

'I will in a minute.' Sarah touches my bottom, pushing me away from them. 'When you come back.' She taps Jo's leg. 'Can you keep an eye on her?'

At the top of the grass bank, I stop to listen for a few more seconds.

Jo starts cheering with lots of other voices. 'Yesss! They've just scored fifty.'

'For God's sake, Jaz!' Sarah's voice is dead angry and quiet. 'You did that on purpose.'

'*What?*'

'In front of her. I want Derrie to have a childhood. Not like –'

'Stop *pecking* my head. It's just a joke. *Christ*. If you laughed, you'd *shit* yourself.'

My fists go all tight when she says that to my mum. But I don't want to hear any more, so I squeeze the money and run. With a pound I can get Sarah some Wotsits as well. I'm speeding so much down the hill, my legs go... too fast. No cars coming, but I have to look right and left loads 'cos I know they're watching me, probably.

These two women push the shop door open for me. From the back, one of them is the same as Jo. Tall with black hair, short like hers. Sarah usually winks at Jo when she sees women like that and says 'Dyke alert'.

I go round the shelves three times before I see the crisps high up. I can just reach. Then I have to wait and wait behind the women because they're getting loads of sweets. I want some too. Thirty-eight pence and another thirty-eight is seventy-four. I'd have enough left for a Milky Way. Better not. Sarah might be mad at me.

The tall woman is whispering so I get closer in to hear. 'It is.'

'You sure?'

'Definitely. "To bathe al fresco." Has to be the weir we drove over, on the way in.'

It's the next clue.

'Sounds a bit too simple. Probably a trick.'

I turn my ear towards them, but they see me move and go quiet.

I want to run back and tell the others but the two women are already out of the door and going quick down the road. I can't lose them. Got to see if they find it. What are Sarah and Jo doing? Still eating. They're taking too long. We won't be able to catch up. If I win, I could get one of those big packets of Pokémon cards with the prize money. The tall one and her friend are turning the corner. Mustn't lose them. Mustn't.

Thirty-one

'So!' Everyone turns to glare at me. Centre stage. Waiting to see what I'm going to do. 'How long have you been planning to keep me out of this touching little occasion?'

Sarah swallows. Shitting herself. Good.

'Listen, Jaz, we didn't know you could...' She stops. Realises. Signals to Somoya. 'There's still plenty of food. Sit down and have something.' Pathetic, the way Sarah thinks she can manipulate anyone. She's so obvious. Can hear her teacher brain working.

'I can't eat.'

They exchange glances. Meaningful. I start smacking two fingers over and over against the inside of my elbow.

'What you *doing*?'

Finally got Somoya's attention.

'Tapping up a vein.' I take them in one by one. 'Well, that's what you think of me. Isn't it?'

Jo mumbles, 'Pathetic.'

Right. That's her as well. I'll have her. Saliva spurts. I lick it, flipping the ring in my lip as I reach for Somoya's shoulders. 'Makes me feel like topping myself.' I can hear them thinking: Go on. Do us all a favour. I scream. 'Where's your sense of community? Thought women were supposed to be different. No one gives a *shite* about me.'

A collective chorus rings out: now we've established that, you can clear off. But no mouths move. Ventriloquists, the lot of them. Limestone faces stare. Ignore them. Steady. Concentrate on something – the wine bottle. My mouth dries, inside cheeks shrivel. Go to neck it, but it's not wine. Elderberry fucking juice. Their eyes get stonier. Now they're not even blinking. Only the flat black and white one knows what I'm on about. Hugging herself on a cushion, whispering, 'what's your poison?'

'Come and sit down, Jaz.' Somoya tries to guide me towards the ground. I shake her off.

'Don't want to sit. Did Somoya tell you we're having a baby?

'Is this true?' Sarah asks Somoya.

I move in on her. 'Course it is. You think I'm a liar? That guy from Napoleon's said he'd be our donor. Start next month. Well, *say* something.' I sing to the tune of Happy Birthday, 'Congratulations to us!' Then I crush Somoya in my arms, lifting her off the ground.

'*Derrie,*' Sarah says, 'Where the hell is she?'

I can feel Somoya's jaw clench against my cheek.

'Don't do this to me, Jaz. Put me down.'

I decide I don't understand English, squeezing her into amnesia. Cold needle points spit from the sky.

Sarah is pulling at Jo. 'You were supposed to be watching her.'

'Please, put me down.' I like it when she pleads.

Have to negotiate before releasing her. 'Come with me then. For a little talk.'

'Okay.' I can see her thinking she'll get me out of the way.

I grab her face. Kiss her teeth through her lips. Thunder rumbles in my head. Feel her up. It might work. Weird. Her breast means nothing to my fingers any more. Just a slack sack. Her pupils glitter and this kind of dry heave forces her throat forward. Reflex action. I make her sick. I know it's true and I wanna throw too. When I drag her towards the car park, she's all resistance. Rigid with fear.

Bullseye.

Thirty-two

Standing still, Jo felt herself speed strangely away. She already knew the fatal consequences of what she hadn't done. She saw Charlotte back under a tree, out of the spitting rain, inspecting the mud splatters on the white heels of her shoes.

'I can't go very fast, I'll hold you up.' Involuntarily, Charlotte's hand fluttered to her groin, then she held her palm out to Andi. 'I'll wait in the car.'

Andi threw the keys in her direction. 'Phone us if she comes back here.'

'I can't find...' Charlotte was absorbed in an unco-ordinated struggle with the contents of her bag. 'My mobile. I must've –'

'It's all my fault,' Sarah screeched and broke into a run.

Sweat stabbed at Jo's armpits.

When she caught up with Sarah, Jo appealed to her, as if it might change the truth. 'It was only over the road.'

'And you were supposed to be watching her.' Sarah's breath came in squeezed sobs. 'Too wound up in your own pathetic self.'

'This won't help,' Jo murmured. Nothing would now. Unable to meet the hatred in Sarah's eyes, she focused on the clammy drops of rain clinging to her own clothes. 'We need to split up and –'

Andi veered off from them. 'I'll ask at the shop if they saw which way –'

'Hurry... up for fuck's... sake.' Sarah began struggling for breath and Jo could only watch her turning in disoriented circles. 'Hurry... up. Someone might have... taken her.'

The village lit up as a white negative of itself.

'It's all my fault,' Sarah repeated.

How can it be yours? This is one of my unforgettable classics, Jo thought. One I'll remember the moment I open me eyes every morning.

Andi raced out of the shop. 'No one's seen –'

A long line of children on horseback trotted by leisurely, blocking Jo's path, their fluorescent yellow tabards printed with black words. Caution. Learner riders. As soon as they passed, she ran blind, hearing Sarah howling their daughter's name. She kept sprinting, while Sarah stopped and gasped the same frantic half questions to whoever she saw.

'Little girl... Blonde...Wearing red?' Scarcely pausing to listen to the answers, to see the shaking heads.

Each time Jo tried to join in, undigested scraps surged from her stomach, tasting acid at the back of her throat. She couldn't ask because she knew the answer. Despite this certainty, she couldn't stop herself pleading silently. Please... Please let her be all right. A chain reaction of calls rang around the village.

She watched Sarah stumble about, asking shopping trolleys, lamp posts. 'Little girl... Blonde... wearing...'

The calling voices were muffled to bird cries by the roar of the rain, but Jo heard Sarah's screams grate across her vocal chords until she felt the rawness in her own throat. In her pocket, a tune vibrated. A tinny rendition of an advertising jingle. Derrie must've been playing with the settings on the phone. The sound pierced Jo's chest, as she realised the new ringing tone might be all that was left of Derrie.

'Gimme the phone.' Sarah's fingertips slid on the buttons. 'Fucking thing. *Fucking* thing. Which one do I press? Phone red sign? Green phone sign?' She jammed the mobile into Jo's hands. '*Do it.*'

Jo answered and passed the phone back to Sarah. 'It's your sister.' Typical fucking inappropriate timing. 'Tell her to clear the line. We need to get through to the others.'

Sarah's flash of loathing acted like G force, pushing Jo a step backwards, but she could still hear Ellie's voice blaring on the other end of the phone, 'Derrie's in trouble.'

'How did you–?' Sarah tried to ask.

'Get to the water.'

'What–?'

'Shut up. The river.'

Without hanging up, Sarah started to run.

Thirty-three

Somoya couldn't concentrate on Jaz's speech, only on her mouth. A moving abrasion, with a glimpse of eggshell teeth as she tried to twist the ring with her tongue. Somoya tuned out until her attention hooked on the word 'baby'.

'… just you and me and our own little –'

She couldn't let her say it again.

'This has got to stop, Jaz. Here and now. It's not goin' to happen.' Her eyes swept the hotel car park, to see if they had any witnesses. No one.

'I know things haven't been right for a bit. But a baby could bring us closer together.' Her tone deteriorated into wheedling. 'You *said* we could do it.'

The sky darkened. Cygnet-grey to gun metal. In the distance, people at the cricket ground were gathering up blankets and other belongings. Somoya sighed, 'That were a long time ago.'

'Well, I haven't forgotten your promise. I'll take you. Come on. Introduce you to this bloke. He's all right –'

'Yer *not listenin'*. I've told you more than enough times.'

With her thumb, Jaz dashed off the ash from her cigarette. 'I've stopped.'

'Yeah, right.'

'I knew you wouldn't believe me. But this time it's *true.*' Jaz curled her finger protectively over the cigarette end in her mouth and a smacking suck hit the air, as she tried to inhale the filter. Then she fingered Somoya's T-shirt. Desperation dampening the material.

Somoya shook her head. All that was left of years was boredom with the lies. She couldn't even summon up the energy to be angry anymore. Couldn't be bothered to answer.

'You *said*. You promised you'd stay, if I packed it in. You can't go now. I'm going to be so ill.' She snorted tear-filled phlegm to the back of her throat. 'I'm doing it for *you.*'

'No. It has to be for yourself.'

'I really don't need this right now, Somoya. I'm crapping myself.' She saw the instruction 'try acting hurt' running through Jaz's mind. 'Every day, you tear another strip off my heart.' Somoya winced at the cliché and noticed the nervous lip-licking speed up.

How could she get rid of her? 'You could do with some rest. You're a wreck. Go home and we'll sort things later, when you're feeling better.'

'I know you're trying to get me out of the way, so you can get busy with that fat arsed – What's her name, Andi? Well, I'm staying.' She dropped the cigarette end and scraped it into fluff under her trainer.

The car park flashed sepia for a second. Somoya realised that she'd have to leave the others and take Jaz home. Large drops of water splattered black against the asphalt. Overhead, the hanging baskets outside the Royal Hotel swayed, rain making tatters of their flowers. She couldn't let Jaz anywhere near Derrie now. Too dangerous...

Derrie. Where was she? Somoya saw the abandoned picnic behind her. Everything getting soaked. She needed to get away and help to look for her.

'I tell you what. You can stay in their car for a bit, keep dry, while I make sure Derrie's all right. Then you can show me where you've parked the Beetle and I'll run you home.' She felt for the car keys Jo had given her earlier, to unpack the last of the picnic, and unlocked the passenger door of the Porsche.

'You're going *nowhere.*' Jaz picked up one of the whitewashed rocks that edged the path to the hotel and slammed it into the car's side window. The drastic shattering rang above the splattering rain. Jaz dropped the rock, then caught Somoya's wrist instead, battering her hand against the solid glass web, as if it might make a better tool for breaking a window.

Somoya waited for Jaz to let her go, then appraised the damage to her hand. It didn't hurt yet. Blood blossomed, dark as raspberries on her knuckles. Finally, the throbbing began... an aching pain drawing the last drops of love from her veins.

'Christ.' She looked up, checking the state of the car. 'They'll make Sarah pay for this.'

'If she can hire a car like that, she can afford it.'

'She's been savin' up for ages and she got my staff discount an' all.'

'All right for those who've got enough money to save.'

'You'll have to pay for it.' Somoya's voice sounded dead. Cold water ran down her neck.

'Ha! What with? My giro? What's your problem? The car's insured.'

'Is it buggery. Not for deliberate criminal damage, it's not.' Seeing the keys still hanging from the car door, Somoya snatched them from the lock.

'You'll think of something.'

'Not this time. I'll get you charged.' Somoya trudged away, pressing numbers into her mobile phone until she felt a pincer grip on her arm.

'What? You calling the police? You wouldn't *dare*, knowing what I could tell them about you.'

'I've got more important things to deal with just now. Like trying to get hold of Sarah... Shit! Engaged.'

Under the rain, several thin red streams ran into pink tributaries along Somoya's arm. It was weird, she thought, how resigned she'd become to the sight of her own blood.

Catching both of Somoya's wrists, Jaz studied the fresh wet red and compared it with the black stitching on the other. 'Now you've got a matching pair.'

Weary, Somoya twisted away. 'There's no way you're goin' to keep doing this.'

Jaz screamed after her, 'Funny, isn't it, how things like this only happen to me when I'm with you?'

Thirty-four

Mustn't lose them. I run as fast as I can to catch up, but make my soles go quiet so they don't slap on the pavement. Have to store the Wotsits packets under my armpits, to stop them crackling. I'll wait here. Press up to the wall, so I'm invisible. They're going down some steps. If I sprint, I could crouch down behind that hedge. I can see them a bit through the gap. The stink of the pissy leaves makes me want to sneeze, so I pinch my nose. Can just see the tall one sitting on a wall, next to some flat water. Must be the weir they were on about. She's reaching down those massive stone blocks to something sticking out. *Yes!* She's got it. Now read it. Quick. Go on, put it *back*. Put it back. Right, now you can *go*.

As soon as they run off laughing, I jump down the steps. I need to walk carefully along the wall. The river looks deep down there. Now, kneel down and lean over the big stones. Maybe this is the right place. Wicked. The card's there, but my arms are just... just not long enough. The stretch is burning my armpit. If I lie down and swing myself lower, I bet I could... My stomach's all squashed on the stone. Hanging upside-down, the moving water underneath rushes like the blood in my head. The water's loud. Keeps saying 'Sh... Sh...' over and over, while it makes bubble bath foam at the bottom. It's a long way down. If Jo was here, she'd be able to reach it. Have to fling myself back up on to the wall again, in case I go swilling over the waterfall.

Wait for the sick feeling to clear. I'll climb down the bank. The card's low down from those rocks. I could reach it if I balanced and stretched across. Just have to trample the brambles out of the way. They well prickle. My sandals are just junk for climbing down here. Cling on to that tree trunk. If I stride, I could get to that... massive rock. These stepping stones are nasty. Slippy and green. Can't stand properly. Keep sliding. My foot's deep under. Freezing. Ankle's stuck. The rock's got me. Pushing me over. Going down too fast. Can't reach... nothing to grip on to. The Wotsits are floating off. Ow! No... please... stop... Ahh! Rocks smashing me.

'Sarah, *please*... Jo!'

Water's in my nose. Blow it out. Mustn't swallow... mustn't. Can hear Ellie calling. How come she's here? How did she –?

'Hold *on*, Derrie. Tighter. Tilt your head up. Higher. I can't reach you.'

'Ellie. Get me... get me out.' It is her. Yellow hair. All cloudy through the water and the sky. A flash makes everything white. Even Auntie Ellie. Fat rain drops hit heavy on my head.

'I said hold your head *up*, you little runt.' Ellie's a wavery yellow blob. '*Please*. Can't lose you now.'

My mouth's full. Mustn't swallow... mustn't...

Thirty-five

Time divided into snapshots. First, a row of cottages, their curved crazy-paved patios lapped by the pool at the head of the weir. Then a single mallard, standing so still it looked wooden. The square church tower overshadowed the river. Through the dense downpour, a pale body swelled in the water, washing in and out of focus. Jo waded in and dragged the white thing out. Slick as a fish. A fish that didn't move. So limp, Sarah knew it must be heavy, but Jo carried it like something lightweight up the steps. Sarah had no idea what to do. She couldn't bargain with a non-existent God to change it back into a girl.

The church clock chimed the quarter hour, ding dong, ding dong, recording the time of death.

'She's dead,' Sarah explained quietly to herself.

'Don't be soft,' Jo murmured, examining her burden. 'She's sound.'

How could she say that? Sarah searched the body for signs. Eyes closed. Face ghastly. Totally still.

'Dead.'

'Stop auditioning for RADA and give us something to wrap her in.'

Jo kissed and wiped the little lips clean with her T-shirt. Sarah ripped more strips of skin from her gnawed fingers: the taste of iron coated her tongue.

'C'mon. Gimme something dry to put on her.' Jo peeled off the small sopping clothes.

What did she mean? Why was Jo acting like this? How could taking her clothes off help now? Couldn't she see it was too late? Something hot spilled down Sarah's cheek and over her tongue. Salt water. Then the sun cracked through the clouds, just as the grey flesh spat out a mouthful of muddy, olive-green river, as if right on cue. What the hell's wrong with me, having thoughts like that now? Not directing a film. Am I?... Am I? Then she understood. The conviction that she'd become childless hammered her. This coughing creature isn't mine. This girl with diamonds dripping from the ends of her hair. She's someone else's. Mine has been washed away by my negligence.

'Your dress. *Hurry up.*'

She saw the thing in Jo's arms give a cartoon quiver. So cold. Sarah pulled her dress off rapidly, relieved to be told exactly what to do, then watched intently as the body turned into a juddering meaty package. From inside, a sibilant chattering emerged.

'She wants you,' Jo told her, taking Sarah's hand and placing it on the bundle. Warm cold flesh vibrated under her palm.

Derrie wriggled. 'S... S... Sarah.'

Sarah couldn't speak, but she leaned in and caught the muddy odour of river from her hair, all the apple scent gone.

'She's here,' Jo soothed, then her head sagged to her chest. An odd retching movement surged through her shoulders. Sarah couldn't tell if she was crying or being sick.

'S... Sarah... Did you find it?' Derrie asked as she sat up in Jo's arms, her trembling bottom lip the only evidence left of the river. 'It's wedged into the moss in the wall.' She pointed to the top of the weir.

'What?' Jo asked, wiping her nose.

'She means the clue. Don't worry about that, Derrie, we've got to get you to Accident and Emergency.'

'We *can't*! We can't just sack it.' As Derrie grasped at Sarah, pink suffused her cheeks. 'The treasure –'

'Forget it, scally, Sarah's right. You've had enough for one day.'

'We need to get you examined.'

'That's dorky. I didn't even swallow any.'

'You nearly died.'

'Stop scaring her.' Jo shook her head at Sarah. 'You always have to exaggerate –'

'She could have smashed her head open.' Sarah eyes were riveted to where the rushing water formed a crystal sheer drop. 'What a stupid place to plant a –'

'Out of all proportion,' Jo continued.

'I'm *all right.*' In demonstration, Derrie threw off Sarah's dress, stood up and spread her arms wide, as if she'd just completed a piece of perfect gymnastics. 'Look!' She wore her nakedness like a designer label.

'Don't even think about it. Here,' Sarah slipped the dress back over the skinny body.

From under the tent of material, Derrie begged. 'Please... We've only got one more clue to find.' Derrie's head crowned the neckline and Sarah eased her hands up inside the armholes, locating her limbs.

'What kind of parents would that make us? Our daughter half drowns and we carry on dragging her round the country.'

'Don't be a puss. I'm fine. Please... *Please.*' Derrie's aria of pleading reached a grand scale.

'What d'you think, Sarah?'

'You can't just behave as if nothing's happened.'

'Okay. What d'you reckon we should do?'

'Don't lay it back on me this time. You decide.'

'Well, she's all in one piece and –'

'And it's your birthday,' Derrie added, 'So you get to choose.'

'That's right.' She glanced warily at Sarah. 'I get to choose.'

They both stared at Jo, expectantly. In response, she leapt up and, sidestepping watercolour puddles, sprinted onto the wall. She snatched the gold card and waved it above her head.

'We carry on.'

'Yes... Yes... *Yes!*' Derrie clenched her fist in triumphant salute and drew it to a controlled stop next to her chest. Jo squinted at the card, pushed it back into the emerald crack between the rocks, then raced down the hill towards them.

'The ducks have got glitter on their heads,' Derrie said.

'You're both *mad*.' Sarah noticed she was undressed. 'So I'm supposed to run round the north of England in my underwear?'

'Lovely,' Jo smiled, admiring her.

Sarah raised her middle finger. 'Sit on that and swivel!'

Jo swiped up Derrie's mangled T-shirt and flung it towards Sarah. 'This should stretch to fit.' It landed in a clinging slap against her stomach. 'Or if you'd prefer, I've got me running gear back in the car... But I'll need that myself.' She flapped at her own wringing clothes then reached to feel the dress wound around Derrie. 'It's not that damp.'

Derrie hugged the dress to her. 'It's mine now.'

Jo's hand flew to her eye as if she'd been stung. 'Something in my –' She blinked at the grit from the river and pulled her eyelid to dislodge her contact lens. When it dropped into her open palm, she felt about blindly with an outstretched arm for the lens case Sarah held out to her automatically.

'Can I have me glasses?'

Sarah had already unzipped them from the side pocket of her bag. They gave Jo the magnified gaze of a bush baby, the spirals of dense glass rendering her infinitely vulnerable. Sarah had an urge to fold her in her arms.

'Don't laugh at me,' Jo complained with an awkward smile. 'I know these glasses make me look ginky.'

'What did the clue say?' Derrie asked as she held out her arms to Sarah, miming her intention to climb on to her shoulders.

'"Change the gender of this watering hole and you'll work out which famous Czech this is."' Jo took off her glasses and wiped them on her T-shirt. 'Then it said something about giving yourself a warm hand to celebrate the end of the trail.'

From her regal ride on Sarah's shoulders, Derrie called down to Jo. 'Charlotte will know the answer.'

'It'll be Navratilova,' Jo replied, obviously pleased at finally solving one of the clues.

'Yes, but which pub?' Sarah asked. 'There's got to be at least ten here.'

'Let's just get you back to the car to change,' Jo said so firmly that Derrie didn't bother arguing.

The renewed rays of the sun began to burn Sarah's exposed skin, making her feel silly. She hoped her underwear would pass for a swimming costume in the village. Derrie held Sarah's head, steering her, and she could sense her daughter's smug delight at being in a brief golden period when she got whatever she asked for.

After only a few steps, Sarah lowered her head, easing Derrie towards the ground, then rubbed at the cramped muscles in her neck.

'You'll have to take over, Jo. She's too heavy for me.'

As Jo hoisted her up, Derrie's royal wave to her imaginary subjects reminded Sarah that she couldn't delay the inevitable lecture any longer.

She fixed the child with a serious stare. 'It's time for you to promise never, *ever* to go off like that again.'

'Yeah, *yeah.*'

The weary, adolescent intonation made Sarah cringe. 'Don't *mess* with me. I *mean* it.'

'Ellie talked to me when I was in the water.'

Sarah wondered if this could be a deliberate distraction technique. 'What? In your head?'

'No, from the bank.'

'You imagined it,' Jo told her.

'No. She had that yellow dress on that pushes her tits up.'

'*Breasts,*' Jo corrected.

Ignoring them, Sarah listened as Ellie's last phone call replayed in her mind: 'Derrie's in trouble... get to the water.' Just now at the river hadn't been the first time. A year ago... the fractured arm in the play-ground. Ellie got there even before the dinner ladies started dialling numbers on the emergency list. But when Sarah had asked how she knew, she just got a casual shrug and an infuriating, secret smile.

Sarah delved further back still, to when Ellie had held Derrie for the first time. Dangled her by the scruff of her neck, like a puppy. Their eyes locked together in a pact, talking adult to adult. Child to child. 'It's about time,' Ellie had said. 'About time you got here.'

Sarah had bitten the inside of her cheek. What did she mean? It wasn't as if Derrie had been overdue.

'Long time no see,' Ellie had admonished her niece.

'What are you on about?' Sarah demanded.

Then came that maddening shrug. The slight smile. 'It's a blood thing.'

'You're *bizarre.*'

Ellie had nestled Derrie along the length of her thighs and leaned into her tiny face. It made Sarah feel like a stranger, as she saw their mirrored features and the ancient amusement spinning in their eyes. She knew she'd been robbed, by an already hardened thief: her sister.

Ellie had pushed their snub noses together. 'It's been a long time, you little runt.'

Thirty-six

There's no power in this fucking Beetle. Makes no difference flooring the accelerator, I can't feel any bite. That roaring sounds like the clutch is going. I told her to trade it in months ago. Don't know why she isn't ashamed to be seen in such a piece of crap. Still, I better not have a go at her about that now, or I'll never get her to talk to me. Can't stand this silence. It's making my nails puncture the plastic steering wheel cover. That kid is the one thing that might get Somoya to speak.

'So? Derrie's not done herself any damage then?' I ask.

It's not working. She's faking being glued to something on the slip road. Too pissed off to speak, 'cos she's missing her little party. Pussy party. She's fuming about acting as my armed escort. Still, she'll get over it. Always does. The engine's racing. Change into fifth. I could try slipping a hand on her thigh. But her leg keeps twitching away as if my fingers are infectious. Maybe they are. Chill. Work her a bit.

'Come on, Somoya. I've said I'm sorry. It's only a window. They can still drive the thing home. I'll pay for it.'

A vicious laugh chokes through her curls. 'What with?'

Right. Got her to speak. 'They've offered me some cash in hand at –'

'Yer in no state. You couldn't hold yourself together long enough to work. Even *you* must realise –'

Fine. She's facing me. 'I know. You're right.' Plead with the eyes. Hook her in. 'There's no way I can do anything until – Ugh.' I have to double up. Difficult to drive. 'I'm getting sick, Somoya. I told you before. I've stopped and I... You wanted this –' Real sweat greases my forehead.

'Jaz, pull over on to hard shoulder.' She's all calm command laced with panic.

Can feel the steering wheel moving on its own. No. Her hand's gripping it. 'Brake, Jaz, for Christ's sake. Slam your feet down.'

Do what she tells you. My head sinks to the sweaty wheel and the stretching yank of the handbrake hurts nerve endings behind my eyes. Stroking my cold shoulder, she sounds out of range. Over the hills and faraway.

'When you're ready, slide over into this seat. I'll drive us home quick sharp and get you into bed. Okay, Jaz? All right, honey?'

A dark answer whispers from the back seat. 'No. Not okay. You're going nowhere.'

'Wha' the...?' Try to twist round. I can't see who it is. Maybe that's where the kid's been hiding all along. 'I can't do this, Somoya.'

The weird whisper's there again. 'At least you know your limitations.'

Shut... the fuck... up.

Somoya squeezes shoulder bones through my thin skin. 'Yes, you can. You've got me to help you.'

Slam, dunk. Ball's back in my court.

Whisper. Whisper. Gravel whisper from the back-seat driver. 'What's a nice girl like her doing with a sad fuck like you?'

Got to silence the bastard before Somoya hears. Can't have this wrecked now we're on track. Back seat's empty. I'm hearing things again. I'm just strung out, that's all it is. Been speeding too hard. That's all. Bit of smack will sort me out. Everything's going to be all right. Back in my court.

'Au contraire.' The invisible fucker thinks I'll be confused by

French. 'Game over. No chance of a re-match. Somoya's starting a new game as we speak.'

Turn to the passenger seat. Also empty. That's not right. That's impossible. Then I know. Somoya's not coming home tonight. She's stayed with them. She never got in the car. My mind's eye takes aim and machine-gun fire makes the lot of them do a jerking puppet dance. But I'm too wasted to reload the ammunition to keep going. I'll sort it all tomorrow. Just got to get back. In one piece.

Mirror... signal... fucking manoeuvre. Slip back into the flow, stay with it. Automatic pilot... right... next... cash... need to work out how much I've got. Surprise, surprise, little Miss Ginger twat short and stout, isn't as clever as she makes out, leaving her purse sticking out of her bag. So accessible. Access. My flexible friend. Let's see what else is in here. Driving licence, library card, sports club membership... that photo must be from way back... hair bigger and redder, face thinner. Luckier. She might actually have used a gym then. For fuck's sake! Doesn't she carry any cash? All right! Zipped in the side. Only sixty. Still, there's plenty of credit. Need to stop at an offy or two before she cancels these.

Thirty-seven

'You got to press charges.' Jo folded a sheet of newspaper into a thick wad and closed it round a piece of loose glass in the Porsche's side window.

'It's only a scrape,' Somoya answered quietly, staring at the gauze Sarah had wrapped around her knuckles.

Jo eased hexagons of shattered glass backwards and forwards and lifted them clear of the frame.

'If Jaz was a man you would.'

Silence.

Clenching her jaw, Jo handed the pieces to Somoya. 'Are you getting something out of this? Is it some masochistic little game?'

The toe of Somoya's trainer paused paddling in a rainbow of engine oil. Her eyes flared, hurt, tears plastering her lashes together.

'OK. *Sorry.*' Jo prised out another chunk. 'Where is she now?'

'Doing her wandering off act. Probably angling for some of the attention Derrie's been getting.'

'We're not hanging round here for her. Derrie's got treasure to find.'

They both glanced across the car park to where Derrie stood, surrounded by handmaidens. Crouching at her feet, Charlotte held open a pair of Jo's shorts, which dwarfed Derrie's waif-like waist. Then she rolled the waistband into a sausage of cloth, making sure it would stay up. Sarah wound Andi's bikini top around Derrie's chest, while Andi shot the impromptu fashion show from several angles.

'There's no missing you in that lot, lass.'

Somoya's mouth relaxed into a small smile. 'New York, Paris, Milan, Hayfield. This season's catwalk chic.'

'Right.' Jo brushed her hands together, her tone final. 'The truth. You want rid of Jaz?'

Crumpling the last package of newspaper and broken glass into a carrier bag, Somoya mumbled something.

'What?'

'I said, I want some peace.'

'Do you want rid?'

A slow exhalation of air. 'Yes.'

'Press charges.'

Sucking her teeth, Somoya combed through her curls with her fingers. 'What good will locking her up do?

'We're ready,' Derrie shouted at them. 'Can we go now? There's a pub up past the post office, where Andi parked. We're going to see what it's called.'

'The Packhorse, it's not the one.' Jo lowered her voice: 'She could get treatment.'

'You know as well as I do, that's not true. I've *seen* people who've been sectioned. It's just more drugs.'

Worn out with words, Jo made a move towards the others, one last try trailing behind her. 'You've got to get away from her, before she kills you.'

Thirty-eight

Love squeezed at Sarah's throat as she regarded Derrie jumping along next to Andi. Derrie looked joyously unscathed. There were no clues to what she'd been through apart from her wet straggle of hair and Jo's rolled-up shorts, accessorised with the stringy top. The effect of the new oversized outfit on her thin frame made her look older and taller.

Sarah shook her head, still amazed at Derrie's resilience. 'Thank Christ she's all right.'

Jo tracked her daughter's every move. 'I wouldn't have wanted to live if anything –'

Sarah's fingers flew to cover Jo's mouth, making her flinch. 'You and me, both.'

'*And…* What *is* happening?' Jo couldn't hold Sarah's gaze. 'With you and me, I mean.'

Sarah had no answer. Shock had locked her brain into freeze frame.

'Are we finished?'

Priorities crept into numerical order. Number one, Derrie was safe. Sarah realised that for the moment there was no number two.

'I can't trust you any more.'

'I know.'

She noticed that Jo's stricken expression had no impact on her. A weather girl provided a curious commentary in her mind. Cold front coming in from the north. She turned away, sheltering from further frost damage.

'You could lie to me again if I gave you the chance. Once the first time's out of the way, I'm sure it gets easier.'

Jo reached for her. 'I never –'

Shaking her off, Sarah spoke with deliberate ice. *'Don't.* I don't want you touching me.'

But her skin had been branded on the minute points where Jo had rested her fingertips. Those polka dots of shoulder knew the truth. They pulsed, spreading a seditious message through the rest of her skin. *You still love her... You still...* She caught the crushed expression in Jo's eyes, just before she lowered them to her running shoe, grinding the grass into mud.

The others were heading for a bend in the road beyond which she wouldn't be able to see them. Anxiously, Sarah walked faster, willing Jo to follow.

Turning the corner, Jo stopped abruptly beside her, gripped by the sight of their little girl on the other side fo the road. While Andi leaned over her, Derrie held out arched fingers at arms' length, squinting through them, to frame a view of the village. Then lifting the camera from round her neck, Derrie steadied her hands and stood stiller than they had ever seen her, to take the shot.

At any other time, Sarah knew that she and Jo would have shared a smile. But Derrie's new skill passed unmarked and anguish took a crying hold on Sarah's throat again.

'Just tell me why.'

Jo swallowed, then grimaced, as if tasting something sour. 'It's going to sound stupid.'

'Probably.'

Raising her head, Derrie saw them watching her. She hung the camera carefully back over her neck and tried to haul Andi towards them. But Andi steered her firmly away.

Jo started slowly. 'I thought... I thought... Is this it? Is this all there is? I mean... Lovely girlfriend...' Sarah warned *'Don't'* with narrowed eyes, but Jo carried on as if she hadn't been interrupted. 'Gorgeous daughter, good job... None of it was enough. Been there, done that. Feels flat. I still hadn't climbed to base camp on Everest. I still hadn't –'

Sarah's throat tightened even more, as a new stream of illicit notes were passed around inside her. Below the surface now. *You still love her...*

'Oh, how very *mundane*. You're such a fucking cliché with your pathetic little mid-life crisis.' As if she were watching herself from a long way off, Sarah wondered what compelled her to say these things. She had the impression that she was acting... cast as an unconvincing character who lurched into a derisive whine. 'Where's all the *excitement* gone? I *know*! I'll have an affair.' For a second, she felt gratified as she saw her words razor at Jo, 'It's so lame it's on crutches.' While she scoured her mind for fresh incisions, she ached to dress Jo's wounds. 'How mediocre can you get? You've an amazing capacity for settling on the ordinary.'

But Jo's deep quiet scared Sarah. Self-interest snaked back. Perhaps she'd gone too far. Some damage limitation might be needed. She remembered there were more serious considerations – Derrie. She had to keep this together for her. Change tack. Think.

'What's stopping you?'

Chancing a wary glance, Jo tensed her muscles, ready to retreat. The question came from nowhere, deliberately out of context enough to throw her off guard.

'Why don't you take some unpaid leave and do this base camp thing?'

Confusion crossed Jo's face. It seemed safer to keep quiet. But now the idea had been planted, Sarah could see it rooting. Already crystal ice sparkled under Jo's feet.

'I earn enough to pay the bills while you're away. Neither of us should give up on things we've always wanted.' Sarah paused for maximum effect. 'Unless this is all an elaborate way of dumping me, because you don't have the guts to tell me you're sick of the sex.'

'That's one thing between you and me that's never been a problem.' Regret splashed from Jo's cheek onto the muddy toe of her trainer. 'If you don't tell me to fuck off now, we'll still be causing trouble in our sheltered accommodation. All the old biddies will be complaining to the warden about the noises coming through our walls.'

'Fuck off.'

Jo's head hung lower. Beaten.

'Look...' Sarah couldn't act any more, as she heard her mild tone betraying her. 'I don't care who you shag, as long as you don't bore me with the details.' Listening to her own words, she had no idea if she meant any of them. 'None of it matters if you love me and Derrie.' She felt as if she'd bought her relationship back from a black-market boot sale, using lies as currency.

Burying her face in Sarah's neck, Jo released snatches of crying speech. 'Thought... you'd hate me... Wouldn't let me... see Derrie...'

Sarah inhaled, sinking into her scent. Acqua Di Gio. Sensuous familiarity. She's a person, too, and deserves my respect. I knew that once. It's taken years to forget.

A little body pushed in between them. 'What's the matter with you two?'

Jo turned away from Derrie to wipe her face.

'Nothing,' Sarah answered. 'We're just being silly.'

'*Huh*! You tell me not to argue.'

Sarah touched Derrie's cashmere fringe. 'It's a parent's privilege to be a hypocrite.'

Derrie shook her head. 'You're not funny.'

'No,' Jo agreed. 'We're tragic.'

Staring at them seriously, Derrie joined Jo and Sarah's hands together and patted them. 'Life's as funny as you make it.'

As the three of them set off, to catch up with the others, for once, they were all quiet. The church clock chimed. In her mind, Sarah heard the muffled refrain of a town crier. Five o'clock and all is well.

She studied Derrie's feet as she skipped haphazardly on and off the kerb and then knew she'd been wrong to relax, even for a moment. Derrie wasn't safe. None of them were. She could feel Colin on the move again. Closing in. This time she didn't try to stop the reel running in her head. She had to know...

'No win. No fee.' The fluorescent promise pasted to the window stops Colin in his tracks. Next to the open door, a sandwich board issues another invitation. 'Free legal clinic here 2.30–5.30.'

Time check. Sarah looks at her watch at the same second he does. Five past five. The script starts racing in her head, too fast to storyboard. Colin enters the building.

The air-conditioning is a relief from the sun. He slides open a glass panel in the wall and sticks his head through, but there's no one at the desk.

'Hello?' In the empty waiting room, his voice is too high. 'Are you still open?'

'Yes.' The receptionist appears, framed in the doorway, wiping her hands on a paper towel. The rough, dull blue, cheap kind. 'Can I help you?'

'Er, I don't suppose you've got any appointments left for today?'

She picks up an open diary from her desk, but doesn't bother to refer to it. 'You're in luck.' With a short smile, she gestures towards a line of plastic chairs. 'Seems like everyone's too busy sunbathing. What name is it?'

Her pen hovers over her diary, while he decides what name to give.

'Preston.'

She prints it in fat loops.

'And what's the nature of the inquiry, Mr Preston?'

'I'd rather... If I could just speak to the solicitor.'

'Fine.' She makes her way down the corridor. 'Let me inform Mr Streatham.'

A fan turns its head towards him, flapping at his shirt. Cooling the clammy patches under his arms.

She's back.

'You can go through, Mr Preston. Second door on the left.'

The door's closed. Colin pauses, wondering whether to knock. His knuckles tap too quietly. No answer. When he opens the door, he stands hunched, half in, half out of the office.

'Erm... I...'

'Please, take a seat.'

The solicitor's cheeks are flecked with angry pockmarks. He doesn't look old enough to be out of law school.

'I was wondering... if you could answer a few questions?'

Pulling a small pad of paper towards him, the solicitor simultaneously clicks his ballpoint pen with his thumb.

'What's this in connection with?'

Colin takes a breath, as he adjusts his glasses. 'A number of years ago... over nine to be precise, I... gave a donation of sperm to an unknown party.' He sounds odd and formal. 'Since that time, I've had no dealings with the mother and child. But now the circumstances have changed somewhat. I happened to discover where they are.' Perspiration beads his temples.

Without glancing up, Mr Streatham jots something down. 'What are the particular issues this raises for you?'

'Well, um. What rights do I have? I mean, if I want... contact with the little girl.'

Both the solicitor's eyebrows rise.

'Was the donation arranged through a clinic?'

'No... Anonymously.'

His pen stops, poised on the page. 'Well, the courts have not grasped the nettle of this one yet. To date, I don't think they've had to deal with anyone in that position.'

'Maybe I could be a test case?'

His eyebrows arch again. 'Private arrangements of this sort aren't governed by the HFEA and –'

'What's that stand for?'

'The Human Fertilisation and Embryology Act, which informs any donors to clinics that they're not the legal parent of a child they may father.'

'But there are other laws. I mean, about fathers' rights.'

'When it's a matter of private semen donation, it's rather uncharted territory. It's yet to be tested by the courts. Natural fathers may be viewed as important by the Children Act, but with a contact application, the court takes many circumstances into account.'

'Like what?'

'Well, the views of the child are considered carefully. So, for example, if she and the mother weren't in favour of meeting and you chose to pursue the matter, it would mean that a Children and Family Reporter would become involved. At that point –'

'Could they persuade her to see me?' Colin drops eye contact to see why his fingers hurt. They're locked in a white grip onto the edge of the desk.

'Er… It doesn't quite work like that. Their role is to undertake an independent investigation, with regard to the welfare checklist. Then to report the outcome to the court.'

'If I asked for a blood test to prove she's mine and the mother wouldn't go along with it. What could the law do?'

'A court can draw inference from a refusal –'

'Yes!' His voice breaks. 'Then she'd have to let me see her.'

'It's only fair to point out that even if you prove paternity and obtain a defined contact order, it can still be extremely difficult to enforce if the mother is determined not to let –'

'I don't understand. If I win in court… If it's the law?'

'Quite, but court orders are sabotaged time and time again. In some cases, a parent may claim their child is unwell every time contact is scheduled.'

'If that happened, I could appeal to the court again, couldn't I?'

'Indeed, though it can become a costly and drawn-out process.'

Colin's sigh is measured. Meant to intimidate. 'What about your "No win, no fee" sign outside?'

'I'm afraid that refers to my colleague's practice. She deals mainly with personal injury law. I'm a family lawyer.'

Colin leans back in his chair, combing his fingers across his threadbare head. Sarah can hear him thinking. He's going to get a second opinion. Hire someone who'll agree with him.

'Of course,' Mr. Streatham continued, 'A client can always find a solicitor who is prepared to take their money, regardless of how viable their case may be.' He grimaces in place of a smile. 'Don't quote me on that.'

'So what are you saying? Going on past experience, what do you think my chances are?'

'It's potentially quite complicated. As you've had no contact so far and if the child doesn't want to meet you, then it would prove hard to persuade the courts otherwise.'

'Surely a kid that young wouldn't be allowed to dictate the whole thing? Especially if the mother is feeding her lines.'

The solicitor propels his chair backwards, glaring at Colin's hand in front of him. Colin stares at it as if he doesn't know how it has formed a fist and slammed down on top of the notepad. He removes it quickly.

'The court would think very carefully about overriding the views of say, a mature nine-year-old.'

'Yes. All right.' Colin shifts, not listening. 'Thank you for your time.'

'If you require any further –'

'Yes. Thanks.' Abruptly he stands up and as he stalks out of the office, Sarah sees the resolute decision on his face. He's not going to waste any time or money. He's going to take matters into his own hands. We can't supervise her one hundred per cent of the time. He'll wait for her. He'd only need to get a few hairs for DNA testing and send them off to one of those American Internet companies. He'll find out what kind of things she likes... get her talking. Then, he'll tell her who he is. Tell her she's got rights too...

*

Sarah started to hyperventilate as she made a mental list. Warn after-school club that she'd seen a paedophile hanging round the school gates. Drill Derrie again about not speaking to strangers... She felt Jo's hand stroking her back.

'It's okay, Sarah. Everything's gonna be all right.'

Thirty-nine

White fluff floated into their faces and Andi rubbed at the scorching itch inside her nose. She watched as Derrie picked a stick from the hedgerow and attacked the source of the trouble – tall purple weeds, weaving into cottonwool seedheads.

'Rosebay willowherb,' Sarah announced with authority.

'We should come out here camping,' Jo said, staring at the horizon. 'It would be brilliant.'

Derrie bounced up and down between them. 'Yeah! Sick!'

Screwing her eyes up into a mask of mock evil, Sarah swung towards Jo. 'Why do you think if you suggest it enough times, I'll change my mind?'

A peevish, barbed scratching started under Andi's eyelids as she exploded. '*Atishoo*... Camping is an invention of the devil.'

Derrie took another swipe with her stick. 'When can we go?'

'Take no notice of those two,' Jo said. 'You and me can go.'

'And Somoya? Can she come? She's got that tent like a space ship.' Andi noticed Somoya hanging back a fair way behind them. 'And what about Adesua? If her mum'll let her.'

'We'll ask them,' Jo promised.

With a dramatic sweep of her hand to her brow, Sarah breathed out a long sigh. 'The relief! I'm finally out of the camping equation.'

'That place we went to with the swing bridge was well good.' Derrie said. 'We did that skimming stones in the river. I got three, but Jo got the most of everybody.'

'Remember me, chopping all those logs?' With her left hand, Jo admired the curve of muscle in her right arm. 'Develops your pecs.' Then she bent down in front of Derrie. 'Just feel that definition. Flippin' marvellous!'

'That weekend has to go down as the worst time in the anus of history.' Sarah's mouth dipped in disgust. 'If sleeping on the rocky ground hadn't put my back out, I'd have had to fake it. Wilds of Yorkshire. Absolutely no boy children allowed. That bridge swinging like an instrument of torture. Christ knows how you'd get across if you were disabled.'

'You stayed lying in the tent the *whole* time,' Derrie accused her.

'At least it meant I didn't have to chop wood or cook disgusting communal cauldrons of soya.'

Andi built up to another eruption of wet sneezes. She checked Somoya for a response. Nothing. I'd even live out here, if it meant being with her.

Across the street, greasing her fingers down the window display of a gift shop, Derrie searched for something among dream catchers, dried flowers and handmade greetings cards.

'No Pokémons,' she muttered dismissively and carried on uphill. 'Anyway, how d'you know we're going the right way?' Derrie's eyes were swollen with sun and fatigue as she nudged Sarah towards a teenage girl passing them. '*Ask* someone, instead of just wandering round.'

'Excuse me,' Sarah said, stopping her. 'Can you tell us the names of any of the pubs round here?'

The girl scowled in concentration. 'Well, there's The Bull's Head, The George... um Hotel, Kinder Lodge, Lantern Pike, The Royal Hotel, The Packhorse, Waltzing Weasel, The Conservative Club...'

'Is there one that's got anything to do with tennis?' Derrie asked, jiggling up and down in agitation.

'Tennis?' The girl's eyes clouded even darker under her long fringe.

'Or sport,' Jo prompted.

'Oh, yeah.' Her face brightened like the sun emerging. 'There's The Sportsman.'

Derrie's jiggling evolved into hopping on the spot. 'Where is it?'

'About fifteen minutes walk, straight up Kinder Road, it's on your –'

'We'll go in the car,' Derrie patted the girl on the back. 'Good one. Thanks. Let's go! Your car's only over there, Andi, can I go with you?'

Just ahead, Andi spotted a clothes rail standing outside a second-hand dress agency. 'I just want to have a quick look through these.'

'Aw… Why do I always have to wait?' Derrie nettled.

'Charlotte, these would be perfect for you. Size fourteen. That's right isn't it? Much cooler than nylon in this heat.' She held up a pair of stone-coloured trousers, which bloused with a collection of pockets along the narrow cut legs. Then she took Charlotte's hand, prompting her to stroke the material. 'Baby-soft cotton.'

'How d'you do that?' Sarah asked, fingering the label. 'A whole rail full of rubbish and you pick out designer wear in two seconds. They're only three pounds. I want them.'

'I want them too,' Derrie joined in.

'They're much too big for you,' Sarah replied.

'Not if I rolled them up. I could –'

'Anyway,' Andi interrupted. 'These are for Charlotte.' She buttoned a pocket that had come undone, savouring the cloth between her fingertips. 'She'll look stunnin'.'

'Talking about me again?' Jo swaggered towards them, an impudent gleam in her eyes.

'It's taking too long,' Derrie appealed to Jo, who pulled her into a bear hug.

Charlotte transferred her weight uncomfortably. 'I don't like trousers.'

'She's not just like this with you, you know,' Jo explained. 'She tries to dress everybody. Last night she binned my T-shirt while we were still out.'

'Really?' Pain pinched Sarah's face.

Tugging at Sarah's arm with real force, Derrie whimpered. 'Can we *go* now?'

'Not long now, you bold lass,' Andi answered. Glancing quickly at Charlotte's knotted calves, she attempted to persuade her in earnest. 'Come on, Charlotte. With your long legs they'll hang beautifully. I'd kill to be able to parade around in these. What d'you say?'

A smile drained from Charlotte. 'I don't know.' Andi saw that her fingernails were hovering over her neck, resisting the temptation to scratch the blotches on her skin.

Andi indicated the area over her own throat. 'Are you all right?'

Shrugging one shoulder, Charlotte lowered her voice to a whisper. 'Oestrogen and sunlight aren't a brilliant mix.'

'Wait for us in the car,' Andi handed her the keys before stepping through the shop door. 'I'll get these anyway. They might grow on you, like.' Then she doubled back, spotting something else on the rail. She unhooked a thin white tailored blouse and laid it against the trousers. Another perfect fit. 'See? New ensemble for a fiver. You can give us a fashion show later.'

'Wish she was my personal shopper.' As she disappeared into the shop, Andi could hear the envy in Sarah's voice. Through the window, she located Somoya. Christ, she's looking at us. Staring in that strange, hard way that pulls at the bloody lump in my chest. Tug-of-love heart in custody battle. I was way off the mark. It's not true you can fall out of love in a second... not true.

'Come on, *please*, Andi,' Derrie squeaked, poking her head round the door. 'Last clue! Jo's gone to fetch the car for us. Last chance!'

Andi handed over a ten-pound note and waited while the owner folded the clothes in slow motion. In no time at all, Somoya will away home and I'll have blown it again. More than likely for the final time. Last chance. Andi remembered. Over the years, she'd often observed the straight lads' ritual agony at closing time. Synchronising their watches. Ten to two, last chance. Swilling down the dregs of their beer, rubbing their palms together and chorusing through grim smiles, 'Ten to two, last chance,' as they headed in the direction of the girl they'd been eyeing all night. Andi's heart always set up its own vicarious thudding. Do it now. Ask her before someone else does, before she disappears forever.

Holding her hand over the counter for her change, Andi studied Somoya still waiting outside. Standing on her own, Somoya surveyed the hills as if she were already up there. How could anybody be designed on such economic lines? She's so precise. So self-contained. How the hell can I catch her? Engage her? Tears swelled in Andi's throat.

She charged towards her car and saw Charlotte drifting to sleep in the passenger seat. When she opened the door and pressed the carrier bag of clothes into her arms, Andi barely registered Charlotte's contained smile. Instead, she continued tracking Somoya striding towards the Porsche. It's enough to make a lass swear, the unfairness of wanting. Strips you of your sense, so you can't do anything. She accelerated away from the kerb, trying to keep the others in sight. Ten to two, last chance. Andi's car made the steep ascent up the narrow road, very gradually. On each side, the cottages were almost hidden beneath a profusion of summer bedding plants, spilling from window boxes. How to work my way into her and stay? Slide into symbiosis. Speedy intravenous panic pumped through her.

Ahead, Jo pulled to a stop and, through the rear windscreen, Andi caught a glimpse of Derrie slapping Somoya with a jubilant high five.

'Do you mind if I wait in the car?' Charlotte murmured. 'I feel a bit... tired.'

As she climbed out, Andi noticed Charlotte's foundation creased along the fine lines in her skin and mascara smudged into weary shadows under her eyes.

'That's fine, pet. We'll not be long.'

Drawing level with Somoya, she lost the ability to speak. How to get her? Make her laugh. Now I want to, I can't. A drift of cigarette smoke reached them, as they passed an old man shuffling under the weight of his soiled suit, coat and hat. Improvise. With which? Jumble sale fashion or tobacco?

Andi inhaled deeply. 'Umm... nicotine.'

Somoya wrinkled her nose. 'You don't smoke, do yer?'

Wrong choice. Calls to mind the chain-smoking girlfriend.

'Nah. I had to pack 'em in. They were giving us piles.'

Derrie pushed in between them. 'Piles of what?'

'Piles of piles on me bum, from dragging so fierce on those ultra lights.' Weak. Beyond weak. I'm dying a death, here.

Breaking her concentration on the black and cream façade of the pub, Somoya frowned at her. That frown.

Desperate measures. From her pocket, Andi grabbed a fistful of popcorn and flung it high over Somoya's head. When the snowfall had settled, sticking inside corkscrews of hair, she spiked Andi with a narrow, cinnamon scowl.

'What did you do *that* fer?'

Andi tried to remain convinced. 'Commit a random act of madness every day.'

'In't it supposed to be kindness?' Somoya asked as she unstuck popcorn from her curls.

Andi pushed into the pub with Derrie and Somoya sandwiched behind. The gloom of the empty interior created a disorientating contrast to the honeyed evening. Jo bowed her head to avoid the low beams and, dazed by the dark, Andi caught glimpses of red velvet and willow pattern.

'This is it!' Derrie's voice echoed. 'Buried treasure.'

The barmaid took her time to finish a pointed scratch at her shampoo and set, then redirected her frosted nail across the room. Still unsure, they scanned around the equestrian prints, hunting rifles and china King Charles spaniels.

'In the fireplace.'

'Thanks for saving us the trouble.' Sarah followed Derrie and planted a kiss on the top of her head. 'This one's worn out.'

'Are we the last?' Andi braced herself against the stone surround, her arm reaching into the loosely stacked logs, then reappearing with the card.

Wiping wet circles around the bar, the woman sucked at her lipstick. 'Last in a long line of long faces.'

'Why?' Somoya asked. 'Because they didn't win?'

The lacquered nail poked into her solid hair again. 'It's all a con.'

Derrie lifted her eyes from the gold card. 'What d'you mean?'

She shook her head. 'Just read it, sweetheart.'

Sharing her grip on the card with Andi, Derrie mouthed the words. Her eyes were red-rimmed with exhaustion.

'What's wrong with it, Andi?'

Derrie's hair fluffed like eiderdown between the pads of Andi's thumb and forefinger. The fine strands were the spun gold of fairytales and she wondered why that colour never lasted into adulthood.

'It means it's a scam, hinney. A trick.' She folded the last clue and handed it to Somoya.

Seeing the others waiting, Somoya cleared her throat: 'Congratulations on getting to end of the trail. Now, phone this number and, if you're the first to call, you can claim your special surprise holiday. Telephone: 0161 666 060606.'

'So?' Derrie demanded, her forehead a miniature furrowed field. 'Let's ring the number!'

Sarah stroked back Derrie's fringe and tried to smooth the agitated skin.

'It's unobtainable.' The landlady crossed the room and closed Derrie's hands round a packet of crisps. 'Here, lovey. These are for you.'

Jo nodded. 'Too many digits, for a kick off. Surprise is, there's no holiday.'

'Woof, indeed,' Derrie insisted. 'There *was*. It says in the letter you got. The holiday –'

'666,' Sarah noticed. 'It's an omen. Like that film about the boy with the devil's mark tattooed on his scalp.'

Jo whistled, descending a scale of disbelief. 'Cheeky shower of shysters. That's...' she paused to calculate, 'forty quid a car... They'll have made quite a bit.'

'Not that much, surely?' Sarah asked.

'Two grand in a day, if there were... say, fifty cars.'

'Doesn't seem worth all the effort.'

'I don't get it.' Grubby streaks radiated from Derrie's eyes as she rubbed her fists around them. 'What about the prize?'

With her arm folded around Derrie, Somoya urged her towards the back door. 'Wonder where they got all the women's names from?'

Andi rushed in front to hold it open for them. 'Might be someone who works for the city council, like, with access to the confidential mailing lists. Probably got lists of men's names as well. A pink pound scam. I don't suppose they bothered with the pensioners' mailing list.'

The white light in the walled garden was blinding, reflecting off several pale canvas sunshades.

Derrie's voice cracked with broken crying. 'But there has to be a prize. They wouldn't *do* that.'

Sarah gathered a handful of her dress and wiped Derrie's cheeks. 'Sorry, love. I haven't got a tissue.' Jo hugged them both against her and her gaze fused with Sarah's. Andi saw their sadness as they realised their lass would have to learn to be canny and not expect the world to be honest.

Disengaging herself, Derrie made her way towards the rock face that formed the back wall of the garden. Selecting each foothold with care, she climbed to the roots of a fully-grown sycamore jutting through the stone. Raising her head, her eyes glinted as she slapped the tree.

'I'm *not* having it.' She held her palm out to Sarah. 'Give me the letter, please. It's proof. I'm going to the police, right. An' I'm going to ring up that programme – the *Watchdog* one. I'm not going to let them do it again.'

In league, Andi lifted one stony fist in the air and initiated a chat show chant, 'Go, Derrie! Go, Derrie!'

'Well, we're shattered. Cheers for today.' Jo slapped Andi and Somoya in turn. 'Catch you soon, Andi. You ready, Somoya?'

'I'm in no hurry to get home.' Aiming her words at the woods, Somoya was barely audible. 'D'you want to stay for a drink, Andi? Or something to eat?'

'What about Charlotte?'

Sarah nudged Jo gently. 'Don't worry. She can come with us.'

Forty

'I can't go back,' Somoya whispered, focusing on a silver sliver of Kinder reservoir shining through the trees. Andi felt relieved to hear her speak, after their silent drive from the pub. 'I can't be dealin' with it.'

'Don't, then,' Andi averted her face so that Somoya couldn't see her expression change. The quiet wood amplified the crisp sound of their feet on the bracken. With the sun still blasting out heat, the brittle ground showed no evidence of the earlier shower.

'I've got to.'

'Why? What d'you have to go back for, like?'

Andi waited, holding her gaze, asking again.

Unnerved, Somoya scanned the path, 'There's all my stuff... I need to...'

'Don't worry yourself. Tell us when she'll be out an' I'll go and pick it up.'

She pinched at the lines creasing the bridge of her nose. 'Sayin' that, it's most likely shredded and scattered around road already.' The dropped word made Andi notice Somoya's accent getting broader with her increasing fear.

'At least it'll save you packing.'

'I can't laugh at this yet.' Somoya pursed her lips in disdain, generating sporadic charges through Andi.

'Aye, I'm sorry.'

'Next week, I might well phone you up and laugh,' she kidded.

Hope fluttered freshly laundered chances in Andi's face. She could see pain spiking through Somoya's temples and she wished she could kiss it away.

'What else?' Andi asked. Somoya's eyes skimmed over her absently. 'What else have you to go back for?'

'Just to listen to the all night bloody garbage about it all bein' my fault, and if only I'd –'

'Have you done? So you're choosing to go back to be tortured?' Andi shook her head in an attitude of mock gravity, while stroking a thumb and finger over her chin. The therapist she had transformed into had a precise Brooklyn accent. 'You're one sick little bunny.'

Somoya's caramel complexion fired up. 'It's not a *joke*, pal! Everythin's so easy fer you. So simple. I can't leave her in that state.'

Jealousy fastened a slipknot around Andi's windpipe, making her speech sound strange. 'Jaz isn't going to be getting any better...' She wondered how stupid it would be to push her conclusion. '... with you there to blame.'

Rounding on her, teeth bared, Somoya gave the impression she could tear out Andi's throat. 'You've got no idea. Just get away from me. *Move.*'

Involuntarily, Andi stumbled backwards. 'No bother, man.' While I've still got some fucking pride left. Bet you wouldn't dare speak to her like that. Unless you fancied having your head caved in. So easy for us? Like fuck. Just because I refuse to stoop to the sympathy vote. Try having a smackhead for a sister, then you'd know that no amount of loving someone like that makes any difference. It doesn't count. Doesn't count over and over, until all that's left of love is how often you open your purse and how often you manage to keep it closed, till all love means is repeat bloody trips to Accident and Emergency to gawk at disposable cardboard bowls overfilling – regurgitated charcoal, floating with Paracetamol.

Andi hurried away, digging viciously in her pocket for her car keys.
'Wait.'

Andi carried on. Some people can't bear being loved. Course, it could be she just doesn't like us. Well, either way, I'm not masochistic enough to hang around to find out. I'm away home.

'How am I supposed to get back?' Somoya shouted.

'Bus.'

Somoya chased after her, snapping through the undergrowth. 'At least drop me at the village.'

'It's a thirty-minute walk, maximum.' I can't get me breath. She was wrong when she said I've no self-preservation skills. I've any amount.

Racing past, Somoya blocked her way at a point where the path narrowed on each side with trees. 'I'm sorry, right. I know you were tryin' to help.'

The pressure around her upper arms where Somoya held her insisted she listened. Tired of the sustained effort of lying, Andi felt her head sway in denial.

'Nah, I wasn't. I was trying to get you to... leave her... I was trying to...' Telling the truth didn't seem to come as an easy option either. She kicked the ground, blinking away shame.

'Go easy. I know. Why d'you think you've been scaring me so much? The chance you give me to jump, we're talkin'... the great escape.' Somoya touched one of Andi's tears. Curious to find out what was happening, Andi glanced up and as Somoya licked her fingertip delicately, a sharp memory shuddered through her. 'Mm... salt.'

Still holding one of Andi's arms, Somoya eased her down to the ground, arranging her carefully with her back against warm bark. The rays gilding the trees seemed brighter and Andi felt tempted to lift her camera, angle the lens towards the sky and steal the scene.

Staring straight ahead at the gold trees, Somoya whispered, 'Stay here for a while.'

'As long as you don't try to have sex with us. I'm allergic.'

Selecting a stick from the ground, Somoya held it up to Andi's navel, threatening to poke it in. Then she flung it high into the air.

'Wouldn't touch yer with a twig. Besides, I've forgotten how.' They both saw the stick land in a slow stream. 'What I need is peace... time to... haven't had any peace for years.'

'Okay,' Andi jumped up and brushed sandy soil from the back of her shorts. 'Howay. I'll drive us back. I could drop you at Sarah and Jo's. They'll put you up as long as you like. Derrie would be ecstatic. I don't know how peaceful it'll be, mind, with her climbing all over you, every waking minute.' Somoya hadn't moved, and Andi could hear herself gabbling. 'That, combined with getting your sleep disturbed by the happy couple. There'll be hell on. Those two have got any amount of making up to do.' Andi felt humiliated by how jealous she sounded.

'Lucky sods.'

Keep going, she told herself. I'm the arrogant bastard who knows what's best for her. S'nothing to do with the awful charred embers in my cunt.

'You know you can stay at mine for a few days, until you find a place.' The unlikely light flushing Somoya's curls distracted her. Andi saw they were the same cellophane colour as toffee apple wrapping. The effect forced another unwelcome burst of honesty from her. 'But that wouldn't work... Wouldn't work with the peace thing.'

Somoya bent a fern towards herself and stroked slow lines with it down her own arm. 'It's peaceful here.'

'Aye.' Andi noticed Somoya's bandage had worked loose, showing the cut on her knuckles already dried dark brown. In her mind, she touched it with her mouth.

Flicking her thumb through fronds, Somoya held the silence for a while. Despite the distance between them, Andi thought she could smell a bitter, grassy perfume on Somoya's hands.

'We could stay.'

'Here?'

'Yeah.' Eyes bright as a toddler's, Somoya picked up the bits of dry wood that were within arm's reach. 'We could mek a fire so we won't get cold.'

Rigid, Andi tried to gauge if too much exposure to Jaz had altered Somoya's balance. Andi had never slept anywhere without a downy mattress, inside the privacy of a room. Even the descriptions of other people's camping trips left her sweating with disgust and the thought of rocks jabbing through densely packed earth made her feet curl inside the protection of her sandals.

'I canna sleep on the *ground*. I'm the original princess and the pea.'

'I'll make you a fine bed, your majesty, from the floor of the forest.' Jumping up and bowing, Somoya began sweeping away pebbles, smoothing soil with the palm of her hand and layering leaves into a miniature mattress. She resembled a demented child, a crazy Girl Scout with her curls raising skyward, full of static electricity. Andi had no intention of spending the most uncomfortable night of her life in this place. Apart from anything else, they could be raped and murdered by some madman out here in the dark, on their own.

'If you really don't want to go back to Manchester tonight, I saw a decent-looking Bed and Breakfast in the village.'

'You know I meant *here*.' Somoya flattened her fingers down into the fairy bed and glared at her, issuing an ultimatum. Here and now. Now or nothing.

Slapping the warm earth, Andi tried one last attempt to get her own way. 'Give over. We won't sleep a wink on *this*.'

'We'll not sleep tonight anyroad.' Somoya met her eyes in challenge.

Andi's heart started to swell. A heart swell of relief from its walnut prison. She'd forgotten it was still there and the expansion hurt after so long being clamped. Now blood forced her heart open, filling her chest again, until it pressed at her ribcage like it had that morning. An age ago, when she'd seen Somoya's finger pause on the map. Andi shivered.

'I'll make a fire,' Somoya said.

She thinks I'm cold. How can she think I'm cold? I'm incendiary.

'Got any matches?'

'Nah. You'll get done for arson.'

'Never mind. I used ter be able to do it other way.'

Andi sat down again and watched Somoya select two sticks, deciding she was kidding. But the serious gathering of ingredients stemmed any wisecracks. Clearing a sandy space, Somoya laid everything out in order – a handful of dried grass, some sweet wrappers from her pocket and a small pile of twigs. Resting two sticks on the ground, she started to rub them together rapidly. It'll never work, Andi thought, that's just the stuff of army survival videos and nineteen-fifties boys' adventure annuals. She needs a magnifying glass, like we used when we were kids. The rubbing went on so long that Andi had to look away. But she felt like she ought to say something. Fill the silence.

Settling back, Andi tried to yawn. 'It takes it out of you, eating cake.' I'm talking to myself here, she realised. I need something that'll get a rise out of her. 'Whatever else happens, you're starting that course. I'll hound you until you do. I'm going to send your notice into that bloody car hire place an' –'

'I wouldn't be able to concentrate.'

'It's exactly what you need to get your mind off everything.'

Creeping sunset drove the shadows into darker relief. Something tickled her inner thigh. An ant. An itch too tiny to ignore. She swept her hand over it and it stopped. Then it commenced its intermittent trek again, this time along the back of her knee and down her calf. When she dared to glance back, she saw Somoya breathing on the grass as if she was whispering. A thin line of smoke whispered back. Somoya blew so lightly on the grass, it didn't move, but a red pinprick of light touched the hairy fringe of the ripped paper. Andi saw a flame suck to life. As Somoya fed it a few more dried blades and sweet wrappers, a smouldering radiance shone against her tanned nose and cheeks. Then, picking up only the spindliest twigs, she threaded them intricately through each other over the tiny fire. In a moment they caught light and Somoya added larger sticks, waiting for the flames to accept each one before offering the next.

An acorn dropped, narrowly missing Somoya's head and nestled next to a tiny oak seedling. If it survives, Andi realised, it could out-live us both several times over.

Abruptly, they were both shy. After aching to kiss her all day, all year, Andi didn't know what to do. Any action would be too crass. Too sudden. If only she could press up against her. If only she didn't need her permission, then it might be easy. I want her, Andi thought, so I take her. Like a dog nosing in from behind. I'd claw in to keep her still. Pin her against the path. Climb on. Clamour and convulse till I come – with her I might be able to.

Wood smoke curled into their clothes, as they focused on the fire, listening to the flames snapping twigs.

Forty-one

Sink's clogged with orange. Wotsits. Sour cheese. Try running the water. Fuck, it's filling up more. If I poke it down – Yeuk. Sluggy egg white, sluggy fucking stuff. Can't do it. Christ, my guts.

'You're supposed to be here for this, Somoya. Ringside fucking seat.'

Ugh. God. Aim for the bath, sink's too blocked. Can't stand, much more, of this.

'*See*. There's your evidence. Swilling right there. Wouldn't fucking believe me, would you? Evidence –'

Christ, my sides ache. Gotta lie down for a bit. *Jesus*, hold on. C'mere, banister. Can't do this. There's no way. I'll have to get out. It was mental to just stop. Need to find Gary. See if he'll make a house call. Probably not. He's still fucking shirty 'cos I owe him. Just lie here for a... Oh... Not again, it's coming. Get something, anything. Dressing gown... coconut... smells of her. Curl it into a well. Coconut well. Open your mouth wide and wait. It'll be okay. Just wait for the hot lumpy roar. Acid squawk. Ugh. God. The *stink*. The coconut cheese. How much fucking longer? Need the phone. Gary might come if he hears what I'm like. Please, let him be in. Find the phone... find the fucking phone... Ugh. My guts... dropping. Journey to the centre of the earth. Need something to... now. Gotta shit bad. Carrier-bag, quick. Open it. Photos. Cards. Maps. Bras? She's packing. She's fucking packing. Ugh... my guts are chronic. Stretch it. Squat, for fuck's sake. Get a load of this, Somoya. Plastic round my arse... Ugh. Pebble dashing your precious... Bluebottle. Weaving round the top of the bag. Off its box on the stench. Come back and get these if you want them, Somoya. Reclaim your left luggage.

Too shaky. Just lie back. Joints crack. Speckled twist pile. Last time down here, I got carpet burns. It did happen... too many years ago... didn't imagine it... had something sweet. The room's mad. Stuff pulled out where she's started sorting through. I'll never find the rent on this place. The social won't pay it all, that's certain. Have to find somewhere. But where the fuck else is there? Can't go back to Mum's. Not after last night...

Every tin of food in the kitchen's stacked out of the cupboards, on the floor. Standing in the middle, Mum's struggling with a can of stewing steak and the tin opener. Her hands fucking covered in tomato sauce. She gives up and goes back to the mess on the table.

'Mum?'

She picks up the last few baked beans from a plastic bowl. Kills them between her thumb and finger, then wipes the mush off on to a full plate. A mini mountain range.

'In here.'

I recognise the road signs. 'Mum. Have you had your tablets today?'

'Rat poison's down tum toilet. Swallowed in one flush.' Finished with the beans, she's back to attacking the half-open steak can with a fork, dragging out strands of meat. A dog food stench hits the air.

'Those ones are just to thin your blood. Where's the others?'

She won't answer. Concentrating on mashing the meat through the same fucking processing plant as the beans. I stare. Her mouth's a permanent pucker of deep cut lines. Hair like a wig... nesting... hatching. Unnatural black, except where she's chopped it jagged at the back. No felt pen marks drawn in today.

'Mum. Where are the rest of them?'

'Gone. Not forgotten.' She slaps a can of sardines and the slippery tin opener into my hands.

For some reason, the food piles are familiar. They make me eight years old again. Sitting in the kitchen with the green-topped table. Blanking Mum's gravy fingers with the alien game. What if aliens did poos through their mouths and ate through their bums? My bum hole opens to suck in a roast potato. I giggle.

'*Open* it,' she screams, sounding much younger than eight.

I'm in deep shite. Don't know what to do. I open the fucking sardines and give them back. A queasy cat food stink smears in with the dog meat. As the fish pulps through her fingers, I wanna shout for help. But there's no one within a million-mile radius who'll come. All the colostomy bags round here back off from me even faster than they do from Mum. Watching the mess spread gives me a dish-rag heart. wrung out, too thin as string to mop anything up. I wanna cry. Cry baby. Gone a-hunting. Momma's gone a-bunting. She shouldn't have been allowed to have me. Somebody should've stopped her. The government, or something. Got her sterilised.

'They've put it in my food 'cos I won't take them. I heard them working it out.' Fish oil streaks down the front of her dressing gown.

Try to stop her hand working. Grab it. 'They couldn't get your tablets in the tins. They're sealed.'

She keeps up her pumping grip on the fish. 'They've got special ways of doing it, so nothing looks tampered with.'

'C'mere.' I show her, smoothing the food mountain with a knife. 'There's no pills in here.'

Her face clears as something filters through. Thank fuck for that.

'Yes. No pills. You're right.'

I nod. Wonder whether to pat her. Something passes across the hallway. People moving in the dark.

'They've ground them up so I can't see them.' She does a kind of lizard dash to the bin with the plate. Most of it slops in, but some muddy rivers down the outside.

Give up. Losing fucking battle. Escape out the front door. Tell her. 'You want locking up...'

No. That's definite. Not back there. Have to stay here. Let them evict me. It'll take a while to get a court order. Close my eyes into the spin cycle. With any luck, I'll be dead by then.

Forty-two

'Hurry up and fasten your seat belt,' Sarah instructed.

Derrie struggled in the back. 'Give me a chance, man.'

'I'm not a man.'

Charlotte held back, still unsure, as the belt refused to connect, until Derrie handed it to her.

'You do it, please.'

The warm evening rushed in through the open window, ruffling Sarah's hair. The sky seemed huge. Carmine. Plump with crushed velvet clouds.

'Cirrus.' Jo tilted her face up. 'Beautiful. And you don't have to pay a penny for it.'

Oncoming headlights caught the silver freckling Derrie's nose.

'Who put that sparkly stuff on your face?' Sarah asked.

'Andi. It's body glitter.'

In the dark, with Derrie safe behind, Sarah felt a song surge through her even before any notes formed. 'Pack up your troubles, flying into evening light...' The melody rang in her throat, perfectly pitched. 'Your luggage got lost, so everything will be all right.'

'What's that song?' Derrie asked.

'Don't know. It just came into my head.'

'I thought it was gonna be...' Jo grinned and began to sing. 'Pack up your troubles –'

Sarah joined in, building to a finale, 'In your old kit bag, and smile, smile, smile.'

Mildly, Charlotte started her own song: 'It's a long way to Tipperary –'

'What *is* a rary?' Dozily, Derrie slid sideways into Charlotte's lap. Sarah groaned. 'Old joke.'

'What d'you mean?'

She was too tired for explanations.

'Tipperary's a place,' Charlotte murmured, sounding far away.

'Yes. I remember. A bookshop.' Derrie patted Charlotte's hand sleepily, timing her words with each touch. 'Everything… is… going… to… be… all right.' Then she whispered, 'I had a *great* day,' just before drifting off.

Sarah shook her head at Jo. 'What is it about the way she says things? Even the unweird things sound… She's just got a way of saying things.' The corners of Sarah's lips curled up as she remembered Derrie's outburst at the end of the treasure hunt. 'I'm *not* having it.' I don't blame you, girl. You keep reminding me what I have to do. She saw the muscles in Derrie's peach cheeks, blank with sleep. The sight prompted a scrambling trail of words through Sarah's head.

Home free,
My little teacher,
Home run
With righteous fury,
Home and dry
Flaunting a finger at fear,
As years get lost
I'll remind you,
So you can remind me.

– Remind me to fight back. I'm not having it either. If Colin comes *anywhere* near, I'll see a solicitor. Get a restraining order against him.

Charlotte cleared her throat, making Sarah wonder what she was leading up to.

'I had a great day, too. I want to thank you for letting me come out with you.'

Her unprompted speech jolted Sarah. The words hung, going nowhere, forming a residue of guilt that left Sarah at a loss for a polite reply. She wanted to say sorry. She knew she needed to say something. She gazed at Derrie, sleeping across Charlotte's lap.

'Doesn't she look peaceful?' Taking in every precious detail of her daughter's face, Sarah remembered what might be waiting for them at home...

His car had a factory reek of overheated plastic – enough to kick-start a headache. From the back seat, Sarah's point-of-view shot tilted over Colin's shoulder, so she could see his fountain pen form pinched letters on a purple greetings card.

Dear Sarah and Jo,

I know that me writing like this will come as a surprise. I imagine you never thought you'd hear from me, especially out of the blue, after nine and a half years. You might not remember my name. It's Colin. By pure chance, I happened to see you going out in the car a few days ago with Derrie and I recognised Sarah. Don't worry. It's no big mystery that I know your names, your neighbour volunteered them. I will keep my promise of anonymity, if you are absolutely sure that's what you want. Don't be alarmed, Sarah, but I knew all along it was you who wanted to be a mother. I could tell that our arrangement was for you, by how serious you were about it. Your little girl looks happy, so I'm sure you are making a good job of bringing her up. But when I saw her, it made me wonder if your circumstances had changed now. Does she ever ask about me? I imagine she would welcome the opportunity to meet up, so she understands more about where she comes from. I'd be more than happy to arrange this with you and I know my mother would be over the moon to meet her.

My intentions have always been altruistic. I was glad to help and, now I've seen Derrie, I'm convinced she must be a joy to you both. She looks like a real little treasure. Maybe I should send a photograph of me, in case she asks who I am and it would be really nice if Derrie wanted to write back, telling me a little bit about herself. Who knows? Perhaps she might like a day out, now and then? My solicitor could draw up an equitable visitation schedule. Please telephone when you've had chance to discuss this (my card is enclosed) so we can decide how to proceed.

With all best wishes,

Sarah didn't wait to see him sign it. Her skull seemed to be punching through her forehead. They'd have to move house. Leave no forwarding address.

Forty-three

The dog rose in Andi again. She wanted to snuffle around in the hair at the back of Somoya's neck. Take panting breaths of that coconut scent. Sniff and lick at the day's salt in the creases of her skin and the roots of her wiry fur. She needed to dig in her claws and hump her as if life depended on it, ignoring the yelping as she howled at the sky. Sinking her incisors in to hold her in position while she worked away till she'd finished.

But she did nothing. Still she stayed still. Not even able to meet her eyes. I'll just be another bloody disaster for her. Exit mad bitch. Enter frigid one. On the edge of her field of vision she sensed a movement. Somoya's bandaged fingers unfurled and slow-motioned towards hers, meeting at the tips. Acute prickles ran down Andi's palm. Their hands slid into a loose link. Andi shut her eyes, feeling the last slanting gold drape a sunny cover over them both. The jittery chafing of crickets grew louder. Even though Somoya had let go, the shape of her fingers stayed imprinted on Andi's. The static bristled again, this time over her chest, tightening her nipples until they stung. She opened her eyes and saw Somoya's hand hovering, an inch above her breasts.

What the hell was she doing?

A solar heat spread below Andi's ribs, then slowed, containing itself. She waited long minutes for the buzzing to calm. Finally, the flint edges inside her dissolved under Somoya's palm. As if she knew, Somoya lowered her hand, barely brushing against Andi and steadied in the air, over her middle. For some reason the words 'solar plexus' entered Andi's head. What was she playing at? She wanted to scream in itching frustration. I want sex. Not fucking healing. Energy charged in rising circles through her stomach, while her mind carried on like a resistance fighter, running underground messages. Humiliating *drivel*. This isn't what she wanted, being played like a puppet. Lost to herself, handed over, wide open and unprotected. How dare she terrify her with this safe and sound stuff. She tried to pull Somoya towards her. Come on. Fuck us and be done with it. Don't try and mess with a soul I never had.

'Don't move,' Somoya warned, resting her injured knuckles in her lap. She lifted her other palm to the exact place she'd just left.

Andi's stomach liquefied. Soon she'd drain into the leaves and biodegrade.

A cuckoo called, then echoed itself. Andi couldn't tell which direction it came from. Somoya's hand drifted down again, still floating, and Andi saw their skin shimmer into a mirage. A sore current kicked in with rhythmic vengeance, pulling her up from the mound of her pubic bone. The hand was too still, cupping the air just above her. Andi badly needed some movement. She wanted to grab Somoya's fingers and squeeze them into a fist to ram between her legs. But then she remembered the black stitches in Somoya's arm.

'Fuck me.' She couldn't believe what she'd said. Her voice all gravel, sounded unlikely.

But Somoya's hand stayed, not moving. She waited until Andi lifted her eyes locking them steadily with hers. Then she smiled. A slight knowing curve, marking the calm before. Leaning down, she touched lips with a brief tip of tongue. Then she stormed, rolling over Andi, gripping her thigh between her own, forcing hard against her. Wrenching Andi's shorts open, one-handed, she painted slow-fisted brush strokes over the rough curls, dampening them tighter. Andi heard her own broken breathing as Somoya's fingers drifted away. She wondered if Somoya's arm was too sore to carry on.

'OK. Stop it now,' Andi whispered, touching Somoya's knuckles. 'You're gonna make these worse.'

Somoya blinked at her hand as if she was wondering what had happened to it.

'No, I'm not,' her eyes smiled. 'Something's taking my mind right off all that.'

She closed each of Andi's eyelids with a kiss. For a moment Andi lay still, until she felt a butterflying over her breasts, touching down on her stomach and lifting off again to dip into her, trailing juice in slight circles over her skin. She nudged at Somoya's thumb as it slicked leisurely between her thighs. Just do it, Andi thought. Push in. She gasped as Somoya did as she was told and Andi wondered whether she'd spoken out loud.

Somoya crooked her middle finger inside, beckoning her forward. Uncurling, then drawing her back. Her whole body fluttering on one finger. A strange deep voice came from her throat, something that sounded like, 'Hard... er ... Hard... er...' and, as she panted with each jagged pull, she heard her voice drowned out by another. She opened her eyes to see where it was coming from. Miles above, the oaks were shifting round, synchronising their speech. Been here. Seen that. Hundreds of years over. It's. All. Going. To. Be. All right.

Picked up and shaken, Andi shuddered against Somoya's hand, not her own, and felt warm spurts leaking from her. This is what it's like, Andi told herself as her limbs levitated towards the upper branches.

Somoya tensed her legs and with a pained frown, ground into Andi. Clenching her teeth into Andi's neck, she breathed rapidly through each word, 'Everything's... going... to... be... all right.'

Forty-four

It's there again. The slug. Flat and black and long as a person. Coming for me. It doesn't wriggle. It jumps, then just waits on the mud, on the hay, gearing up to spring. It'll bite me if I don't get... here it comes. My back presses against the wall. Hit it. Hit it off! It's left a slimy print thing on my arm. I can see it getting its strength back. It's ready to spring again. But Ellie's charging across the farmyard. She gets her body in front of me. Sticks a knife right in the slug, lots of times. I can feel the blade sticking in the gristle, then tugging 'cos the knife won't come out. Something gungy bobbles through the holes in its skin, but Ellie pulls me away so I don't have to see.

She takes me over to the hayloft. There's no slugs in there, so we'll be safe.

Her hand squeezes mine. 'I've got a challenge for you.' She's pointing to the bales of hay laid out in tunnels, piled on top of each other, up high. 'Get through the maze and you'll find out something smart.'

Can't wait to get in. I crawl fast, racing, but there's loads of dead ends and the hay's scratching my knees. I go slower trying to remember which way I've already been. It's really dark now that I'm in deep and my eyes needle with itching. I hit my head against another prickly wall. The hay smell makes me sneeze loads, like I can't stop. It's too small in here. I try to go back, but I'm stuck. I don't like it. I shout. 'I want to get *out*.'

'Get out then,' Ellie calls back.

She's making me mad now. 'How?'

'Imagine you're finding the way out.'

'I don't know what you mean.'

'You used to tell me things before you were born. At least I *listened*.'

I start to cry. The air's being squeezed flat out of me by the bales weighing me down.

'I am... listening. I just don't know what you're on about.'

'We're nearly over the threshold. Hold your arms out, so I can reach you.'

My eyes are so stinging I have to shut them, so the light in front is red. She's got both my hands. Pulls me through the tunnel like a jet. Pressing us together, shooting upwards. Into fresh air. Cool.

'C'mere, you little runt. Remember how we used to blaze about? Missed you like a hole in the heart. Like a heart in a hole.'

Her body curves me into her... fits exactly... same as the other times. And her electric hair sparks with mine.

Ellie's whispering tickles my neck. 'We leave our imprint on each other, our cells chain linked twice over.' She rushes through me. 'My nearly first born.'

I know what she means. Kind of. Her face goes babyish, like one of the kids in the infants.

'Link pinkie fingers,' I say. 'Touch tongues and make a wish.' That theme tune comes back, singing in my chest. 'Do you ever... ever find, weird stuff happens? Are you going out your mind?' I hold Ellie's face to make her look at me. 'Is this the threshold?'

'Over it.'

I'm floating. Spinning. 'Makes me dizzy, staying on for the same ride so many times. You can't keep going round again, pulling me with you.'

Ellie snorts, a sort of laugh. 'Remember it was *you* that said that, when you come back next time as a frog.'

'Cheeky, man! There's no way I'm going backwards. If all this stuff's real, I mean. I'm gonna evolve, like a Pokémon. Like Kakuna changes into Beedril.' I rocket up, leaving her behind, but somehow she's there, out in front, waiting.

'You've got to keep pace with me,' she says.

'Why should I?'

Ellie streams through me. 'I've reminded you enough times, you little witch. You and me are –'

'Unfinished business. Yeah, I know, but why?'

'You're the one who's going to love me back to life.'

'Miss Lester said that the Egyptians put all tools and food and favourite things in people's tombs. But that's stupid. When you're dead, you're dead.'

'You've just forgotten, Derrie.'

'Thingy, right, it's true. So you can't chat. You rot and make things grow. That's what Sarah says. That's the only energy left. The rest is made up, because people are so scared to die. She told me.'

'Your mother doesn't know everything. You'll work that out soon enough.'

'But she loves me.'

'You're the love of her life.' Ellie does a tired sigh. 'She always gets what's mine.'

'Can we go back down now? I want to see her. An' I wanna see Jo.'

'Weird, really. Every time we're grounded, we keep asking, "Why can't we fly?" Then when we're airborne again, we can't wait to get straight back down.'

Underneath us I can see black. Black getting smaller.

Ellie pulls. 'C'mon, hurry up. The threshold's narrowing like a mine...'

I can feel the car slowing down, even though I keep my eyes closed.

'Well... Thanks again for letting me... muscle in.' Charlotte moves my head dead carefully from her lap, trying not to wake me up.

'Don't worry,' Sarah tells her, 'She'll have to climb out soon, anyway. She's getting too heavy to carry.'

The car stops and I make my eyes into slits, so I can see the white railings outside Charlotte's flat. As she eases herself out, she whispers, 'Bye.'

Jo lifts her hand off the steering wheel in a sort of wave.

Sarah smiles. A real smile, 'Look after yourself.' As the car door slams, she whispers, 'See you.' Charlotte slots the key in her front door and while I snuggle my head against the soft leather, another bit of me runs after her...

The trapped heat in the flat rushes at us when she opens the door. It kind of wraps us up together, like we're in a baby's blanket. She scrubs the back of her neck with her knuckles, as if she's torn a muscle, or something. An overlapping cooing noise comes out of the chimney. There must be some pigeons nesting up there. It sounds like they're welcoming us, saying, back in, back in. Charlotte's face looks all dragged down, as if she wishes she could be back in forever. Sleeping like she's had a needle before an operation. What's it called? Anaesthetic. So she never has to open the front door.

She switches on the kettle, then picks a teacup covered in roses from the glass cabinet over the sink. What's she holding it up to the light for? It's see-through. She flips open a small square paper packet, gets hold of a cardboard tag thing and lowers the tea bag into her cup. Her shoulders sag as if it's a lot of effort. The kettle clicks and when the boiling water hits the bottom of the cup, blackcurrant and apple float up to my nose. It makes a pool fill under my tongue. She sips for a bit, then lets out a long stream of air. At the same second she lowers her eyelids, I watch something downloading. All our flickering faces. Even mine. I wonder if I'll see her again? Don't s'pose Sarah will let me.

Her breathing sounds all tight, as if her chest's wound round with wires. She struggles to strip her cardi off, but she's suffocating inside the nylon neck stuck over her head. I want to help, but my hand would just go right through.

Fur strokes my ankles in a silk figure-of-eight.

'Georgia.' The cat answers Charlotte with a squeal. 'Here you are.' She aims a cardboard packet over the bowl by her feet and biscuits hammer out like hailstones. 'Sorry, honey. No meat yet.'

I can see there is a tin in the cupboard. But, maybe Charlotte can't face the dead stink of it. I follow her to the bathroom. She gets a small bottle from the cabinet, then forces the bath plug in and turns the taps on full blast. As she shakes a few drops into the water, I lean over to read the label. Tea tree. A medicine smell breathes through the air.

I can feel the nerve endings screeching between Charlotte's legs. With both hands, she protects the new flat skin, stretching as it tries its best to heal. Through the steam, I can see a massive painting. A pink and yellow iris curling in on itself. Sort of like wrinkled folds of flesh. Charlotte rubs away the tears in her eyes, before they run over. When she stops, she sees flashing lighting up her bedroom and walks towards the red messages. Her finger connects with the answering machine and for a second, there's a loud hissing.

'Hello, Charlotte? It's Mum. Are you in? Hello? All right then, let's see. I hope you had a good day, it's always nice to get out in the countryside. Anyway, this is just to let you know that your dad's leg is a lot better since he's been on the new tablets, so we decided not to cancel the party. Never thought I'd make it to golden with that daft old devil. Well, um. What was it I wanted to... Oh yes. We'd like you to design the invitations, you're so good at that sort of thing. Anyway, I better go. I love you.'

It's nice seeing Charlotte smile. A loud beep makes us jump, then another voice starts. Quiet and sweet.

'Hi... Charlotte. I'm ringing with your phone... Sorry. You left it in my bookshop in Stalybridge. Sorry... My name's Sammy. Well, I thought... as I'm in Manchester on Wednesday, I could give it you back. I know you must be busy, but maybe we could... Well, you know your own number. Give me a ring.'

Charlotte breathes in deep. Her lungs didn't know they could expand this far. Her arms remember the spreading chestnut tree. Flung really wide. Then she's hanging from a branch, trembling, flaking off bits, unfolding into clean lines, damp, but drying in the breeze. Her arms float as if she's pushed her hands rigid against a doorframe for a long time and now she's let go, they're rising of their own accord. Buoyed up by those things in the wind. Thermals. I can hear her thinking... I'm gossamer, shimmering, prepared for take-off.

She presses replay, skipping past her mum's call. The words are kind of breathy. They make Charlotte remember his gentle fingers holding her earring. The red light keeps blinking at the room. The phone slips in her wet hands and the numbers muddle up in front of her eyes as she tries to dial. Her hand slams down as if someone else has forced it.

When she lifts the receiver again, I can hear the conversation in her head, while the phone does a low buzzing in her ear.

'I'm a bit lost in the big city.' It's Sammy's soft voice. 'Maybe you could show me some places you know?'

I'll show him the village, like it's mine, Charlotte thinks. Escort him down Canal Street. Sit outside in the sun with martini and lemonade. He'll ask me where we could go to eat, pointing a sparkling finger at the chrome and plate glass of the Slug and Lettuce, and I'll say, 'We could go there, if you want, but it's full of shoes and shirts.'

He'll ask, 'Who?'

'You know... Suits.' No. Not like that. Not big city know-it-all. I'll tell him the truth. I'll say, 'I'm a bit lost here, too.' Ask him if we can explore with our arms linked like old friends. Like tourists...

'Here we are, Derrie,' Sarah whispers. 'Home.'

I keep my eyes closed, pretending to be asleep.

'Come on.' She pats my leg. 'I can't lift you out.'

I stay still.

'It's all right,' Jo says, 'I'll carry her.'

As she hoists me up, I feel a bit guilty, but I don't want to open my eyes. It's well good being a baby.

Forty-five

'Where were we, before we were rudely interrupted?' Fully clothed, Jo perched on the edge of the bed.

Sarah pulled the covers over her head. 'Sleep in the other room.'

Pitching a tent around them both with the duvet, Jo moved in, skimming her teeth along Sarah's shoulder; tightening the flesh into bites as she reached her neck. Electric flickers coursed through Sarah's stomach, while her mind replayed an extreme close-up of Jo's mouth on Tara's throat. Same position. Exact angle. Perfect continuity.

'I'm too tired.' Sarah rolled over, stonewalling with her back.

She felt Jo waver, then close in. The mattress lost altitude, taking Sarah's stomach with it.

'I just wanna kiss you goodnight.'

Liar. Liar. 'Go to sleep.'

'Okay,' Jo paused. The, 'Love you,' sounded sad, in mourning, as she ran her hand down Sarah's spine, half hesitant, half self-assured.

Turbulence thundered through Sarah, wrenching them both back up, then dropping them twelve hundred feet.

Jo's confident palm smoothed infinitely slow loops over her behind, till a stab shot from Sarah's stomach to a direct hit between her legs. Jo squeezed a stinging handful.

'I said *No!*' Sarah hadn't meant to shout so loud.

Through the wall, they could hear Derrie calling out the soundtrack to her nightmare. 'The rock's got me. Can't reach... can't reach the side. Don't swallow. Mustn't... Ugh... It's gonna get me.'

They both froze, waiting to see if she would wake. Their cheeks touched, making Sarah aware of the heat coming off Jo's skin. She grasped Jo's biceps, making sure it hurt, pushing her away diamond-hard, hoping Jo would carry on forcing towards her. Go on, then. Make me. Cunt burn set in. A cornfield patch, slashed and torched, waiting to be turned over.

Sensing her weaken, Jo pressed her mouth hastily against Sarah's, then lifted her face to test her telepathy.

Sarah flung her head back, groaning in anguished defeat. 'Bastard.' Wide open. Streaming. Screaming. Make me, you bastard.

Over her in a second, Jo's solid weight slammed in.

Incensed, Sarah started to struggle. 'Get... off... me.'

Smiling, Jo caught Sarah's fists, pinning her wrists to the bed.

'I... said... get... off.' As she tried to wriggle free, humiliated heat itched through her.

'Make me.' Jo chanced a sea-grey wink, twinkling with conceit, then increased the pressure on Sarah's wrists to unbearable.

As she strained chaotically underneath, she felt Jo's coarse cotton jeans searing inside her thighs. 'I'm going to kick the *fucking shit* out of you,' Sarah hissed, as she started to spill on to the sheet, slick with need.

With a derisive laugh, Jo fused their foreheads together. 'An' who you gonna get to help you?'

Sarah snarled, embedding her teeth into Jo's neck. Rearing away, Jo dug her fingers into Sarah's shoulders to hold her at a safe distance and Sarah noticed with satisfaction the livid marks on Jo's throat.

'You're pathetic,' she taunted.

With a flush of adrenaline, Jo flexed her body, crushing into her, denim and hard bone chafing. The erratic rhythm drew Sarah in, making her push up to reach the bucking against her. Bruising their mouths together, Jo bit Sarah's lips apart gently, prising her tongue through clenched teeth. Sarah listened as Jo's strained breathing changed into deep complaints. Arching her back, Jo clasped Sarah's breasts and rammed into a frantic, flamboyant collision. Repeat collision. Sarah came achingly close to oblivion, jerking automatically as she saw Jo's face transform with distress.

A self-conscious clearing of the throat sounded from behind the door. They stiffened apart.

'What's the matter, Derrie?' Jo asked through quick breaths.

'The slug. The giant one jumped at me in the water, biting me. And Ellie didn't come. She didn't kill it.'

Jo pushed herself off the mattress. 'It's all right. I'll get you a drink.'

Sarah moved over to create space. 'Come here, honey. We'll have a cuddle, then I'll take you back to bed.'

Derrie centered her chill, skinny body against Sarah's side and released a slow sigh. The small adjustments she made sent tickling messages along the surface of Sarah's skin.

'Here you are. Sit up.' In the dark, Jo made her way carefully towards the bed. As she tucked a pile of envelopes under her arm, Sarah caught a telltale flash of transparent paper windows. Bills. Jo felt for Derrie's hands and steadied the glass of apple juice between them.

'Why have you brought those?' Sarah asked.

'I didn't see them before, behind the door.'

'Jo, it's the middle of the night. I'm sure we can wait till morning to start opening bills.'

'No. There's a purple one as well. Probably another card for me.'

Sarah took the envelopes from her and slid them under the bed.

The mattress rocked as Jo jumped back in. Nestling in for the night, Derrie pulled Jo and Sarah around her like two halves of an oyster shell, then stretched up to place a ticklish kiss on her mother's lips. 'Pass it on.'

Sarah lifted her face and passed it on.